Heir in Exile

Danielle Bourdon

For grandpa Judd
You are missed

Chapter One

Chey knew this particular brand of bliss, the kind that came wrapped in golden skin, strong hands and passionate kisses, couldn't last forever. Well it *could.* Today, however, she was out of time for ecstasy.

Rolling onto her stomach, sheets twisted around her hips, dark hair tangled around her shoulders, Chey surfaced from the haze of desire and ignored the lusty look her fiance was giving her.

Sander, all male, with his golden hair, rough whiskers and appealing broad shoulders, acted like they didn't have a day fraught with tension, strife and possible danger ahead. He cocked his elbow into the pillow and rested his temple in his palm.

"What?" Chey asked, giving Sander an accusing look. He shouldn't be so sexy, so...infuriatingly masculine. *Hot.* That's what Prince Sander Darrion Ahtissari was.

And hers. All hers.

"It's not like you to quit before you co--"

"*Sander.* We don't have time for all that." Chey rested her flushed cheek against the pillow.

"But you had time for two hours of--"

"It's almost eight o'clock. We're due at the castle at ten." Chey cut him off before he could remind her, again, what they'd been doing for the last two hours.

"If I use my tongue, it only takes you four or five minutes to rea--"

"*Sander Darrion Ahtissari!*"

"Quit cutting me off." He reached over to pinch her shoulder before untangling from the covers. Sliding out of bed, he got to his feet and shook his hair out like a lion shakes his mane. Grinning like the rogue he was, he strode for the bathroom in all his naked glory.

At six-foot-three, there was a lot of naked flesh for Chey to enjoy. She lingered over his thick thighs, taut buttocks and tight stomach. Until he swerved out of sight, that is.

Chey kicked off the sheets and followed. After the morning just past, she felt wonderfully nimble and sleek. Sander had a way of bringing everything feminine about her to the fore. Although many inches shorter than him, she carried herself with statuesque grace, bare feet silent on the stone floor.

Catching sight of herself in the long mirror, she glimpsed the riot of dark hair tumbled around narrow shoulders, the modest indent of her waist and shapely legs that had not so long ago been wrapped around Sander's hips. She crept up behind him while he ran the water in a shower that could easily fit eight people standing upright. Sliding her arms around his middle, she pressed several kisses between his shoulder blades and made a low noise of pleasure when he reached back to stroke calloused fingers across her outer thigh.

"You sure you don't want me to--"

"Just get in the shower." Laughing, Chey bulled him under the spray. He was incorrigible.

While they washed their skin clean of sweat and the scent of sex, Chey allowed her mind to roam over the last month and a half.

Since his proposal on Christmas eve, they had been inseparable. Except for meetings and other Princely duties,

Sander and Chey had hidden away on the island of Pallan a few miles off Latvala's shore. The brutal winter season, well under way, made it difficult to do any serious traveling or sight seeing. Never mind that Chey was in the country illegally, hiding out from the King and Queen. Only members of Sander's personal staff and a few others knew she was here.

Chey hadn't minded exploring the castle and the island, what they could reach of it, with Sander. He'd taken her hiking on the mountain, skiing on gentle slopes and snow mobile riding through meadows and valleys. He'd proven time and again what a skilled outdoorsman he was, handling the equipment like a seasoned pro. He also knew the island well, giving them the advantage when he took her adventuring.

So far, no one knew of their engagement. They kept it hidden even from Mattias, Sander's younger brother, a man both trustworthy and able to keep secrets.

Now, however, her presence in Sander's life, if not their engagement, was about to come out. He had a ball to attend in Dubai in three days and he insisted she go with him. It was time, he'd said, to break the news to the King and Queen so they didn't find out through photos of the event that Chey was back in his life.

Rinsing suds from her body, she gathered the shampoo and attacked her hair next. Sander kissed her on the shoulder on his way out of the shower. Finished before her, he snagged a towel from the holder, shook out his hair, and toweled dry.

Chey watched him while she finished a routine that included a skin scrub, shaving her legs, and the use of a pumice stone on her heels. By the time she was done, Sander had changed into a pair of black slacks, white button down, and a suit jacket that he paired with an ice blue tie.

"That looks nice on you. Decided to dress up for the occasion, huh?" she asked. It meant she needed to find something equally fitting to wear. Not that she would have gone in jeans or something too casual. But now she needed a semi-formal dress or suit so she didn't look out of place for the announcement.

"For some reason, I always think they

take me more seriously when I wear a suit," he said, glancing up after he pulled on socks and a pair of polished shoes.

"I'm sure." Chey wrapped the towel around her body and stepped over to 'her' sink. There were two, one of which was surrounded by a bevy of organizers holding all her feminine accoutrements. She kept it neat and tidy, so it didn't overflow the long counter top.

Just as she reached for a comb to pull through the wet strands of her hair, a bout of nausea hit. She stilled, one hand bracing against the counter. Her nerves must be getting the better of her. Breathing in and breathing out, she steadied herself.

"You all right?" Sander asked from a bench in the middle of the closet.

"Yeah. I think my nerves are starting to kick in." It was bound to happen some time.

He rose after fixing the hem on his pants and walked over to stand behind her. Dwarfing her in height, he set a hand on her towel covered hip and studied her face in the mirror.

"You sure? You look a little pale."

"Just nauseous. It's not bad." She smiled at his reflection and picked up the comb. While she sorted the tangles out, Sander regarded her with a dubious expression.

"No, we don't need to put it off," she said, anticipating his protest. "We need to get it over with, then I won't be nervous about it anymore."

He hovered at her back, protective and skeptical. "We can delay three or four hours, if that'll help."

"I'll be all right, really. Promise."

Giving her hip a squeeze, Sander stepped to the side, leaning against the counter. Watching her.

"Are you going to stare at me the whole time I get ready?" she asked, amused despite the pitch and roll of her stomach.

"I might."

"It's distracting." She put the comb down and picked up the blow dryer.

"And?"

"And you should go busy yourself with something else until I'm done. I can't concentrate," she retorted around a laugh. Chey turned the dyer on, mouthing *I can't hear you* when he complained. She didn't want him to leave, but the idea of puking in front of him was too mortifying to contemplate.

He snorted and smacked her on the

backside before exiting the bathroom.

Relieved, Chey braced a hip against the counter and swallowed down another bout of nausea. Maybe she needed to nibble on toast.

You're stronger than this, Chey. Don't let them get to you. Easier said than done, she thought, as she dried her hair before taking a curling iron to it. Making quick work of applying a thin layer of make up, she put everything away when she was done and went into the expansive closet. She'd filled 'her' side quite nicely after the recent shopping trip.

What she chose from the racks was a heavy, throat to mid-calf dress with long sleeves and a modestly scooped neckline. It was ivory, with baby blue piping on the cuffs and collar. Very suitable for winter. A baby blue overcoat as long as the dress went with it. She added taupe boots with a flat sole and stuffed gloves into one of the over-large coat pockets.

If Chey had learned anything in her time here, it was to dress for the weather. A slinky, satin creation with high heels would have landed her half frozen and probably skiing on the helicopter pad before the day was through. She enjoyed the heavier clothing anyway, at least while the snow was knee deep, and didn't mind bundling up in several layers.

Exiting into the suite, fixing the collar of the coat, she saw Sander slathering a piece of toast with butter and a dab of jelly. He'd ordered up a quick breakfast between the time he'd left the bathroom and now.

"Here. I thought this might help," he said, handing her a small plate with several slices of prepared toast.

Chey took the little plate and picked up a slice right away. "Thanks. How did you know? It's like you read my mind."

"Isn't this what people usually eat if they're sick to their stomach? Toast, crackers, things like that?" He arched a brow and bit into his own piece.

"I suppose it is. I couldn't have stomached a really big breakfast anyway. Not today." Not with the meeting looming over their heads. She took little bites of toast and sipped hot coffee that he'd poured her. Sander thought of everything.

"I know it's a lot of tension. I wish there was another way around it," he said.

Chey also heard what he *didn't* say. That she'd known by agreeing to stay that this was the way it would be. This was his life, replete with unpalatable situations that she needed to learn to work through.

"I know. I'll get through it." She wanted him to know that her constitution was still strong, that she could face adversity and come out intact on the other side.

He cut a quick smile her way and finished the last bite. Sander hadn't eaten much.

Chey noticed that his mood was moving into that stage between bare tolerance and forced diplomacy. It was his default demeanor lately whenever he had to face the King and Queen. She wouldn't have called it a black mood, per se, just one where he didn't smile as deep or as often. Sander was prone to longer stretches of silence during these times and a strict expression that did not invite jokes or games.

Little by little, Chey was learning all his subtle nuances. She knew it was better to keep her rambling thoughts to herself until they were out of the meeting and back on more familiar ground.

"Ready?" he asked after swinging a longer, heavier coat around his shoulders.

"Yes." Chey set the plate down with just one half slice of toast remaining.

Already her stomach felt better.

"Remember to take the ring off," he added, throwing a scarf around his neck.

Chey frowned. She hadn't removed it since he'd proposed on Christmas Eve. "What if I just wear my gloves the whole time?"

"I'd rather not take the chance. It's not time yet to divulge our engagement." His tone indicated he wouldn't budge on this issue.

Chey slipped the ring from her hand and walked it over to him. She looked up into his eyes. "Keep it safe for me?"

Sander palmed it and slid it into the inner pocket of his overcoat. "Done."

"Thanks."

He extended an elbow to escort her out, shoulders squaring, expression waning neutral once more.

The time for facing down the King and Queen was upon them.

. . .

As the helicopter flew over Ahtissari Castle, Chey stared down at the turrets and spires with bittersweet nostalgia and a wealth of unease. She'd met Sander while staying there. Had almost lost her life. Within those walls, she had grown and matured as a person, learned that not everything was always as it seemed. She felt stronger now, more ready to deal with the unpleasant aspects of dating a man whose parents strongly disapproved of her.

Accepting Sander's hand out of the aircraft when it landed, she followed him to the waiting limousine and slid inside. Her stomach somersaulted with a fresh bout of nerves. There was no turning back now. Already she could see the curious glances some of the security were giving her, puzzling over her presence with Prince Dare.

Sander grew more grim and quiet on the short drive through the gates and up into the courtyard. Once parked out front of the steps, he disembarked and held a hand down. Chey accepted the aid and gave his fingers a faint squeeze before hooking a hold under his elbow.

Allar Kusta, one of the original security members who had come to Seattle for Chey, waited near the open doors. He clipped a wink at Sander that must have had some underlying meaning. She just didn't know what. Perhaps Allar had made sure that Chey's arrival remained unexpected until the last possible second, giving the King and Queen no time to prepare any ugly surprises.

Sander stalked through the doors with her on his arm as if this was *his* castle, as if *he* were already King. His presence grew and expanded right before Chey's eyes, until the air all but crackled with his animal magnetism.

Two advisers standing near the open doors of a parlor glanced, then glanced again. One bristled, shoulders stiffening under the fine lay of his clothing. Both bowed their heads in deference, however, giving respect where it was due.

Sander returned a brief nod of his own and that was all. Like a freight train, he led Chey into the parlor full steam, ignoring one of the advisers blustering attempts to call out and warn the King and Queen at the last second.

Aksel and Helina, perched in chairs that resembled small thrones, both had drinks in their hands. Each wore decadent clothing for the meeting, replete with fur mantles and a crown for Aksel's head. The King was going all out. There was no denying this was a man of power and authority; he wore his regal nature like a second skin, with shrewd eyes and a jut to his whiskered chin that suggested no small amount of arrogance. Helina lounged, as she was wont to, resonating a bored air.

The second Aksel and Helina saw Chey, the proverbial gloves came off. Chey recognized the change with the narrowing of Helina's eyes and in the sudden flare of anger in Aksel's.

Sander was pushing their buttons left and right.

"What," Aksel asked with a breathless pause. "Is the meaning of this?"

Sander brought Chey within ten feet of their seats and bowed his head.

Chey dipped the expected curtsy.

"Father, Mother," Sander said with no small amount of mockery. "I'm sure you remember Miss Sinclair. She will be my official date to the ball in Dubai. After the Valentina scandal and my ensuing annulment, I felt it in my best interest to take someone I could *trust.*"

Chey forced herself not to cringe. The palpable tension in the room made goosebumps break out along her arms and down her legs.

Aksel never looked away from Sander. He set his glass on a small side table and rose slowly to his feet. The blood red cloak he wore swished around his booted ankles as he approached. Coming face to face, Aksel and Sander stared each other down. Sander had a few inch height advantage over his father that he used to its full potential.

"So this is what has kept you so busy. I wondered," Aksel said. "I should have known you would run back to the most inappropriate woman available. You, Sander Darrion, are a disappointment as a son. Not only have you failed to take a fitting, proper wife, you have failed your country."

"Not nearly as badly as you have failed as King," Sander replied, nonplussed. "You put this country in jeopardy with your greed and your ignorance. Allowing a mere Princess to use you to such a degree—it's a wonder you can look at your own reflection with any amount of pride." He paused while Aksel sucked in a furious breath, then added, "I'm here, yet again, doing the right thing. Presenting the woman I intend to court, which will be made public knowledge at the ball in Dubai. In this, you have no say."

"She is banned from this country and should be arrested immediately," Aksel said when he got his breath back. "What, are you going to take on the entire military?"

Chey felt a stirring of fear. Maybe Sander had misjudged the King after all. Would Aksel go so far as to call in the military to arrest and detain her? He had already detained her once already. Her fingers shifted on Sander's arm.

"If you so much as raise your pinky in gesture for the armed guards, I will invoke an Heir's First Right on the grounds of impairment and take the throne right out from underneath you." Sander took a threatening step forward. "Go ahead. Try me."

Helina's glass hit the floor and shattered. She broke into a tirade in their mother tongue, skin pale, hands fluttering wildly.

Chey had never seen the woman so distraught. What was this Heir's First Right? Did Sander really have that kind of power?

Aksel snarled just as several security members swarmed into the room via the open door. They stalked closer, looking warily between faces.

"You," Aksel wheezed in fury at Sander, "have just gone too far. What befalls you from here is your own doing."

He retreated with a swirl of his cape and a snap of his fingers at the guards. Whatever he bellowed was in a language Chey didn't understand. Tense, expecting them to fall on her and wrest her away from Sander's side, Chey tightened her grip and glanced over her shoulder. The security didn't come for her, they came for her and Sander both.

Sander, refusing to budge until he was good and ready, stared at the back of the King's head. Finally, he pivoted, Chey's fingers trapped under his elbow, and stalked out of the parlor under his own power. No one, Chey noticed, dared touch him. Either of them. Regardless that the King wanted him removed, the guards treated Sander with the respect his position demanded.

Instinct warned Chey not to speak while they were in the castle itself. Shocked at the vehement display, she wondered how long tensions had been this high between Aksel and Sander. She waited until they were back in the limousine en route for the helipad to dare ask any questions.

"Sander, what happened?" She glanced sideways. His face was a mask of anger.

"I threatened to have him yanked off

the throne, that's what. Suggesting he has become too impaired to make sound judgments for this country." Sander clenched his teeth, a muscle flexing in his jaw.

"By that Heir's First Right? What is that?" Chey whispered, as if she feared the driver and accompanying guard beyond the divider window might hear.

"It's a special addendum that allows the official Heir to the Throne—which I currently am—to over ride the sitting King if there is proof that the King is showing signs of obvious impairment in regard to ruling the country. I believe I can do that, considering he married me to a woman carrying another man's son. In court, I will win that fight. It's an extremely grievous error, him allowing a pregnant woman to persuade him to give her the ascending Heir. Should a bastard take the throne of Latvala, it could change *everything.*"

Chey studied Sander's profile as he talked. A muscle kept flexing in his jaw and several of his words clipped tight past his teeth. Sander meant every word he said. She wondered if anything this serious had ever happened in the Ahtissari reign.

"Would you really do it?" she whispered. "Have him removed?"

"If he called the military in to arrest and detain you? You bet your sweet ass I would." Sander paused, then said, "Some of this animosity goes back before you ever arrived. He is a tough man, and a tougher father. Some of his decisions regarding our stance for other countries have not been in Latvala's best interests. There has been mild tension between Aksel and the council members, his advisers and others before. He and I do not always share the same line of thought."

"I see." Relieved that she wasn't the whole cause of all the tension between father and son, Chey relaxed against the seat. Her stomach had taken to doing flips once more, and she rested a hand against it over the coat. They arrived at the helipad before Chey could really delve into the subject and with Sander's aid, made the transfer from car to aircraft with little trouble.

Soon they were flying over the choppy water toward the island.

Chapter Two

Dubai was unlike any city Chey had ever seen. Tall skyscrapers scratched the underbelly of the atmosphere, commanding and ultra modern, while businesses in glass buildings crowded close to a waterway that snaked between commercial districts. She felt like she'd been transported to another world, in a future century, where everything was new and on the cutting edge of architecture.

To accentuate the foreign nature, patches of raw desert could be seen from the air, tucked between highways and new construction. It made a striking contrast butted up against the greenery, foliage and palms lining the water.

Once on the ground ensconced in a sleek silver limousine, the effect intensified. To her utter amazement, she saw three robed men on camels meandering through the sand in the heart of the city.

"Pretty amazing, isn't it?" Sander

asked. He sat beside her, resplendent in a black suit, the snowy shirt beneath open at the throat to expose a swath of golden skin.

In the three days since their disastrous meeting with the King, Sander had been brooding and quiet. He hadn't neglected her; to the contrary, he was possessive, attentive and at her side more often than not. He chose to express his distaste of the situation with his father in thoughtful silence, which Chey was more than happy to give him. She didn't need endless conversation to be comfortable in his presence.

"I feel like I'm on another planet," she admitted. "Did you see those camels?"

"It's a common enough sight here," he replied, looking ahead rather than out the windows.

Chey glanced over to Sander. "I wonder if I'll ever be able to look at all these new things with the same casual regard you have. When does it become 'normal'? Or is it just that you've grown up around it and expect it now?"

He finally met her eyes. "It's funny that you wonder if you'll ever be indifferent—and I often wonder what it would be like to see it through *your* eyes. I get a glimpse now and then being around you, but yes, I expect all this now. It's never been any other way, hm?"

Chey hadn't thought about the situation in reverse. It surprised her to think he envied anything about her. "How many times have you been here? Wasn't it new when you first came?"

"I've watched it grow over the years. It takes some of the edge off, though I do remember being impressed on my first visit. As for how many?" He tongued the edge of his teeth. "I've been here ten or so times."

It occurred to Chey then that she didn't even know how old Sander was. Obviously older than her, which explained why he'd been around the world more than she'd first thought. "How old *are* you, anyway?"

He laughed. For the first time in three days, he actually laughed. "Thirty-three. And you're twenty-four, twenty-five on April twenty-second."

"How did you know my birthday?"

"I made it my business to find out."

"Well, aren't you resourceful."

"I can be."

She scoffed. Several resources came to mind, all right, but they had nothing to do with information gathering. Color stained her cheeks for the thoughts that rioted around her head for a moment.

"You're blushing. That means--"

Chey cut him off. "I'm not blushing."

"Yes, you are. I always know when you're thinking about *that*."

"Do I have a neon sign on my forehead?"

"You might as well. Right now it says, *what he did with his tongue last night--*"

"You're so full of it," she said, laughing. Her face felt like it was on fire.

"But you enjoy it," he pointed out, with no small amount of mirth and conviction.

"Yes, *yes* I enjoy it when you're being a rogue. Okay?" She brushed a wayward strand of hair away from her cheek and tugged on the shortcoat of the cream colored suit she wore. Her lips continued to tremble with the urge to suppress another smile.

He caught her chin between his fingers and gently turned her head away from the window. His eyes, such a vivid blue, were intent and focused on her own. Without any more warning than that, he kissed her. Slow, reminiscent of other kisses in recent days that had preceded a hot night of passion.

When they parted, her breath was short in her throat, mind aswirl with all sorts of sordid imagery that had no business being present under the current circumstances.

"Quit it, you're distracting me," she said, pinching his thigh.

"We'll have a few hours this afternoon before the gala this evening. I'm sure I can think of some way to fill them." He smiled, more wolf than man, fingers grazing her chin before falling away.

Chey snorted. Then she dropped her voice to a sultry purr. "Oh, so can I. In fact, one word nicely sums it all up."

"Really," he said. "And what word is that?"

"*Shopping.*"

. . .

The *Royal Regency* lived up to its name. Everything about the hotel catered to the ultra rich, the ultra famous, or the ultra elite. Sitting right on the waterway, rising thirty-four floors above the ground, the structure was a study in Arabic architecture, glossy marble, gold accented columns and lush potted palms.

Men and women of power and standing

came and went through tight security at the front doors, guarded by their own detail on their way to and from the building. Four of Sander's men formed a loose circle of protection from sign in all the way up to the penthouse suite. The suite had its own personal foyer outside the doors for security purposes, as well as an alarm system and panic button.

Arabesque archways led to other bedrooms, an office, a full kitchen and theater room. The furniture had a distinct Mediterranean flair while retaining a modern theme.

After Chey marveled over the view out of the floor to ceiling windows, she unpacked a few belongings and prepared for the shopping trip Sander promised her.

Every retail store, from the ones in the *Regency* to others lining the water, were as upscale as the hotels that surrounded them. The clothes, souvenirs and other items had price tags to match. Sander goaded her into buying things she wouldn't have otherwise looked at twice, and when she came across a dress that felt like liquid in her hands, he insisted she get it. Red, made of intricately sewn sequins that shined, the floor length gown had a scandalous slit up the leg, a snug bodice and an open back. A red ruby dangled from the nape all the way to the low spine. Adding shoes to match, along with a slim clutch, they departed the store ten thousand dollars lighter than when they went in.

Light headed at such expenditures, Chey lunched with Sander in an open air restaurant overlooking a tropical water display. The weather, a temperate seventy-four degrees with cloudless skies, was enjoyable after the two foot snows of Latvala.

In higher spirits once they returned to the room, Chey hung up her dress, sent the other purchases to be laundered, and spent the remaining two hours before the gala in Sander's arms.

As evening fell, and the lights of the city glittered to life, Chey showered and changed into her gown. She admired the way it streamlined her curves and accentuated the shape of her shoulders. Wearing her hair up in coils and curls allowed the dangling ruby to swing unhindered down her back.

Stepping out into the main living area in search of Sander, Chey stopped dead in her tracks. He stood with a glass of what looked to be whiskey in his hand, the other in his pocket, staring out at the glittery cityscape beyond the windows. The black, tuxedo length jacket matched slacks of a fine cut and cloth, and overlaid white-on-white layers beneath: white brocade vest, white shirt, white tie. It was a handsome suit by itself; on Sander, it was staggering. His shoulders filled out the jacket to perfection.

What stood out more than anything was the loose way he wore his hair. Instead of combed meticulously away from his face and caught in a low tail, as usual, he'd opted to wear it down. The golden strands brushed a couple inches below the collar, giving him a rakish look. He could have been a high class stripper in a club that catered to women, except for the debonair mantle he wore that would have surely set him apart from the rest. There was no mistaking his confidence or importance, and certainly no mistaking his allure.

"You're staring," he said without looking over.

"As any red blooded woman would," she countered.

He took a drink. Glanced aside. His gaze raked her head to toe, glimmering with a resurgence of passion. Then, he smiled. A devastating smile that changed his whole face.

"You're a devil," she decided, attempting and failing to control the hectic pace of her heart.

"Ironic, considering you're the one wearing red. And wearing it well, I might add. Turn around, let me see if there's a tail." He narrowed his eyes in anticipation.

"You just want to see my backside."

"Is that a surprise?"

"Not really."

"So turn around and indulge me."

"You're impossible." Chey turned around. Slowly. She swore she felt his gaze caress the naked length of her spine. The dress, Chey decided, was worth every penny. When she finished her turn, she found Sander standing directly in front of her. Towering over her, swirling his drink in the glass. He smelled like heaven. Masculine, musky, with a subtle bite of spice.

"I don't know. Maybe we can skip the gala. What do you think?" He lifted the glass and drained it.

"What? After all this? You're crazy. Besides, we *just* spent half the afternoon in bed."

"Not *half.* More like a quarter."

"You're greedy, that's what you are." She flirted with him from under her lashes.

"I don't hear you complaining."

"You always say that. Like I'm going to ever complain." She laughed at the very idea.

He took a step closer. "So is that a no, then?"

"We can't just rip these clothes off now!" Chey eyed him to see if he was joking. Surely he had to be kidding. "Aren't you required to show up to this shindig or something?"

"I'm not *required,* but I *am* expected." His expression gave nothing away. Sweeping a hand low around her back, he splayed his fingers across her spine.

Chey shivered at the contact. Damn the man. He was distracting her well and good with hardly any effort. "Then we should go."

"Should we?"

Chey felt her resolve weaken. She started to have wild ideas about taking his clothes off with her teeth. Peeling away one decadent layer at a time, until he was beautifully naked and at her mercy.

With a sudden switch, he smiled. Charming, boyish, *devilish.* "Gotcha," he whispered.

Chey backhanded his chest. "You just wanted to see me get all, all..."

"Yes," he said, interrupting her with easy charm. "I wanted to see you get *all* swoony and moon-eyed. You're very alluring when you do that, and it puffs up my ego to think I can sway you without even a kiss."

Chey scoffed a laugh. "Like your ego needs any puffing up. *Please.*"

Grinning, he applied pressure with his arm and escorted her toward the door. "C'mon, Slinky. Let's go tear up the town. Later I'll let you have your wicked way with me."

Chapter Three

The gala in the grand ball room of the *Royal Regency* put the party in Monte Carlo to shame. Here, a ceiling arched high over the glossy floor, done in white like the walls, table linens and high backed chairs. Gold was the accent for everything, from the rims of real crystal glasses to the edging on plates to the medallions decorating arabesque carved niches. Even the polished marble they walked on had thin gold veining. Waiters and waitresses wore white as well, with gold piping the collars and sleeves.

All the color came from the clothing of the guests, which ranged the full spectrum of the rainbow.

Escorted to a specific table with Sander's name and title on a placard, Chey discovered they shared the space with three other couples. One, of some Asian descent, another definitively Spanish, and the third was German. To her surprise, Chey found each set to be accomplished conversationalists with cultured, easy to understand accents. The topics remained in the safe categories of the host country's ample assets, the weather, and the reliable shopping district, of which Chey could at least speak with a little knowledge. Her fears about keeping up with such elite company faded as the dinner wore on, until she was smiling and chatting as if she'd known the women, at least, for much longer than an hour.

When the men excused themselves for a more obvious session about business, Chey retreated to one of the lounge areas with the ladies. From there they could see the dance floor and the expansive skyline beyond the arching windows. Wary of a repeat from Monte Carlo, she declined any drinks that waiters brought by on trays, instead choosing to order direct from a specific one that Sander sent over.

When the women started discreet rounds of gossip, dropping famous names left and right, all Chey could do was smile and listen. She didn't personally know this Royal, or that Princess. Nor did she have the slightest clue what those four A-List actresses were up to. It wasn't until the Spanish beauty turned a curious look on Chey that she realized *she* was about to become the hot topic of the evening.

"I hear you're something of a minor celebrity in Latvala, is that true dear?" the Spanish lady asked.

Chey arched her brows and tempered her reply. "Me? No, of course not. If I am, no one has made me aware."

The women tinkled polite laughter.

"Sometimes," the Asian said, "it is best if we turn a blind eye to certain things. You aided in a rescue on a dock however, did you not?"

"Oh, yes. I did. But it was only what anyone else would have done. Hardly noteworthy." Chey honestly felt that way.

"And modest, too," the German added. "It's no wonder he snatched you up again the second he was free of Princess Valentina."

"Yes, what a terrible situation," another said.

Chey wondered if the elite of the world were delivered all the raging gossip by their employees for just these kinds of occasions. Put on the spot, she frantically sought a way to address the comment and remain politically correct. Sander had cautioned her earlier about leaving her ring in the safe of the room so it didn't spark questions and controversy. She was thankful for his foresight.

"It was unfortunate that his marriage ended the way it did," Chey said first, buying herself some time. "Prince Sander and I have always been fond of one another, however, so I saw no harm in accepting his invitation to attend the gala."

"Does this mean you're not actually dating then?" the Asian inquired.

"Shame, I rather thought she fit well into the circle," the Spanish woman added.

"We see each other now and then. I'm definitely not adverse to dating the Prince, though," Chey added, diverting from her stoic reply for a bit of honesty. After all, she *was* engaged to Sander, and at some point, the knowledge would hit the rest of society.

The women laughed while they eyed her. None were unkind, and none seemed to judge her harshly. Another surprise for Chey, who knew some of the women in these circles were more like piranha than not.

"I cannot imagine many women being adverse to such a thing," the German said, proving she was more blunt than her companions.

"Indeed. I've heard several notable Princesses have expressed interest now that he is single once more," the Asian remarked.

"And that one brash American—sorry dear," the Spanish lady said, pausing to excuse the fact that Chey herself was American. "The supermodel who just dumped Leo of all people for a shot at the Prince's affection."

"I haven't heard anything about it," Chey said with a tepid smile. She took a sip from her glass and began to contemplate excusing herself for the bathroom. Maybe the conversation would move on to some other member of high society by the time she returned.

"Speaking of Princes," the Spanish lady said, and cleared her throat.

"Excuse me, ladies. I'm here to claim Miss Sinclair for a dance," Sander said, arriving just in the nick of time.

The women smiled broad and full and gave their genteel *glad to have met yous* while Sander helped Chey to her feet. Chey echoed the sentiment, and it wasn't a lie. Yes, some of the topics had been uncomfortable to deal with, but overall, she found the trio pleasant and polite company.

Setting down her glass, Chey let Sander lead her from the lounge to the dance floor, where she eased into the rhythm with an exhale of relief.

"Getting to you?" Sander asked near her ear.

"Not really. 'We' came up, and that's when I started to squirm."

"You hid it well. I couldn't tell by watching you from a distance."

"That's because you were distracted by the slit in my dress."

He laughed. "You make it sound like I have a one track mind."

"That's because you do."

"I do not." He feigned affront.

"Really? Then what was that whole two hours after the shopping trip, and the sexy little attempt to keep me in the room before the party?" She arched her brows, staring up into his eyes. Chey contained a smile with effort.

"I thought of many things *between* all that. None of them had to do with sex. Take my recent side out with the foreign gentlemen over there." He glanced toward the group of men he'd been speaking with who were still collected together in a circle.

Chey caught a glimpse during a turn in the dance. "You actually concentrated on business?" She pretended surprise.

"Well, I *wasn't* thinking about the slit in your dress or the way you were moaning my name earlier in the hotel room. So yes, I actually concentrated on business."

"Did you get anything accomplished?" Her lips trembled at the corners again with the want to smile. Sander's banter never ceased to amuse her.

"We discussed a few trade options, imports and exports, things of that nature. You could say we made progress." He slowed the pace of their dance when the music shifted into something with a more mellow beat.

"Don't you have people who negotiate all that?" she asked.

"Yes. But I like to get my hands dirty with it. You know, make some of the decisions, talk to the people we'll be in business with. Sometimes, these are the first steps of many. Really, it's just an excuse for a bunch of really wealthy people to congregate, show off their jewels and money and write all this off as some expense or another." He snorted.

"Now that sounds a lot more like what

I'm seeing here. The congregate and gossip angle."

"The men don't gossip."

"That's ridiculous. Of course they gossip." Chey scoffed.

"Not like the women do."

He stumped her; Chey had no good comeback.

Grinning, he pulled her closer and flattened his hand low on her spine. The warmth of his skin felt like a brand, a welcome one as far as Chey was concerned.

They danced two more dances, heads close, bodies closer. Chey enjoyed his presence, liked the way he hid nothing of his interest in her. She knew people were talking and didn't care. Let them talk. Most everyone seemed to think Sander had been wronged anyway, which gave him more leeway than if he'd simply left Valentina at the altar or some other ungentlemanly maneuver.

Sander broke away once more for another session with the men, promising to come collect her in a half an hour. Chey retreated to the restrooms, which were set up with entire lounge areas for women to recline, talk, fix make up or smoke in peace. She chose a divan in the corner and put her feet up, more than happy to have some down time. Fishing her phone from her purse, she pretended to have a text conversation while in reality, she perused wedding dresses.

It never hurt to just...look.

The wedding was probably years away, but this relaxed her and took her mind off everything else.

Before she knew it, an hour had gone by. Gasping in surprise when she looked at the time, she shut her phone off, tucked it into her purse, and exited the restroom. Sander was probably thinking she'd gone slinking away with some man again.

Out in the main room, she paused to get her bearings and find the group he'd been speaking with. The circle was no longer there.

Fantastic. She threaded her way through the milling guests, on the hunt for Sander.

. . .

Chey started to worry when she didn't find him after fifteen minutes of searching. Maybe he'd needed to use the men's room as well and got caught up in unexpected conversation. If his security detail was here, Chey had a difficult time pinpointing them. There were others dressed in typical black and white suits, making it hard to differentiate who was who. If there hadn't been a hundred and fifty or so faces to scan, it would have made her task much easier.

"Lost, little girl?" Sander said from behind, next to her ear.

Startled, she twitched a look over her shoulder. "There you are. I was about to go into the men's room and see if you were there."

"I dare you," he said, laughing.

"I don't have to now. You're here." She smiled and faced him. "Did you finish your talks?"

"Yes, and I'm ready to blow this party if you are." Sander offered her his elbow.

Chey slid her fingers under the crook and let him lead her through the room. From nowhere, his security appeared out of the throng and took up flanking positions. So they *had* been somewhere in the room. Or at least two of them had.

Sander passed off a few goodbyes on their way through the enormous arabesque arch. He led her along a hallway, then into another where the VIP elevator banks were located.

Pressing the button, they waited until the doors slid open and he guided her inside. The security situated two in front, two in back.

Chey slipped little glances aside at Sander as the carriage began to ascend. It was a smooth, quiet ride, with a light flickering above each number as they passed the floor. In no time, the final ding rang through the cabin and the elevator doors hissed open.

With a sudden flurry of motion, dark clad figures rushed in. Although it was night time outside, each wore sunglasses that gave their faces a bug like appearance. Sander's security had no time to unsheathe their weapons or block the blows that landed a moment later. Silencers, several of them, swept the carriage while someone shouted for everyone to freeze.

Sander shoved Chey behind him and batted at a silencer, grabbing the long muzzle with one hand while kicking at the first man's knee. Two other men swarmed in from the hall, grappling in the small space.

Chey screamed and fought off an assailant that wrapped her by the throat with an arm. Bodies of guards dropped like flies to the floor of the elevator and were summarily dragged out into the corridor.

Catching glimpses of Sander fighting for his life, Chey wrestled with the man who trapped her against his chest. He had the advantage in height, strength and experience. Bulling her forward, he guided her through the foyer of the suite and in through the already open doors.

Someone had planned this well.

She dropped her clutch on the floor when the man, rather harshly, forced her down into a chair.

"Do *not* move," he snarled, brandishing the gun to show her he meant business.

She screamed, a high pitched, blood chilling sound that caused the assailant to backhand her hard across the cheek. Tasting blood, she choked, swallowed and went silent. Fuzzy bees blurred the edge of her vision, swarming in and out in a dizzying pattern. She blinked them away, desperate to regain full control of her senses.

The shape of Sander, arms wrenched behind his back, came into sharper focus when the assailants shoved him into the suite from the foyer. Blood spattered the once pristine white vest, shirt and tie. It took four men to subdue him. Several more staggered in wearing split lips, wounded arms or legs, and abrasions to their faces.

The man in charge yanked his sunglasses off his eyes and kicked the penthouse doors closed with his boot.

"Now then," he said with a heavy mid-eastern accent. "That will be enough of that."

Each member of the unit had sun-dark skin that placed their heritage in the nearby vicinity and thick black mustaches that Chey might have thought were fake if only because they all looked exactly the same. The men wore goatees as well, trimmed precisely alike. The crazy thought that the tans and accents were part of a disguise stubbornly persisted.

Shoved down into a chair adjacent to Chey, Sander said nothing. He glared, however, gaze raking over the men while he tongued his swollen lip.

Chey knew he was assessing, calculating, looking for weakness and openings. Waiting for one person to slip up so he could make a move. She knew it as well as she knew the sun would rise tomorrow. Sander, not of pampered gentry, was able to fend for himself. Skilled and cunning, he wasn't afraid to get his hands dirty in a fight. The only question was—would the men shoot to kill? Chey thought the motive here was clear; the King, after warning Sander something else was coming, had made a major move. *What befalls you from here is your own doing.*

Surely he wouldn't kill his own son. Not the firstborn, heir to the throne. It was too radical a step even for Aksel. Wasn't it?

She was another matter. Chey had no illusions that Aksel would do away with her for good this time. It made her stomach queasy, made her light headed. They had taken a chance by confessing their relationship to the King and Queen and now they would pay.

The leader of the group approached Sander, gun held down at his side. He tucked his sunglasses into a front pocket on his shirt.

"I will make this as short and painless as possible," the man said, making eye contact with Sander.

Sander still said nothing. His face was set into stoic, neutral lines, eyes cold and flinty.

"You will return to Latvala as soon as we are finished here. There is a meeting arranged between you and the King, where he will immediately, and permanently, send you into exile," the leader said.

Chey stifled a gasp of shock. Exile? Aksel was willing to give up his first born, the natural heir, because of all this? Killing, as she suspected, was too extreme. Permanent exile was not.

Sander showed no reaction. He didn't scowl, or snort, or argue.

The leader arched his brows. "You *do* hear me, yes?"

Sander remained stoic. No agreement, no nod.

"I know you are not deaf," the leader said. "You will accept the exile and leave Latvala for a distant holding in another country. The point is, you will be stripped of your ranking, your privileges and your title, along with your money. For all intents and purposes, you will become a commoner, forced to live under the protection of the ruling family if for no other reason than they wish not to deal with ransom situations."

Silence met the leader's mocking

announcement. The man looked briefly annoyed and gestured at Sander with his gun hand.

"To press the point home, in case you are thinking of an escape, or that you might somehow salvage the situation, know that should you fail to do exactly as I have said, *she* will become a casualty of the human trafficking trade." The leader gestured Chey's direction while he paced closer to her chair. "She will be absorbed into a system that, as you well know, tends to make citizens disappear with alarming speed. The Chey Sinclair sitting before us will cease to exist and become some sheik's plaything in a harem until she loses whatever appeal she might have. Then she will become someone else's plaything, or used to generate income in a manner I don't think either of you would approve of."

Chey listened with growing horror. This went far beyond being detained in a musty cell below the King's castle. They meant to make her disappear for good, in a way that would ultimately be worse than death. She glanced at Sander. He wasn't looking at her, but at the leader of the group. Following the man with his eyes. Chey couldn't tell what he was thinking, although he must still be planning an out. Some kind of escape.

He would not allow her to be sent off and get lost in any human trafficking system.

"Do you understand? This is non-negotiable, Sander Ahtissari. You *will* be exiled, and she *will* become a victim of trade if you do not do as you're told. Accept your due, and she will be returned to her old life." The leader of the group circled Chey's chair twice, flicking a piece of her hair with a finger. He came to stand in front of their chairs once more, looking between them.

"I can see from the look in your eyes that you need more convincing," the leader finally said to Sander.

"He has always been stubborn like that," another, familiar voice said from around the corner of an archway.

Chey snapped a glanced that direction. A cold chill gripped her spine.

Mattias stepped into view, leaning a shoulder against a marble column. Dark eyes shifted between Sander and Chey with careless disregard. He said, "But I'm guessing he didn't see *this* coming."

Chapter Four

Not Mattias. Chey repeated the mantra while shock held her immobile in the chair. She heard Sander hiss to her right, the first sign of reaction since the leader began speaking. Glancing between brothers, Chey found them staring at each other with impossible to read expressions.

No matter how Chey tried to reason what was going on, her mind simply refused to accept that Mattias had a hand in this. He couldn't have been stringing Sander along the whole time—could he? Was it all a lie? Mattias stood next in line to the throne; he had the most to gain if Sander was ousted as heir.

The man she'd come to know, had lunched with, conversed with, confided in, would not do this to his brother. Yet there Mattias stood, looking for all the world as if everything was falling neatly into place.

"The cat seems to have got his tongue,"

the leader said to Mattias, in regard to Sander's silence.

"He won't say anything. It's his way," Mattias replied. His attention returned to Sander. "What the man says is true, brother. Unfortunately, Chey *will* find that unlucky fate as her own should you not return of your own accord and accept the terms of exile. The sooner, the better. Chey is scheduled to be transferred this evening to a holding cell before finding her way onto a bus bound inland in the morning. If I were you, I would get moving."

Sander pushed up from the chair. Several armed men brought their guns up, muzzles aimed at Sander's chest.

"Careful boys," Mattias chided. "Dead bodies are messy. See him out."

Sander looked away from Mattias to Chey. For the first time, she was able to read the gleam in his eyes. His held promise of retribution, of rescue. He would do everything in his power to free her.

She inclined her head, a subtle motion of acknowledgment. Sander turned his gaze on Mattias once more as he started for the door of the suite. He pointed a finger at his brother, the kind of gesture that also promised retribution.

Mattias, if Sander's gesture could be believed, had not seen the last of him.

Chey felt sick. Her stomach churned and clenched. She watched Sander depart the room with two armed men in his wake. They kept a careful distance, leaving the door open behind them. Once Sander was on the elevator heading down, the men returned to stand guard with the others.

"All right then. This just got easier," Mattias said. He pushed up from his lean. "Have her transferred as we discussed," he ordered the leader. "Report to me as soon as she's gone in the morning."

"Yes sir." The leader gestured to the man closest to Chey's chair.

"Let's go, *Princess,*" the man said. He hauled Chey to her feet with a rough grasp of her elbow. His taunt over a title she would never have drew a derisive laugh from the others. The men snorted and muttered unkind things about how much time she would soon be spending on her back.

Swallowing bile, Chey stabbed a hot look of anger at Mattias. He smirked with half his mouth, apparently nonplussed at the accusation in her gaze.

Two of the men escorted Chey out of the suite, past the foyer and the elevator bank, to a locked door leading to the utility staircase. One produced a key and guided her onto a dimly lit landing.

They were taking no chances allowing her anywhere near the public or other hotel employees. She started down the metal stairs; thirty-five floors seemed an impossible descent in these heels. Stumbling, one of the men snarled, gripped her elbow tighter, and righted her balance.

"Try anything funny and you *will* eat a bullet," he said. "Messy dead bodies or not."

Chey decided Sander had the right of it, and remained silent. She concentrated on getting down the steps one at a time without falling and breaking her neck. At some point, her hands had started shaking. The nausea was worse, causing an uncomfortable lump of bile to rise up the back of her throat.

What would happen now? Would Sander call for reinforcements once he was in the hotel lobby? She'd been surprised that the men had allowed him to go free, with no escort and no guard. Perhaps that would have been too risky, given Sander's propensity for self defense. Or, maybe, they thought he would do exactly as commanded to keep her safe. By the time he left Latvala after being exiled, she would be too far gone for Sander to find.

After three floors, one of the men guided her into one of the utility elevators only used by hotel employees. The gunmetal gray interior lacked the polish and opulence of the others used by guests. It was a spartan carriage with plain buttons and bare metal walls.

Chey watched the numbers illuminate on their way down. It didn't stop until a light pinged on over a button marked *G.* The doors opened onto a broad basement garage obviously sectioned off for special deliveries. Here there were vans and sedans with the hotel logo on the doors instead of luxury vehicles that might have belonged to guests. That section was somewhere out of sight, likely accessed by the V.I.P. parking attendants rather than regular customers.

Screaming would do her no good here. Even if she did shout in the hope of attracting an employees attention, she feared another blow to the head might knock her completely out. She wanted to be aware and coherent so she could memorize the route the men took.

Bustled toward a waiting van, the men paused long enough to secure her wrists in front of her with a length of thin rope. After the sliding side door opened, she found herself pushed into a seat. At every opportunity, she looked for escape. Waited for their attention to divert just enough to make a break. A break that never came. The men hovered too close, smothered her with their bodies, guns openly displayed.

Upright in the seat, Chey wondered where she would be taken from here. Blinking away the sting of tears, she focused instead on her anger. Anger helped keep the panic at bay. There was still time. Sander would reorganize, find help, and locate her before any transfer took place in the morning. Never mind that she didn't intend to be a passive participant. There *would* be an opportunity, at some point, and she intended to exploit it for all she was worth. The men would get lazy, or distracted, and she meant to use the lapse against them.

In the meantime, she stared out the windows as the van exited from the garage onto the street. She intended to keep track of the turns so that she might find her way back here again, or at least use the hotel as a point of reference should she go on the run.

Darkness made it difficult. The van turned three times, then hooked two lefts at alternating stop lights. Chey twisted in the seat, looking back, fixing the route in her mind. Already it was a bit hazy. Familiar landmarks she might have recognized from her earlier outing couldn't all be seen under the cloak of night, leaving her to fixate on clusters of buildings or lighted signs instead.

Damn. The van took a right. A left.

By then, her confusion was complete.

Frustrated, she clenched her teeth until her jaw hurt. Her gaze dropped to the floor of the van in search of something, anything, to use as a weapon. The only thing she saw was a collapsible umbrella.

Fat lot of good that would do her. It was small, to boot, without even a spiked tip to use for stabbing. She wondered if the handle was thick enough to cause a decent blow if she struck the driver or passenger with it.

In the meantime, she worked at the

rope binding her wrists. The men hadn't been very thorough in this, at least, and the more she wriggled her hands, the looser it became. Small favors. She hid the action from the driver as best as she could. He kept glancing in the rear view mirror, shifty-eyed and menacing.

A moment after that, she got the rope completely free of her wrists. That was when the idea to use the rope struck. She could choke the driver, cause him to crash, and then, with any luck, she might escape before the men could detain her.

Discreetly, she toed off the heels. They would only hinder her later. If she got desperate, she might use one. Aim for the eye or the jugular.

Before she could solidify her plans and act, the driver spat a curse at the windshield.

Chey looked up from her lap, fearing the driver had seen her free the ropes from her hands.

With a jolt, the van picked up speed. A lot of speed. The driver wasn't paying attention to her, but something behind on the road.

Chey twisted around to glance back.

A sleek black SUV was coming up fast, a heavy duty grill guard in place. It impacted the back bumper of the van, sending the vehicle into a small fishtail.

Chey gasped. Could it be Sander already? How in the world had he found them?

The driver of the van cursed again, this time in another language, and corrected the fishtail. He sped ahead, stomping the gas pedal.

Chey decided it was now or never. If it was Sander, the least she could do was help slow the van down. Wrapping each end of the rope around her hands, she lurched forward and hooked it around the driver's neck. She jerked back with all her might, one foot braced against the seat.

In the next second, all hell broke loose.

. . .

The van swerved hard to the right, throwing Chey's balance off. Overcompensating, the struggling, choking driver veered back the other way, grappling with the steering wheel while attempting to reach back and grab Chey's arm.

Tenacious, she hung on. Right up until the passenger clocked her in the cheekbone with his elbow. Stunned, she slumped back against the seat, losing her grip on the rope.

The SUV banged into the back of the van again, harder this time.

Shouting curses, red faced, the driver whipped the wheel between his hands, left and right, fighting to regain control. The van shot forward again and screeched into a hard right turn at the looming stoplight.

Chey reached down, feeling around for the umbrella, fending off the irate passenger who had twisted between the seats to try and subdue her. He snatched her hair, eliciting a cry of pain. She scrabbled for his eyes with her fingers, returning the favor. Bastard.

She scratched harder while unsnapping the clasp on the umbrella. Shoving it up between the seats, she pressed the button and the thing shot open, causing the passenger to fall back against the dashboard. Using the sharp little ends, Chey caught some on the driver's face and pulled.

Lights flashed through the back windshield as the SUV closed in. This time, the SUV pulled alongside in the other lane and rammed the van on the driver's side.

Chey yelped and dropped the umbrella.

The next thing she knew, she was wedged between the front seats, console digging into her ribs. Disoriented, she felt around for a hold on something. Anything.

What had just happened? The van was no longer moving. She heard a hiss, and ticking, and a buzz that replaced it in her ears. Chey felt like she was underwater, moving much slower than she thought she was.

The side door of the van opened with a screech of metal. Two men in suits reached in to extract Chey from the seats, hands gentle yet firm. One of the men fished a phone out of the driver's pocket before they were through.

"What happened? Sander?" Chey sought their faces as they pulled her free of the van and got her feet on the ground. Woozy, she stumbled. A hand shot out to wrap her waist and provide something sturdy to lean on. She saw the van had crashed into a lamp post, the entire hood crumpled in over the engine. The driver and passenger were slumped against airbags, unconscious.

Guiding her forward to the SUV that had sustained minimal damage thanks to the grill guard, the suited men loaded her into the back seat with all due haste. One climbed into the front seat, another behind.

Chey glanced across the seat.

Instead of Sander, she found herself staring at Mattias.

. . .

Gone was the aloof man who had appeared so indifferent in the hotel room. This Mattias wore concern in his dark eyes and a vague frown on his brow. Chey stared at him, head swimming from the impact of the van with the lamppost. She didn't even remember the crash.

"Are you all right?" Mattias asked. "We have a lot to discuss. Things, obviously, are not what they appear to be."

"Obviously," Chey said. She didn't know if she was all right or not. Her body was numb, her thoughts scattered. She didn't know who to trust or whether she should be trying to escape yet again.

"It's a long story, one I will fill you in on when we meet up with Sander."

"We're meeting up with Sander? Was he in on this, too? I don't understand." Nothing made sense to Chey. It was too complicated, too perverse. One brother pitted against the other, a King with murder on his mind, an heir headed for exile.

"No, he knew nothing. It had to be this way. I needed the men in the hotel room to report back to the King—and for the King to believe them. It had to be real, at least in the moment." Mattias paused to touch her shoulder, a gentle splay of masculine fingers. "I had men waiting to intercept Sander before he left the hotel. We're meeting up at another hotel not far."

"Someone could have gotten killed," she snapped, patience at an end. She didn't brush off Mattias's hand, even if she wasn't sure she could trust him.

"Yes. Any one of us, should the King have discovered my duplicity. We'll be there shortly." Mattias removed his touch and engaged the driver in their mother tongue.

Chey didn't know what to think. She stared out the window, rubbing her ribs with a palm. There would be bruises, no doubt. Otherwise, a spot on her leg hurt, and one of her shoulders, but that was all. No blood that she could see. The seats had spared her the worst of it.

Brooding, she crossed her arms over her middle and watched the glittering city of Dubai fly by out the windows. She couldn't appreciate the glamor or the beauty after a night like tonight. And it wasn't just tonight. It was the entire thing. The whole shebang.

Was this really what it was like to be a part of Royalty? Did these extremes go on all the time? She recalled reading about this chase or that kidnapping or other horrors regarding the elite of the world. Stories that had seemed so far removed from her reality in Seattle, Washington. Chey understood things happened, and that there were people who would see harm come to leaders and the ruling class. This happened to be the *King*, however, acting against his firstborn son. Was it normal? Were the children of Royalty really forced to bend to the will of their superiors and elders?

It was mind boggling.

Sooner than later, the SUV pulled into an underground parking garage not unlike the one she'd left not long ago. It tested her nerves, put her patience on edge again.

Parking near an elevator bank, the suited men disembarked and came around to help her to the ground. Barefoot, the concrete cold on her skin, she padded to the elevator with Mattias hovering at her back.

They rode up in silence.

She wasn't sure what hotel they were at, or where they were in the city. The chase and chaos had totally obliterated her sense of direction.

The light chimed above floor number *20.* Opening onto what appeared to be a regular floor of a well appointed hotel, Chey allowed Mattias to guide her to a set of double doors with a gold plaque on the wall listing the suite as number *204.* She noted there were few other doors on this floor as well; perhaps it was one of the private floors reserved for celebrities or the like.

One of the guards opened the door with a pass card, stepping back to allow Mattias in first.

Chey followed on Mattias's heels, immediately searching for Sander. The suite was not as elaborate as the penthouse of the *Royal Regency,* but it was nevertheless a five star appointment. Rich mahogany paired with tapestry covered furniture and leather to create an almost Victorian feel.

Sander paced through the room, agitation clear in the line of his shoulders. Once he saw Mattias and Chey, he cut across the space and gathered her into his arms.

Chey slid her arms around his neck, relief making her knees weak. Thank God.

Mattias hadn't lied. Sander was in one piece, albeit banged up from the confrontation with the armed assailants.

"You look a bit of a wreck. Are you all right?" Sander asked near her ear.

"I'm fine. Just a few bruises." Her cheek sported a good one from the backhand, easy to ignore for now. Later there would be time for ice, maybe a hot bath to ease the ache starting to collect in her muscles from the crash. "What about you?"

Sander leaned back and cupped her face in his palms. "Fine, fine. Come sit down." He led her to a plush sofa and helped her down into the cushions.

"I'd really like to know what's going on," she said once she was settled. What she wanted was a change of clothes and something hot to drink. Maybe even something spiked.

Sander perched on the arm of the sofa

at her side and looked across at Mattias.

"You know," Sander said. "If I hadn't known for sure you were on my side, I would have sworn you'd been baited to work for the King."

Mattias poured himself a drink from a sidebar. "As I told Chey in the car, it had to be real. The men had to believe I was on his side, not yours. It's still very important to keep that charade up for now."

"What the hell is going on, Mattias? What's this about exile? He has to know I'll never agree to that."

Mattias kicked back a healthy swallow before speaking. "I overheard him talking about these plans in his private parlor. He didn't realize I was there. He's furious, ready to denounce you and remove you entirely from the line of successors. Exile is a good way to prevent you from ever being able to ascend in his wake. If you do it on your own merit, it allows him to save face in front of our people, you see."

"I have a hard time believing he would go to this extreme just because of who I choose to date."

"It's not just that it isn't their choosing —which is a lot of it, you know how they are—but that she's American. A foreigner with no standing, no family, no political advantage. And you seriously pissed him off with the threat of removing him from the throne. He's on a tear, ready to do whatever it takes," Mattias replied.

Chey cringed inside at how cavalier it sounded. She might not have all those things any longer, but she was still *human* for crying out loud, still compassionate and caring and good-hearted over all. Didn't that account for anything? She squeezed Sander's hand when he reached down to grasp hers. As if he knew, rightly so, that it might be hard for her to hear.

"Why didn't you just confront him in the parlor?" Sander asked. "Wouldn't it have been easier to try and change his mind?"

"There is no changing his mind. Not only that, he made a peculiar statement that has sat ill with me ever since. He said, *Sander will go into exile—one way or another.* It was his tone, the absolute certainty he could make it happen. I started to think he has some other ace up his sleeve and decided on the spot that I would intercept the carrier and insert myself into the plans. They undoubtedly reported back to the King that I did so, that I'm here under my own power, with the intent to see his plot through for my own gain. The throne will be mine, technically, if you go into exile. What I'm trying to do is buy us time. I want Aksel to believe I'm pushing for the same agenda he is." Mattias leaned against the side of a couch and glanced between Sander and Chey.

Sander stroked a thumb across Chey's knuckles while he listened. He said, "What else could he have though, that would force me into exile? I can't think of anything."

"I can't either, but that doesn't mean there isn't some secret he's been keeping. He and mother have a wealth of them, you know that."

Sander grunted. "Yes."

"So what does this mean, then? What is your plan from here?" Chey asked.

"It means we will allow the others to think you have been handed off—which reminds me. Byron, use that phone and send a text to the others saying Chey has been secured for the night. In the morning at seven, send another text that she has been handed over to a man named Saul." Mattias glanced over his shoulder to one of two suited men still in the suite. Men obviously working for Mattias and Sander, or at least loyal to their cause.

Byron inclined his head and fished out the phone to send his text.

Mattias picked up where he left off. "Anyway, we want them to think you are on your way to some sordid trafficking center while Sander goes back to Latvala. What I think should happen is that you have a meeting with the King, brother, and try to force him to expose whatever other ace he's got up his sleeve so we can deal with it."

Sander rubbed his fingers over the ridge of his jaw. "That's really all I can do at this point. If I don't show up, he'll try and track Chey's whereabouts down to make double sure she's not with me, and our cover will be blown."

"Exactly. I will be there as well, with any luck, by invitation of the King. I expect he'll want to enforce the idea that I'm working with him and that I am ready to accept the official position as Heir. It keeps me close to him, in case he decides to confide in me. We'll work him from both angles," Mattias said.

"This seems impossible," Chey said. "Has it really come to this? He's your father. I have a hard time wrapping my head around the fact he can be so callous as to throw his own son out of his life. Out of the country, for that matter."

Sander and Mattias turned their attention on Chey.

"Remember, I mentioned that the tension goes back beyond this. Further than you. I think it's a culmination of things. Never mind he's pissed that I threatened to throw him off the throne and take his place *now,* before his time as ruler has passed. That alone might have made him take more aggressive action," Sander said.

"True, very true," Mattias agreed. "He is possessive of his title. Most monarchs are. Few will give it up until they're absolutely forced to."

Chey recalled that the Queen of England, quite late on in her years, had yet to hand her title down to her son. She wondered if the Queen would continue to rule until her death, or until she became mentally incapable. Perhaps there were laws in place preventing her from handing power down before then. Chey couldn't be sure.

"You would be surprised at what goes on behind the scenes, Chey," Sander said. He lowered his voice, watching her face as he spoke. "Some are far worse than my father, who thinks he is in the right to press his hand. Maybe he is, but it's not in my nature to bow to that kind of pressure. They groomed me to be King —and that's what I will become."

Chey regarded Sander's determined expression. He was a different man now than the one who had sat so stone faced in the hotel room. Yet she detected gears turning underneath his calmer exterior, working out ideas and plans in the back of his mind. She believed him, too, when he said he would one day become King.

"I guess I *would* be surprised, though I shouldn't after Elise's failed attempt to kill me and your father's order banning me from the country," she said.

"All of this will make you stronger should your relationship with Sander progress," Mattias said. "One thing you *must* remember, however, is that my loyalty, without question, is to Sander. No matter what I say or do, no matter what you see, there will always be a reason for it. Sander knew this evening before he ever left the hotel room that I was fronting and covering."

Chey wondered what Mattias would

think if he knew that Sander had already proposed. "I had a hard time believing you would do those things," she admitted to Mattias. "It just didn't seem like the man I'd come to know. After the Viia thing, though, and the Queen—one just never can tell. I'll remember."

"Good. Because it means my loyalty is also to you while you're with him," Mattias added.

"Which will be for a very long time. I've already proposed, and she said yes," Sander said, putting the news into the open.

Mattias arched his brows and reached into the breast pocket of his coat. From it, he withdrew a little velvet box.

Her ring box.

"That explains my surprise when I found this in the safe in your suite. I thought you meant to propose on the trip. Congratulations, then," Mattias said.

Sander inclined his head. "Thanks for thinking to sweep the room and check the safe. I would have rampaged if that fell into the hands of those hooligans."

Chey, relieved beyond reason, stood up off the couch and approached Mattias. He handed the box over to her with a smile.

"Thanks," she said, taking the ring out.

She hated taking it off for any reason. It went back onto her ring finger for now.

"You're welcome, future Queen of Latvala."

Chapter Five

I should not be writing any of this down. It isn't even on a page in my real journal, which is locked away at a castle I do not currently have access to. This is a scrap of paper I salvaged from one advertisement or another. Right now I'm sitting in a hotel in Dubai and it's 3:47 in the morning. I haven't slept yet, for good reason.

Earlier, Sander and I were accosted in the elevator by a group of men with guns. Just as I had let my guard down a little, just when I thought any danger like that was past. I should know better by now. It turns out Mattias infiltrated the group and he managed to waylay the more sinister plans they had for Sander and me. The King is the ultimate culprit—and I'm definitely not surprised about that.

He wants to send Sander into exile, strip him of his titles and his right to the throne. After all, Sander threatened the King with the same. It was a brazen move on Sander's part, but I honestly think Sander is doing it for the good of the country and not because he has empowerment issues.

This has become a tedious mess, the whole of it. My nerves are shot after a hair raising car chase (and resulting crash) through the city. Some of these bruises are going to be here a while.

To make matters worse, I'm sick to my stomach again. Who can blame me? Any time there are eight or nine guns pointed straight at my head, I think I'm entitled to a little nausea. As well, the idea of being carted off to become a whore in a human trafficking ring does not exactly sit well.

Aksel is a ruthless man. More ruthless than I realized. Death is nothing to him. Life means little unless he gets what he wants out of the deal. I don't know how Sander and Mattias are going to come out on top of this one, and while I have faith, and I think they are clever, wily men, the unstable actions of the King leave me worried.

Tomorrow we leave for Latvala with a plan in place, though the more I think about it the more upset my stomach becomes. Everything hinges on too many *delicate details. Mattias and Sander have arranged to hide me in Latvala, not far from the main castle so that they have easy access to me in case things go south with Sander and Aksel's meeting. I am okay with that. Staying close to Sander at this point is important to me.*

I think my journal venting is over now. I wish I could say it brought me some peace.

Chey

Chey stared at the paper in her lap with a pensive frown. Her chicken scratch was barely legible as handwriting, the slant sharper than usual and angled funny due to lack of light and carelessness.

She didn't care. It wasn't like she was keeping it anyway. Setting the pen aside on the nightstand, she flipped the paper over—there was a local club advertisement on the back—and proceeded to wad it into a ball. Sliding out of bed, careful not to wake Sander, she approached the fire place and tossed the ball in over the grate. Although the fire had eased to smaller flames and crackling embers, the paper caught and burned within seconds. She wasn't sure whether she felt relieved or dismayed it was gone.

"What are you doing?" Sander asked. His voice was low and raspy with the affects of slumber.

"Just getting warm. I'm coming back to bed," she said, turning away from the fireplace. Thanks to Mattias's quick thinking, both she and Sander had pajamas to wear for the evening. He'd grabbed not just their personal belongings from the other suite, but also some of their clothes.

The high slit, slinky red dress she'd been wearing dangled from a hanger over the door, replaced by yoga pants of gray and a faded pink shirt. Her tennis shoes sat on the floor at the edge of the bed in case there was a need for a hasty departure.

Climbing between the sheets, she shuffled down until she was prone, one hand sliding over Sander's back. He turned his head on the pillow to face her, golden hair tousled around his head.

"Can't sleep?" he asked.

"Not really."

"Are you hurting?"

"A little. It's nothing serious though. I

got lucky in the accident." Chey stroked her fingers lightly over his muscles. Reassuring herself, perhaps, or reassuring him she was all right.

"You sure there's nothing else?" He propped his head up an inch and peered at her in the gloom.

"I'm sure." She didn't need to tell him about the nausea and her incessant worries over the King. One would resolve the other anyway, and that couldn't happen until Sander had his meeting with Aksel.

Reaching out with one arm, Sander pulled her closer to his body. He turned onto his side, bringing her flush against him. "I know it's a lot to deal with. A lot to handle. Once we subdue the King, I think things will settle. It won't be like this every day."

"I hope you're right." That was as close as she felt comfortable confessing what was truly on her mind. Chey pressed her cheek against his chest, listening for his heartbeat. His skin was warm, scented lightly with musk, and comfortable.

"Life as a Queen will never be like your life in Seattle. Once you gain the title alongside me, then we'll have to worry about random assassination attempts, political tricks and traps and dealing with the weight being a ruler brings. It will settle to a point, but you'll never again walk the streets with immunity or without being recognized. Even I won't be able to go among the people without protection after I become King. It's just too risky. Doing so is to invite some foreign crazy across the border for a kidnapping and extortion event. It sucks, that part, I admit," he said.

Chey thought about it. About forever being a target, never knowing from which side someone might strike. Some citizens might hate her for being American, or because of the color of her eyes. One could never tell what might set another off. She discovered that she wasn't put off by the thought of constantly watching her back. These last weeks, she'd done so anyway. It was becoming ingrained to pay closer attention to sounds and shuffles and smells and gut instinct. She was learning, slowly, to absorb the shocks and to be resilient in the face of fear. Striking back at the driver of the van earlier had come naturally in her unwillingness to be their helpless victim.

Maybe, she thought, it would do her good to attend self defense classes. The idea intrigued her.

"I think I'm learning with each thing that happens," she whispered. "To deal with it better, to cope faster, to not dwell too long after a catastrophe. I *will* feel better to know that someone isn't actively after us, like the King. This is still a *right now* situation, whereas taking up the titles will be a more long term, watch over our shoulder deal than a constant, immediate threat."

"I'm glad you feel that way. Eventually it will come as second nature to you. The longer you're Queen, the easier it will become." He kissed the crown of her head. "You should try and get at least a little sleep. It'll be dawn soon and time to leave."

"I'll try." It was the best Chey could offer. She closed her eyes and tried to relax.

Sander skimmed his hands up and down her back, soothing circle shapes paired with brief massages near her shoulders.

It felt so good, Chey stopped thinking altogether and just enjoyed his touch.

Before long, she was asleep.

. . .

Disembarking in Latvala was a clandestine affair; Sander cut away for one of two helicopters sitting on different helipads, glancing back at Chey while she headed for the other with Mattias.

She smiled, a quick flash, before allowing Mattias to hand her into the back seat of the aircraft. She buckled in while he did the same, glancing out the window as the helicopter carrying Sander lifted off and swung away over the landscape. Although there was a heavy amount of snow on the ground, the skies were currently clear, the sun shining down on a cold Latvala day.

Seconds after the first, their helicopter took flight. Mattias had explained the details several times on the way home from Dubai and Chey went over it all in her mind as the craft sped them toward their destination. Below, patches of forest stretched for miles, breaking open onto farmland swathed in white. A river cut through the terrain, snaking away into the distance.

Chey knew, after looking at a map, where her general location would be. Sander had explained the importance of direction in case she should find herself on the run. Doubtful, he'd said, but not impossible. So she had memorized, to the best of her ability, certain landmarks to use should it become necessary.

Not many minutes later, the helicopter slowed and positioned itself to lower to the ground. There was no helipad here, no cement square with guiding lights or lines. The pilot set them down on a stretch of shale cleared of snow from the rotor blades.

"Now remember, you only have the phone I gave you," Mattias said, raising his voice. "It rings my number and no other. If I don't answer, it's because I can't. If it's an emergency, leave a text. If you don't have time, keep the phone on you. I'll have it—and your whereabouts—traced. All right?"

"I got it. I know what to do," she replied, picking up the straps of the lone duffel bag Mattias allowed her to keep. Citing the need to travel light, Mattias had suggested she pack the bare essentials.

"Good. You know the way from here?" he asked, using a finger to point away toward the woods.

"I know right where to go." She touched his arm, then climbed down after the guard in the front passenger seat opened her door. Chey waved to Mattias, ducking instinctively while she ran out from under the whirl of the blades. At the edge of the trees, which lashed back and forth from the choppy wind, she lifted a hand to Mattias and disappeared into the forest. Before she was ten feet under the canopy, the helicopter lifted off.

Breathing the scent of pine, fresh snow and other woodsy scents, Chey centered herself and stayed on her path. There was no trail among the sparsely spaced tree trunks, but she didn't need one. The homestead she sought should be no more than fifty yards ahead in a clearing marked by an old fashioned windmill.

Mattias had given her a key with the information that the vacant home sat on Royally protected land and would not be disrupted by random passersby. Never mind it sat by itself off the beaten path. It had several bedrooms, working plumbing and the shelves had been stocked by Mattias himself. She was to wait there while Sander had his meeting, safe from prying eyes and attention, until Mattias sent her a text.

Breaking into the clearing, Chey spotted the home as well as the windmill.

A path for cars leading to and away sat on the other side, snaking toward a road or intersecting path not visible with the naked eye. It was at least a half mile from any main thoroughfare. A newer dwelling, with a peaked roof and broad porch, the home itself was of a cabin-like design. It reminded her of what she might find on a trip into the mountains or a luxury ski resort.

Chey approached, digging out the key, attentive to the woods around her. She wouldn't grow lax simply because she *thought* she was safe. Nothing moved, nothing seemed out of place.

At the door, she used the key and entered with no trouble. Inside, the house proved as cozy as the exterior suggested. It was not as affluently appointed as Sander's cabin, though the furniture was well made and looked relatively new. She locked the door behind her, set the bag on the floor, and pulled out a handgun that Mattias provided her with. His short instructional had been thorough enough to see her through this venture.

Checking the safety, she prowled the house, inspecting each bedroom, bathroom and closet. The back door was bolted from the inside and none of the windows were broken. All good signs. Ones Sander and Mattias insisted she check first thing. After examining the pantry in the kitchen, Chey pulled the blinds on all the windows and turned on the heat. She forewent any lights, seeing that it was daytime and she didn't immediately need them. Breathing easier, she set the gun on the kitchen table and got a bottle of water from the fridge.

Her stomach wouldn't handle food right now. Drinking half the contents of the bottle, she set it on the table next to the gun and fished her phone from her pocket. It was a simple black device that had no new messages waiting. Now that she was in the house, she turned the volume up just loud enough to hear.

She wondered how Sander was doing, and whether the meeting was going as planned.

Chapter Six

Sander entered Ahtissari castle stone faced and resolute. He said nothing to any of the guards, even the ones who greeted him with subtle nods. After buttoning up his suit coat, he checked the knot on his ice blue tie and headed up the stairs to the third floor. His shoes made quiet clicks over the polished marble on approach to the private parlor where the King would be waiting.

Striding through the open door, Sander came to a halt.

Instead of the King sitting in his throne-like chair, waiting, Sander found a suited security member standing next to the seat.

"The King?" Sander asked, cutting to the chase. He subdued an initial flash of annoyance at the delay, surely planned by Aksel to get under his skin.

"Apologies, Prince Dare. The King has asked for a morning meeting. He took ill an hour before your arrival."

Sander's lips thinned. Ill his ass. He about faced, stalked out of the parlor, and marched down the hallway toward the private Royal rooms. Two guards stood on either side of the King's chamber doors. Both men stepped away from the wall and blocked Sander's path.

"The King is currently--"

"Step aside, or I'll *move* you aside," Sander said, giving each guard a threatening glance.

One guard set a hand out, jarring Sander's shoulder. The other reached for a weapon.

Sander cocked his shoulder back out of reach and brought a foot up to shatter the knee of one guard, while snaring the wrist of the other. Wails of pain filled the hallway. He brought a hand down hard enough to crack bone across the second guard's arm; the gun flew to the floor and skittered away. Shoving the guard from the door, ignoring the shouts of agony, Sander grabbed the handle and entered.

The private domain of the King was a glut of luxury. Gold trimmed every piece of furniture, veined the floors and accented paintings on the walls. The chamber was the size of a small house, with other rooms and halls branching off the main area.

Aksel swiveled around from his spot near the roaring fireplace, frowning. He yanked the pipe out of his mouth.

"You look recovered enough to receive me, *father,*" Sander said with a mocking bow. He halted near the edge of a divan as the guards, groaning in the hallway, called for back up. "Worthless are the guards who can't protect you from one simple man."

"I don't figure they expected my own son to strike them. How dare you, Sander. But that is your preference of late, is it not? To defy me?" Aksel said. He tapped out the contents of the pipe and set it on the fireplace mantel.

"Save your speech and let's get down to business. We both know that's why I'm here." Sander crossed his arms over his chest. He had little patience for games. It took a wealth of willpower not to rain hell down upon Aksel's head for what he'd done in Dubai.

In his own domain, the King wore black slacks and a white shirt with the first three buttons undone. He appeared to be in between meetings, paring the suit down to its thinnest layers until he was required to present himself once more.

As other guards and military arrived, Aksel held up a staying hand. "Retreat until I call for you," he said.

The security members, wary and alert, receded into the hallway.

Sander never glanced back. He continued to regard the King with a confrontational air. "Well?"

"I have had the papers drawn up for your official exile," the King said. "More details than that I am not prepared to give you. As my man said...I am under the weather and will go through everything with you in the morning."

"The hell you will," Sander snarled. "You'll do it *now--*"

"Do not take that tone with me!" Aksel shouted. "Who do you think you are, ordering your King to do *anything,* boy?"

Sander laughed. A derisive sound lacking respect for authority. He glared into his father's eyes. "The man who will snitch that throne right out from under you, my liege."

Aksel strode around the divan and came toe to toe with Sander. "Those are a traitor's words, punishable by death. You're very lucky you are of my blood. It will see you into exile instead."

Sander, with a few inch height

advantage, closed the distance by half. Close enough to see the striations in Aksel's eyes. "So I've heard. But I've seen the blood on your hands, I *know* some of the secrets you keep. What a pity if those nasty things ever came to light."

Aksel's face paled. His lips pinched into a furious frown. *"How dare you speak to me of--"*

"Murder?" Sander interrupted, whispering. He glanced with ill disguised discretion toward the open doorway, then back. "Should I say it a little louder, father? Or do you have no care for your reputation? Perhaps you've gloated about the little maid whose life you took, hm?"

Aksel struck Sander hard across the face with the back of his hand. The heavy, ornate ring adorning his finger left a small gash on Sander's jaw.

Head snapping to the side, Sander accepted the blow and cut a knowing look at the King. "I was what? Thirteen? A young age to come across my father on the back end of a tryst with a butcher knife in one hand and a dead maid in the other. But I've kept your secret—that one at least—under wraps all these years. So don't stand on ceremony with *me,* acting as if you're a paragon of virtue."

Breathing hard, Aksel narrowed his eyes. "No one would ever believe you."

"No? But I know where you buried her. We'll just dig up her bones."

Aksel threw his head back and laughed. Full of apparent mirth, he turned away from Sander. One finger lifted to tick-tock in an *I got you* fashion. "Oh, but no. No, you won't. Because I moved her. *Scattered* her."

Sander's nostrils flared. The place where his morals lived protested violently at the grisly image Aksel's descriptive word sent through his mind. "I should have known."

"Yes, maybe you should have." Aksel paused to pour himself a drink from a side bar. His hands shook. A splash of hard liquor landed on the counter before it hit the glass.

"I still remember her name. I remember too many details to discount. Either way, you're guilty and we both know it. That's just one of several sins, should I go on?" Sander only paused for a moment, then he continued. "The point is—you are not sending me anywhere. Not off the throne, and not into exile. I won't allow it."

"You remember her name?" Aksel said, ignoring the rest.

"Yes. Siona. She was one of the nicer women in the employ of the Royals at that time."

Aksel lifted the glass and took a stiff drink. And another. After, he chuckled. It turned into a laugh. The kind of laugh that tilted his head back and made his stomach quiver with the force of his mirth.

"What could possibly be funny?" Sander asked, frowning. Not for the first time, he wondered just how unhinged his father really was. He had no doubt of his father's steady decline, though he suspected Aksel hid the truth of it from everyone. Even his wife.

"How lucky you are that we won't be burying you beside her. She must be resting in twelve different spots, at least." Aksel laughed again.

Sander stared hard at the King. Aksel's sanity, at this point, was in serious question. Perhaps the idea of ripping the King off his throne before his time had more merit than Sander realized. "And why would you do that? Because I am the only witness?"

"Because, *you fool.* She was your mother."

. . .

Sander stared at the King with a blatant look of suspicious disbelief. The implications, if true, could be potentially devastating. "You're lying."

"No, *son,* I'm not. Siona was your mother. It wasn't a tryst we were having when you found us in the dungeon, it was an argument. She wanted you to know who she was, promised to keep it a secret if she could just have a mother and son relationship with you. Of course, that would never work. Secrets like that get out when they're in the wrong hands, and it wasn't a secret we could take any chances with." Aksel finished off the entire glass and set the tumbler down with a sharp crack against the table. He used the side of his wrist on his mouth, smearing away stray droplets.

"I don't believe you. The Queen--"

"Helina had no choice. She went along, faking the pregnancy and birth. Only a very select few knew of the ruse. Everyone else in the castle believed it to be true. When Siona went into labor with you, Helina went into fake labor and shut herself away for the better part of a day until the baby could be smuggled in through the hidden passageways to her room." Aksel straightened his shoulders and faced Sander, chin lifted as if in defense of his actions. As if, somehow, he believed he had done Sander a great honor by not proclaiming him a bastard.

"I've seen my birth certificate," Sander said with a snarl. "It was signed by witnesses that I am the rightful heir. The firstborn."

Aksel laughed. Another of those unnatural laughs born of a man forced to keep secrets that weighed down his soul. "Bought off. The 'official' witness, the head nurse who supposedly birthed you. She and a second nurse knew, and both readily agreed to keep their mouths shut."

"I want proof. I want a meeting with each one--"

"They're dead," Aksel said, using a tone that chided Sander for not knowing better.

"Dead?" Sander, hands clenched into fists at his sides, stared at Aksel with renewed disgust. "You again."

"No, they were made to look as accidents—have you not been paying *any* attention, or were the snow jobs just that good?" He chuckled, a mocking sound of bemusement.

"A boy—for I must have been that when you decided to take their lives—would hardly suspect such games," Sander growled. He thrust a hand through his hair and paced through the room. Agitated. He didn't know whether to believe Aksel or not. There was a certain dark truth to his father's confession, blithely cavalier, that made his gut instinct sit up and take notice. On the other hand, Aksel was an accomplished liar, both by habit and necessity.

"Helina will tell you. Or will you not believe her, either?" Aksel paused, then rocked back and forth on his shoes. "What will be interesting now, is whether you keep this information to yourself or whether, in the *best interest of the country,* you go into exile and allow the proper heir to take over."

Sander shot a look of utter loathing across the room. Thirty-three years he had been groomed for this role. To become King. Having his whole existence and the reason for it brought into question after all this time made him sick. Would he believe Helina? He didn't know.

Aksel faced down the stare, finding a calmer facade to present at this stage of the conversation. "That is what you threatened me with, yes? To yank the throne out from under me for the good of Latvala? Hm? So now what, Sander? To continue on makes you look like a hypocrite for dumping Valentina because in taking the throne yourself, you are doing exactly what you accused her of. Putting a bastard in to rule."

"I am still *your* son," Sander shouted. "The Ahtissari name belongs to me."

"It just makes you half a bastard." Aksel gestured toward the side table. "Drink? You're looking a little peaked."

Sander spat an ugly curse that wrought a laugh out of Aksel.

"It sucks to have the tables turned, does it not?" Aksel asked.

Sander paced, hands flexing through a series of clenches. He argued with himself, pitting what his heart told him to do against the reality that Aksel might be telling the truth. How convenient the timing was, though. That Aksel could yank his bloodline right out from underneath him when it suited him most. Finally, he prowled to a stop near the fireplace and faced the King. "I'll need more than your word. More than Helina's. At this point, to prevent yourself from being ousted off the throne, I wouldn't put anything past you."

"There is no one left! Don't you see? We have covered our—and your—tracks well!" Aksel turned to pour himself another drink. His hand shook less than last time.

"Convenient," Sander said. "Too convenient. I will not be going into exile--"

"Yes, you will," Aksel said. His voice lowered, grew soft. Sure. He took a drink.

"You would have to announce this to all of Latvala to strip me of the title of Heir, and I know you won't do that," Sander said. A vein stood out in his forehead.

"I won't have to. Come back tomorrow. I believe Helina may have something that will prove to you once and for all that you are Siona's son. If her confession is not enough, which it should be, then I think there is one other way." Aksel stared toward the windows, mouth quirked into a pensive curve.

"What way is that?" Sander asked.

"Tomorrow."

"*Now.*"

Aksel just smiled and lifted the

tumbler for another sip. He hissed on the exhale.

"You have tried to stall this meeting since I got here. Now you want me to come back tomorrow. Why?" Sander said with a sudden frown.

"As I said. I am feeling ill today." Aksel didn't meet Sander's eyes. Didn't glance away from the window.

"Lies." Sander turned on a heel and stalked out the door.

He didn't look back.

Chapter Seven

Chey waited until the gloom inside the cabin grew too dark to see before she risked turning a light on. The remains of a bowl of soup sat on the counter along with an empty bottle of water, proof she had at least attempted to eat something for dinner. Washing the bowl, the small pot and the spoon, she set the dishes to drain, dried her hands, and fished out another bottle of water from the fridge.

She wondered where Mattias and Sander were. She knew both men would be back here at some point this evening, and that they planned to take every precaution to throw any followers off their tail. Chey trusted them both not to lead anyone back here.

Just as she approached a bookcase along one wall, she heard the door knob rattle. Crossing back to the kitchen, she slid the gun off the table and thumbed off the safety. Facing the door, she watched it swing open, mentally preparing herself to shoot-to-maim should someone enter who was not Mattias or Sander.

Mattias came first, followed by Sander. "It's us," Mattias said when he saw her standing ready.

"I was beginning to think you wouldn't show tonight," Chey admitted. She put the safety on and set the gun on the table. Right away she knew something was wrong. Sander's expression was a hard mask, lips pressed tight, a muscle flexing in his jaw.

Mattias closed the door behind his brother and followed Sander into the living area. "We took special care to make sure no one followed us here. One of my meetings ran over as well."

"What's wrong?" Chey said after Mattias finished explaining.

Mattias perched on the arm of a sofa while Sander paced, hands on his hips, glaring at the floor.

"I got here just as he did," Mattias said. "What happened, brother?"

"You were right. He's got something else up his sleeve. If he's telling the truth, then he has put me in a position I cannot wrap my mind around." Sander spat a curse and thrust a hand through his hair.

"Is it as bad as all that?" Mattias

asked, frowning.

Chey stood near Mattias, arms crossed over her chest. She regarded Sander with growing concern. She'd never seen him so agitated. A vein pulsed in his forehead, and every so often, he exhaled a sharp breath as if he was struggling to calm himself.

"It's worse," Sander said. He scratched the short edge of his nails along a subtle layer of whiskers starting to fill in along his jaw. "He is attempting to get me to exile myself on the grounds that I am not rightful heir to the throne. Helina, if he is to be believed, is not my mother."

"*What?*" Mattias shoved up out of his casual lean.

"Sander, why would he say such a thing?" Chey frowned, not understanding what was going on.

Sander looked at Chey, then met Mattias's eyes. "I too have secrets. When I was around thirteen years of age, I caught father in what I thought was a tryst with a maid. The back end of a tryst, I should say, because when I actually discovered them he had just murdered her."

Mattias burst into their mother tongue, pacing away from the couch closer to

Sander. He switched to English as if he realized Chey wouldn't be able to understand. "You actually *saw* him with a weapon? How can you be sure it was him and not someone else?"

Chey's stomach flipped over. She covered her lips with her fingertips, stunned into silence.

"There was no one else in the dungeon with them and he was still holding the bloody knife," Sander said. He raked a hand back through his hair again, clearly unsettled. "Aksel said they weren't having a tryst, they were having an argument. She wanted permission to admit to me who she really was. Aksel disagreed."

"Wait—that woman, the one he killed, was your mother?" Chey asked on the back of a gasp.

"Impossible," Mattias said with an edge to his voice. "He's lying."

"That's what he wants me to believe," Sander said, meeting Chey's eyes before looking at Mattias. "I said the same thing. He's lying. The King insists it's as he says. I threatened to find her grave, except he says he *scattered* her around."

Chey groaned at the implication. *Scattered her around.* Her body parts? It had to be. Or perhaps he dug her bones up and moved them all about later on. Sick at heart, disturbed in ways she couldn't believe, Chey curled her fingers near her mouth and fought to refocus on the conversation.

"What about the people who birthed you? There will be witnesses," Mattias said.

"Dead," Sander replied with a specific look at his brother.

Mattias looked disgusted. "So he's attempting to use this to force you into exile. Yet I would wager ten years of my life that he will not publicly announce this. He's going to try and twist your arm and make you do it yourself, using whatever excuse you come up with."

"Exactly. He says I'll do it because otherwise, I'm a hypocrite for dumping Valentina for attempting to put a bastard on the throne—which is what he says I am."

Mattias's expression took a grim turn. "Technically, the title would go to *their* firstborn—his and Helina's—instead of his child with another woman. Except they publicly accepted you as their own all this time, and to renege on that now will cast their trust into a shadow they might not be able to shed later."

"I still think it's an excuse to get me to do what they want, without either of them suffering backlash for it," Sander added.

Chey glanced between brothers as they hashed it out, tension making her shoulders tight. For herself, she didn't care if Sander took the throne. It would save her thoughts of becoming Queen—a title she did not feel suited for anyway—and allow them to have something of a more normal life together. Yet Sander being forced to exile himself against his will rubbed her the wrong way, and seeing him so agitated tugged at her compassion.

He was a good man, who cared about Latvala and its people. Invested mind, body and soul, no one would rule with as much passion as Sander. In Chey's eyes, he deserved to ascend the throne, even if Helina wasn't his mother. But she'd learned, if nothing else, that Royalty had their traditions and rules, and should they chose to exercise their right to enforce Sander's status as a bastard, they might keep him off the throne after all. Sander, she thought, would not find an easy answer here.

"I'm with you. I would need some other kind of proof. After all this, it *does* seem far too convenient as far as timing is concerned," Mattias said.

"He says I'm to return tomorrow. That Helina, along with a confession, might have something that will convince me. No matter how I cajoled, he would not be swayed into showing or telling me today." Sander slouched his elbows back onto the fireplace mantle, a recline that should have made him looked relaxed. He appeared restless instead.

"What could she possibly have that would sway you?" Chey asked. She scoured her mind for ideas over what it might be.

"I can't think of anything," Sander admitted.

Mattias remained silent, gaze cast to the floor in thought.

"What I want to know more than that, even, is *why* Helina agreed to accept me as her own. If this is all true, I would have imagined her to simply shun the maid and the baby, turning them both away from castle life to live elsewhere. Why did she choose to raise me as her own?" Sander asked.

"That, brother, might be the million dollar question." Mattias lifted his gaze and stared at Sander.

"I have to agree. She doesn't seem the type to graciously accept her husband's child from another woman unless she was forced to," Chey said.

"Aksel specifically stated that Helina 'had no choice'," Sander added. "Under what circumstances would that be, I wonder?"

"Unless it's all the lie we believe it to be, and she wasn't forced to do anything. She really is your mother, and all they want is an easy fix for your exile. He's pulling out all the stops," Mattias said.

"He's also stalling. I can't figure out why. He tried to refuse to see me when I arrived, claiming illness. He was not ill," Sander said with a snort.

"Now he wants you to come back tomorrow," Mattias said in agreement. "Yes, he's stalling. It bothers me."

"Yeah, it bothers me, too. He's up to something." Sander shoved off the mantle and went to pour himself a drink. The crystal decanter clinked against a tumbler as amber liquor sloshed inside.

"All we can do is wait until tomorrow. I will endeavor to be there for this little meeting, playing up my part if I can," Mattias said. He stepped toward the door. "For now, I will return to the castle and sleep there. Perhaps he will summon me tonight if he drinks enough or decides he wants to speak with me about my 'interception' of his plans in Dubai."

"Good. If you find anything of immediate importance, make sure you get word here," Sander said. He lifted his glass to Mattias in silent salute.

"Be careful, Mattias," Chey said, mind spinning with implications and conjecture. Already she felt a headache coming on.

"You two as well. I believe you're safe enough here, but keep an eye and ear open, just in case." Mattias bade them goodbye and let himself out through the front door.

Chey followed behind and snapped the bolt into place. Turning her spine to the wood, she leaned against it and regarded Sander across the room.

He finished off a first glass, watching her eyes, then poured a second. After a moment, he said, "If Helina *does* produce irrefutable proof, what then? Do I become the hypocrite he suggests if I fight for the throne, or do I bow out and let Mattias take over?"

"I don't know, Sander. I just don't know."

. . .

The complications of the situation seemed insurmountable to Chey. Every twist became more gut wrenching than the last. She crossed the room after Sander downed his third drink, took him by the hand, and led him through the home to one of the bedrooms. She paused to douse the only burning light and to bring the gun along with them.

Sander put up no resistance or argument. He paced at her flank, silent, and allowed her to begin stripping his suit and shirt from his shoulders.

Chey let her gentle touches and the whisper of her fingertips do the talking right now. Too paranoid to strip him totally naked, she only removed the clothes on his torso, leaving the pants intact. If they needed to move fast, she wanted them both to be at least half dressed.

Leading him to the bed in the dim room, she guided him to lay on his stomach. He did so with a grunt, sinking his considerable bulk into the mattress. Chey set the gun on the nightstand and straddled his hips. She could see the knots of tension across his shoulders, along with angry red lines running parallel under his skin.

He stretched his arms above his head, giving her unimpeded access to his entire back. Chey set her palms right on either side of his spine and began massaging languid circles over the muscles, attempting to ease some of his discomfort. She could tell he was tight and taut, unable to really relax. Even after three drinks. Allowing the silence to stretch, she worked each section until she felt a little give in the sinew. Up near his nape, she leaned down to press several kisses at his hairline. Rewarded with a shiver from him for her effort, she repeated the gesture then sat up once more and continued kneading.

She didn't kid herself for a second into thinking he would get any decent rest tonight. Chey wouldn't be getting any either. Not even with the possibility of an unwanted visitor so distant.

But they could rest, and gather strength for tomorrow.

She sucked in a surprised gasp when, without warning, he twisted just enough to reach back and snag her off his body. He brought her down to the bed with him.

She landed on her back at his side, hair whipping out across the pillows.

"Thank you," he said, words muffled.

"I thought it was the least I could do. Besides, I haven't seen you naked yet today, and I have a quota, sir, that must be met." She tried for a little levity to combat the dark situation they found themselves in.

"I knew it was all about the body," he rumbled.

"Exactly."

"When do I get to see *you* naked? I think it's only fair."

Chey could hear the disturbance in his voice. Despite the easy banter, Sander was not comforted or distracted by it. Dropping the subject, she said instead, "I'm sorry you're dealing with all this. Just know that no matter what happens, I'll be right here at your side."

"I'm glad to hear that," he said, obviously pleased at the topic change.

Chey skimmed her fingers over the arm he laid across her ribs. "Your title, or lack of one, doesn't change a thing about what I feel for you."

"Good. For some women, it would make all the difference."

"I'm not most women, but then you

knew that when you met me. I suspect it's why we're still together." She reached over to brush a few strands of hair away from his face.

"One of many reasons," he assured her. One vivid blue eye came into view. He stared at her, lids low. "There could be a lot of scandal involved with this by the time it's over."

"You make that sound like a warning."

"It is, to an extent. I just don't want you burned so bad by it all that you decide it's not worth it."

"You'll always be worth it," she whispered. "Sometimes it takes me a little while to adjust to something new or shocking, but I *do* adjust. We'll get through whatever comes our way. I have faith we're strong enough together to deal with the fallout."

He grunted. Finally, after ten minutes of comfortable silence, he said, "You should get some sleep. I'll stay awake, keep watch of things."

"I think I'll be able to rest if we take turns. I won't do it unless you let me return the favor later. You need to recuperate so you're on top of your game tomorrow," she said.

"We can trade off keeping watch," he

agreed.

"All right. Are you feeling okay though? I've never seen you so openly distressed," she mentioned, wanting to give him the opportunity to speak about the things that troubled him.

"I'll get through. I'm very disturbed however by the thought that the throne is not mine by birthright. Even the idea, the slightest chance, really puts a burden on whatever choice I make from here." His gaze went distant.

"It's probably exactly what he wants. To make you doubt and to make you suffer," she said.

"I don't like the idea of becoming a hypocrite. Yet the desire to fight for the title of Heir is strong. It's what I've grown up my entire life believing. That it was mine by right."

Chey smoothed her fingers over the skin of his shoulder. She could hear the conflict in his voice, see it on his expression. It made her furious at Aksel for placing doubt in Sander's mind. The King was getting his way again, using nefarious means, and it galled her that Aksel might get through all this unscathed.

"We'll concentrate on believing that

he's lying and deal with the consequences only after irrefutable proof has been found to back his claim. Okay? I know that doesn't ease your concern or make you think about it any less, but the likelihood that he's being untruthful is strong." Chey, like Mattias and Sander, thought the King was using the situation to his advantage.

"Yeah. You go ahead, take first shift for sleep." He met her eyes, indicating that he was ready for a stretch of quiet to think about the shift his life might take on a more private level.

"Wake me in a few hours," Chey said, resting her hand on his back. She closed her eyes and tried to blank her mind. She wouldn't get any sleep at all if she allowed herself to fret and worry about things she could not change. Tomorrow was soon enough to begin the process again.

Chapter Eight

They took turns sleeping and standing watch through the night. By dawn, they had showered, eaten a quick breakfast of bagels and cream cheese, and were ready to say their goodbyes. Sander, dressed in a new suit provided in one of the bedroom closets, hadn't bothered to tie his hair back or shave. The rasp of his whiskers reddened Chey's skin when he caught her face between his hands and planted a kiss square on her mouth.

"I'll be back whenever we're through and I have time to make sure I lose any tail he might put on me," Sander said. He kissed her once more and released.

Chey stared up into his eyes, fingers smoothing the lapels of the steel gray suit coat. "I'll be waiting."

He released her, walked to the kitchen, and opened one of the cupboards. "Mattias left some emergency rations here. Make sure you pack a few things in your duffel after I leave, along with a few bottles of water, all right? That way, just in case, you won't be caught outdoors with nothing." He grabbed a box of trail and protein bars from the shelf and set it on the kitchen counter.

"I saw those last night. I'll make sure I stock up," she promised. That particular task had already gone on her To Do List for this morning. Chey, in the same jeans as yesterday with a new, plain hoodie of beige, snagged her duffel off the floor and set it on the kitchen table.

"Good. If, *if* Mattias calls and tells you to vacate, that phone he gave you has a GPS system in it, so at least you'll know whether you're going North, South, East or West. If you go South, you'll eventually hit the shore, which means you'll run into civilization faster." Sander took out a few bottles of water from the cupboard as well and set those next to the trail bars.

Any other time, Chey might have smiled over his mother hen tendencies where she was concerned. She knew he had a load of things on his mind, yet there he was, making sure she had what she needed in case of an emergency. Leaving nothing to chance.

"I'll remember. I looked at the phone last night while I was waiting and got familiar with everything it can do," she admitted.

"Did you check the weather, too?" he asked, coming around the counter. His features were unusually stoic and grim. "It looks like a storm might move in this morning. Make sure you have a coat with you at all times. That hoodie won't protect you against fifteen degree temperatures."

"It's right by the door," she said. "Mattias left several coats in the closets here as well. I have my choice."

He glanced at the rack by the wall, then down into her eyes. "Excellent. It's about time for me to go. I need a couple hours to wind my way from here back to the castle, come in at a deceiving angle."

"I know. Good luck with your meeting today. I hope it turns out like we think it will," Chey said. The best outcome would be that Sander and Mattias caught the King in a lie.

"Mm." Sander hummed a pensive note while he drew on a heavier overcoat. His fingers made quick work of the buttons. He watched her the whole time, expression sober and serious. Finally, he stepped closer. Instead of touch her, he maintained eye contact for several long minutes.

Chey, refusing to break the tether of their gaze, fought down goosebumps and a stray shudder. Without putting a finger on her, Sander had the ability to affect her on the deepest levels.

He pivoted away and stalked to the door. After a quick glance back, he unlatched the bolts and stepped out into the day. The sun hadn't quite risen above the horizon yet, leaving many pewter shadows clinging around the cabin and the trees.

Chey followed, closing the door in his wake. She engaged the bolt and the regular lock. Moving to the window, she watched him walk across the snowy clearing toward the path that cut through the forest. He must have parked somewhere between the house and the nearest road. She watched until the foliage swallowed him whole.

Stepping away from the window, Chey moved back through the room to the table, checked the gun, then began packing a few trail bars and water bottles into the duffel bag. There were small, single serving packets of beef and turkey jerky, also, as well as a few packs of carob, chocolate, peanut butter and almond mixes. She didn't overload the bag to the point it was too heavy to carry, or would slow her down too much if she had to depart the house. She didn't expect that to happen at all. Mattias or Sander would come for her, even if the King handed Sander news he didn't want to hear. They would see her safely to some other safe haven while the brothers sorted out what plans came next.

In the middle of nibbling on a pack of carob mix, her stomach somersaulted and protested the food. Nausea hit hard, sending her into the bathroom for fear she would puke all over the floor. Surprised at the sudden bout, she hung her head over the rim, scraping her hair back into a ponytail to keep it away from her face.

Fantastic. She wondered if she had caught the flu.

Now just wasn't the time.

Although it was a close call, she didn't end up vomiting. Relieved when the spasm passed, she exited the bathroom and put the rest of the mix away.

Perhaps hot tea would settle things down. She made a cup, glancing at the crack in the window curtains as dawn gave over to a new day. Yet the sky didn't lighten in the way it should have if the sun had access to the landscape.

The storm must be moving in, ready to dump another several inches of snow on Latvala. After packing her duffel and zipping it closed, Chey took her tea to the living room, sat on a sofa, and sipped the hot brew.

Waiting. Wondering. Hoping for the best.

. . .

Sander went twenty miles out of his way after leaving the house, snaking through backwoods terrain, narrow paths that barely cut through the foliage, and overland where there were no roads at all. The SUV handled the rough passage well, bouncing over snow slick rock, frozen mini-streams and hard packed dirt lanes that had not been plowed.

Once he hit a main artery, he picked up speed, glancing at the overcast sky. The snow would start any time. It mattered not at this point if anyone picked up his tail. They couldn't trace him back to his origin of departure, and that was all that mattered.

Still bothered about the obvious stalling tactic of the King, he drove toward the family seat with too many things on his mind.

First and foremost, the question of his birth. He would never admit to anyone just how sick it made him to think he might be stripped of his title. Years upon years he'd been groomed for this role, a role he accepted, embraced and looked forward to.

What would he do if Aksel proved he *was* the son of a maid? The idea of pressing forward, hiding his true heritage, lying to the people of Latvala was not a route he wanted to take. Aksel had hit the nail right on the head suggesting Sander would be a hypocrite to go forward and take the throne after dismissing Valentina for thinking to seat a bastard there.

That's what Sander would be. A King's illegitimate get.

His hands tightened on the wheel.

Did he owe it to the people to fight for the throne, or to back down and pass it off to the rightful heir? Mattias would be a good ruler. Sander had no doubt of his brother's ability. They thought a lot alike, would lead the country almost identically no matter which man ascended the seat of power.

Paavo would not. Paavo, despite his

good intentions, had already shown a propensity to be cowed by foreign pressure. He did not have the experience nor the backbone of Mattias or Sander. Paavo was also loyal to the King rather than his brothers's cause, in constant disagreement when matters of the state came up. He could not be allowed to take the throne regardless of the outcome.

Approaching the main gate, Sander passed through the check point and drove more slowly up the drive toward the broad steps at the entrance. Leaving the SUV behind for the attendants, he stalked through the doors and into the castle proper.

His boots thudded over the floor on his way up three flights of stairs toward the private parlor where the meeting was *supposed* to take place yesterday. Sander pressed his lips together as he strode past guards who inclined their heads in respect and welcome. Turning into the parlor, expecting to see a guard in the King's place with some excuse for a delay or another on his lips, he discovered instead that both his mother, father and Mattias were waiting for him.

Helina sat in her throne-like seat with a medium sized white envelope on her lap, a mug of steaming liquid in one hand. Dressed regally in elegant slacks of dove gray and a loose fitted shirt with an empire waist the color of peacock feathers, the Queen regarded Sander with slightly glassy eyes and a pensive expression.

She did not look especially happy to see him.

The King paced behind his throne chair, hands clasped at his back, a cape of red with a dalmation spotted mantle on his shoulders worn over a navy colored suit.

Sander might have snorted any other time at the blatant display of Aksel's title and power. The cape, he knew, was one more angle of psychological warfare.

Mattias, also in a suit, gave Sander a condescending smirk when he saw him. Playing his role to the hilt, he stood near the King's throne with his hands casually inserted into his pockets.

The King glanced from Sander to Mattias and back again.

Sander made sure to frown vaguely at his brother, as if disappointed to see him siding with the King. Appearances were everything, and Sander understood the importance of playing his part equally as well as Mattias. They needed to sell their discord with one another to pull this off.

"Right on time, I see," the King said. He gestured to a chair opposite his throne. "Have a seat. Helina? Would you mind informing Sander of his true heritage?"

Instead of taking a seat, Sander stood next to the chair, using his height advantage to look down at his mother.

Helina, not to be hurried, sipped from her cup before setting it down on a small table at her side. She folded her hands over the envelope on her lap.

"I am *not* your biological mother," she said straightaway. "I took you in as my own right after your birth and have not looked back since."

Sander stared at her, watching her eyes for clues of deception or lies. "You'll forgive me if I don't believe you, not after what you two have pulled recently to get me to hand over my title."

"Do you really think we would go to this extreme?" Helina asked. "I can assure you, neither Aksel nor I would do so. But since you seem to need more proof, I think I can provide it. Brace yourself, Sander."

"Yes, actually I do think you would go to this extreme. I think you would even go further," he replied.

Helina tisked and opened the envelope. She withdrew a photograph, glanced down at it, then up at Sander. Finally, she offered it over with a knowing look on her face.

Sander didn't immediately move to take it. This was a big step. Whatever he did or did not see in the photograph might change everything as he knew it. Reaching out, he took the photo from Helina and turned it around to view the image. What he saw there made his breath catch in his throat.

A petite blonde woman stared off into the distance with the castle as a backdrop. She was on the front steps, near the entrance, dressed in pants and a pale shirt that differed from the uniforms of today. Not by much, and he couldn't tell precisely what colors since the image was in black and white.

There was no escaping the similar shape of the cheeks and angle of the eyes. Sander looked so much like her that some sort of relation was simply undeniable. This woman, Siona, was a feminine version of him, built sturdy but fragile, with a sweet expression and a sharpness to her gaze that suggested not much got past her.

Sander's jaw tightened.

"See?" Aksel said. "I told you. Even you cannot dismiss the resemblance."

Sander said nothing. He stared at the photo as the implications washed over him like an incoming tsunami. The throne was not his to fight for. Not according to the laws in Latvala. Not according to the laws in many countries, for that matter, existing under a Monarchy. Bastards did not step up to rule before natural born, legitimate children, of which Aksel and Helina had three.

Of all the secrets he knew his father and Helina to keep, this was the most staggering on a personal level. Disappointment at never knowing—*really* knowing—his mother put a temporary ache in his gut.

"Well. Hasn't this just gotten even more interesting," Mattias said. He sounded smug, confident and all but gloated at the turn of events.

Sander snarled at him.

Aksel's mouth trembled with a smile he managed to curtail. "I did try to tell you yesterday, Sander. Now...what *will* you do? Save face in front of millions and retreat in exile, as I have commanded? Or expose your true heritage to the world in a vain attempt to keep what the council and legislators will not allow you to keep?"

Try as he might, Sander could not come up with a reasonable argument at the moment. He handed the photo back. Helina accepted it and slid it into the envelope. Instead of keeping it, she laid it on the chair Sander stood next to. Indicating it was his to have. He was sure this wasn't the only copy.

"I need time to come to a decision," Sander said. He didn't want to make a hasty move without thinking everything through.

"Unfortunately, time is not something I am willing to give you," Aksel said.

"Of course not," Sander said, a growl in his voice. "You want to force me to do it now so that you can start covering your tracks one way or another."

Aksel said nothing and did not deny it.

"What if I won't decide right this minute?" Sander said.

"Then I'll choose for you. Either way, when you depart this room, you *will* be headed for exile. Take the path of least resistance, that's my advice," Aksel said.

He paced behind Helina's chair, the edge of his cape dragging the ground.

"What I don't understand," Sander said, looking at Helina. "Is *why* you went along with it in the beginning. You are not that kind of compassionate woman, and I know as well as I'm standing here that your jealousy must have known no bounds. Yet you took me in—*why?*"

Confronted so bluntly, Helina at first did not reply. She glanced down at her hands.

Sander took that to mean he was right, that something else had driven her to accept her husband's bastard son. For the life of him, he could not figure out what it was. Perhaps Aksel had threatened her. Maybe, Sander thought, they had tried to have a child of their own and she hadn't then conceived, leaving Aksel panicked about an heir. It explained why he had wanted to keep Sander under his roof, why he pressed Helina into making Sander her own.

"She did it for me," Aksel said, stepping in. "Because I asked her to."

"Or forced her to?" Sander countered.

"*Asked* her to. You were a healthy, strong child and regardless of who your mother was, you are still of my blood. As

125

you so succinctly pointed out."

"Yes, I can see how much that means to you now," Sander retorted with a snort. Blood didn't mean so much to Aksel when he had three other heirs to fall back on.

Aksel lifted a shoulder in careless abandon. "Kings do what they must. I am protecting the throne, *our* bloodline, at all costs."

"Yet you were ready to seat me in your place, a bastard by all accounts," Sander said.

"No one would have ever known the difference. And let's face it, Sander. The people love you. It was a risk worth taking. Had you not been of my blood, then of course I would have never allowed Helina to keep you."

"It's a bitter pill, is it not, brother?" Mattias said. He rocked back and forth on the soles of his polished shoes, looking for all the world a man quite satisfied with the turn his life had just taken.

"Hush," Sander snarled at Mattias before looking back to the King. "I will not announce my exile to the people of this country. If you want me gone, then I'm gone, but I will not be going before the public on television."

"So be it," Aksel said. He raised his

voice. "Guards!"

Six security members swarmed into the room.

"Remove Sander from the palace. From Latvala altogether. Drop him in the Caribbean at the holding on Barbados. He is not to leave the island for the next two weeks while this sorts itself out. He is now in exile," Aksel said. He added, "Your phones and bank cards will not work once you leave here. The money in your accounts revert back to the crown upon exile, as I am sure you're aware. If you have money in offshore accounts, that's what you'll have to use if you need something while you're in Barbados. If you decide to immerse yourself into the dregs of 'normal' life, you are required to have security at all times. I won't be paying out ransom money because you were careless enough to get snatched off the street."

Sander cut a look over his shoulder at the approaching guards. "Do not touch me."

Several guards hesitated, glancing between Aksel and Sander.

"Also, send someone for the other little guest. Be rid of it once and for all," Aksel added. With a flick of his fingers, he set the guards into motion once more.

Sander, alarmed at what the latter order meant, suddenly felt sure Aksel had discovered Chey was in the country. That was why he'd been stalling all this time. Gathering intelligence, closing the noose around everyone's neck. Sander dared not look at Mattias to convey his thoughts. He knew Mattias would alert Chey at the soonest possible second.

Turning on a heel, Sander strode from the parlor without goodbyes or a reply to anyone. The sooner he was gone, the faster Mattias could warn Chey.

The guards flanked him in the hallway, providing tight security as he left the palace for the last time.

Chapter Nine

Chey studied the pictures and foreign words in a magazine she found near the couch. It kept her mind busy to try and learn a little of the Latvalan tongue in her down time. Just past noon, she saw flurries turn into all out snowfall, the flakes spiraling faster beyond the windows.

Rising from the chair, she walked over and peered out the crack in the curtains. The sky looked ominous and foreboding, promising to dump copious amounts of the white stuff before dark.

Just then, the phone went off. She retraced her steps back to the table and picked the cell up. A text message flashed across the screen.

Leave the house immediately.

Chey read it again. Alarm sent a rash of goosebumps down her arms under the protective hoodie and made the back of her head tingle. Shoving the phone into the front pocket of her jeans, she yanked the coat off the back of the chair, pushed her arms through the sleeves, and zipped it up the front. Swinging the strap of the duffel bag over her head, she let it settle at a slant across her body so her hands would be free. Picking up the gun next, she checked the safety and slid it into the pocket of the coat. Last, she pulled a beanie over her head for extra protection against the cold. Grabbing one extra bottle of water from the fridge, Chey turned off the lights and exited the house, closing the door behind her.

Wary of being caught, she jogged off the porch and into the snow, relieved that she could still make her way across the ground without too much struggle. A condition that wouldn't last with the speed the snow was falling.

Less than ten yards into the woods, she heard the distant sound of an engine. Startled, she gasped and increased her speed, brushing limbs out of her way with her hands. Mattias wouldn't have warned her to leave if he or Sander had been able to reach her first. The incoming vehicle must be guards or police or the military.

When she glanced behind to see if she could see the clearing she'd left minutes ago, Chey spied the tracks she was leaving behind in the snow.

It would lead them right to her.

Cursing under her breath, she lengthened her stride and started looking for a way to make the trail harder to follow. Several patches of ground under the heavier boughs of trees lacked any snow at all, and she headed into those small swathes of needles, dead leaves and other debris. She feigned leaving the patch in another direction, backtracked, then hopped to another bald spot, hoping anyone getting this far would think she diverted and went the other way.

It was the best she could do. Hurrying through the canopy, protected from the worst of the wind and snow at the moment, she made her way further from the cabin, listening all the while for sounds of someone in pursuit.

Please, please let them think someone drove me away.

Then, somewhere behind her, she thought she heard a shout. Pausing mid-step, she twisted to look behind her. Uncovering her ears from under the beanie, she listened again. Panic made her breath come in shallower puffs.

Another faint shout echoed through the woods.

They were coming. The men in pursuit had found her trail leading into the woods and they were not far behind.

Pulling the beanie down, she started ahead, once more attempting to lose the trail by passing through bald patches and back into the snow another direction. In the open areas where branches didn't overlap, snow fell harder. The wind kicked up, too, reducing visibility to less than thirty feet.

Well, if she couldn't see, then her pursuers couldn't see either. Maybe the new snowfall would obliterate her tracks, making it that much harder to find her.

In short order, Chey's world narrowed down to a distance of feet rather than yards. She darted this way and that, losing all sense of direction. Warning bells cautioned her not to keep going without checking the GPS on the phone. She might wind up in the endless forests and rough terrain Sander once told her about. In that vast wilderness, she would be exposed to wildlife as well as the weather, a combination that could prove deadly if she was out in it too long.

Pausing to get her breath, she leaned against a tree and pulled the phone out of her pocket. She pulled up the map utility and caught a glimpse that said she was headed East when suddenly the map flickered and froze. It appeared the GPS had ceased to work, probably because of the storm.

Chey hissed, turned the phone off to preserve the battery, and was about to lurch forward away from the tree when she heard the snap of twigs somewhere beyond the other side of the trunk. She couldn't decide how close or far it was. Either way she stilled, holding her breath, wondering how in the hell they had found her this fast.

Sliding the gun from her coat, she thumbed the safety off. Would she really be able to shoot? *It's your life or theirs. They won't hesitate to end you where you stand. Are you just going to allow them to without a fight?*

No, she decided. She wouldn't. Swinging out from behind the tree, bringing the gun up level to the ground, she sought a target. Twenty-odd feet away, a deer, as frozen with surprise as she, suddenly leaped high to the left, bounding through the underbrush in a panicked, zig-zag pattern.

A deer. It was just a deer. Chey searched the immediate area anyway, watching for shadows that were not a natural part of the terrain. She saw nothing else move, heard no shouts or voices.

Sliding the safety into place, she pocketed the weapon and continued on. She pulled gloves out of the duffel and slid them over her hands, unable to stand the biting cold turning the tips red any longer.

For the next hour and a half, she traversed the woods, single-minded in her desire to put as much distance between herself and anyone still following. Inevitably, after checking the phone several times to find the GPS was still out, she had to admit she was lost. The weather had deteriorated to a step above blizzard conditions, and she knew by nightfall that her circumstances were going to become dire. She couldn't survive out here in a blizzard. Determined to find some sort of shelter, she pressed on.

Forty minutes later, Chey stumbled out of the forest. To her surprise, a high wall loomed fifty feet ahead, marking the perimeter of some sort of building. The shape of a large home, or an Inn, could be seen above the wall itself. Several lights burned in high windows and smoke streamed out of a chimney. It appeared to be an older structure, perhaps made of stone like the castle.

The stream of smoke was familiar, though Chey couldn't figure out why. Just now, she was more concerned with finding shelter out of the storm than anything, and this place seemed her best shot. Crossing the clearing toward the wall, she began searching for a way in. It was too tall to climb over, even with the help of a tree.

Thirty feet down, she came upon a bramble bush sitting next to an iron gate. Approaching with wary caution, Chey peered through the bars of the gate and felt around for a latch.

Beyond, the warmth of the structure beckoned. The lowest level was well lit, with almost every window spilling warm light through the panes. It reminded Chey more of an old girl's school or orphanage than it did a house. With its many levels and obvious large square footage, it could have once been a mental ward or other institution.

To Chey's surprise, she found no lock in the latch. Undoing the mechanism, she eased the gate open, cringing when a hinge screeched. Moving slower, she eased inside and closed it with less noise. Pausing to get her bearings, she tried to decide whether to go around to the front door and plead for a room, or find another, less noticeable way in to hide away for the night. If the people were loyal to the King, and if Aksel had put out her picture on the television or some such thing, then she might find herself right back where she started.

No, she decided, caution was the best option.

Creeping along the back acreage, which was considerable, she sought a basement door or some other out building. There were several trees inside the walled barrier, too, which provided a little cover as she went. A back door nestled into the structure under an overhang, closed against the encroaching evening. It was a main entrance or exit, not preferable for her needs.

It was so cold now that Chey couldn't feel the end of her nose or her chin. Ahead, she spotted a slanting set of stairs leading down into what must be a basement. Hoping against hope, she headed that way, using the cover of trees until she came even with the stairs. Darkness was only a half hour away, if that, and she was running out of options. This had to be a way in.

Checking the yard and windows, Chey stepped out from behind the trees and ran toward the stairs. Thankful for the railing attached to the low wall, she held on while traversing the slippery steps to the bottom. There she found a small alcove hidden under part of the building with a door that proved to be locked when she tried the handle. Stifling a curse, she felt around the top of the door frame for a key. It was a long shot, and Chey wasn't surprised when she came up empty.

The alcove at least provided protection from falling snow, but not the cold, which meant she needed to get inside somehow. Using her shoulder, she banged against the door, counting on the building being too big and the basement being vacant to hide the noise. She bounced off with no luck and tried again, this time with more force. Closed tight, made of heavy wood, the door didn't budge.

Exhausted from her long trek in bad weather, Chey leaned on the wood for a second and got her breath. Her bones ached, her stomach demanded food and water, and she was sure that if she didn't get the door open, she might die in the alcove of exposure.

Stepping back, she kicked at the door near the lock. A hard, sharp kick that rewarded her with a slight splintering sound. Two more kicks was all it took to bust the latch. The door creaked inward.

Chey put her shoulder against it and opened it further, stepping into the gloom.

. . .

The basement, this section of it anyway, looked to be used only on rare occasions. There was a large pile of cut firewood against the far wall, several benches with remnants of craft projects on the surface, and a few metal tool chests half as tall as Chey. Bins that appeared to have holiday decorations lined another wall, each marked by the color of the lid.

Squinting into the shadows, Chey figured the basement to be as big as her apartment back in Seattle, with several doors leading to different sections and one that, miraculously, opened onto a bathroom. With extreme caution, she explored the basic layout, finding the space clean if dull. The concrete floor lacked dirt or debris, which told Chey that someone came down here at least once a month to sweep.

The small bathroom, with only a sink, a toilet and a cupboard was in working order. Chey took care of business quickly, glad to have some relief where that was concerned. After drying her hands on a few paper towels, she exited the bathroom and sought a pile of moving blankets to raid. She dragged one into a shady recessed area and curled down on it, desiring a buffer between her body and the cold cement. Bringing the duffel bag around to her lap, she eased the zipper open and rooted around for water. She'd consumed one bottle during her trek; three remained. Gulping half the contents, she set it aside and ripped into one of the trail bars, hugging her arms around her while she chewed. It was cold down here. Not as cold as the outside, but frigid enough to make Chey wonder how much protection the basement would provide. The hem of her jeans was wet and unlikely to dry unless she found some place a little warmer.

For now she ate, consuming a piece of beef jerky after the trail bar. Stuffing any trash back into the duffel bag, she zipped it closed and wrapped her arms around herself, desperate to chase the chill away. Wary of discovery, Chey found it difficult to sleep. She knew she needed to rest while she could, before going back on the run. It was daunting when someone upstairs might decide on a whim to visit this part of the basement. The thought of being at fate's mercy wasn't an enticing one.

Chey wondered where Sander and Mattias were. What happened that they sent her fleeing from the safety of the cabin? She imagined all manner of horror, compliments of the King. Aksel must have had some other trick up his sleeve like the brothers thought. Chey didn't know whether to head for the coast or to stay lost for another few days in the forest region. If the storm persisted, it would make travel, and survival, difficult. As soon as the weather cleared enough, she should be able to raise the GPS and find her way to the shore. The question was whether Aksel knew she was here— which seemed likely, considering the voices she'd heard in pursuit—and would be waiting, anticipating her arrival in the busier coastal cities.

In the middle of debating, she fell

asleep.

What woke her some hours later was a snap of light and the rustle of clothing. Jolting upright, neck stiff from where her head had been leaning against the wall, Chey blinked away confusion. The weak spill of light didn't quite reach the recessed curve she was nestled into, instead illuminating the middle sections of the basement and fading the closer it got to the corners and walls.

Clarity returned with the uncomfortable realization that someone might bump across her down here. She heard movement again; someone was in the basement with her.

Biting her tongue, considering pulling the gun in case she needed to defend herself, Chey listened for more clues. Which direction was the person heading? Her way, or over to the firewood pile?

She hoped the latter. Chey could see the stacked wood from her spot if she leaned forward enough. The heavy thud of boots on concrete came next, marking the person's path through the room. Afraid to breathe, Chey closed her eyes and wished the person away. *Let them leave. Make them hurry and go back upstairs.*

Opening her eyes when the rustle of

clothing stopped, she tried to gauge where the person was in the basement. Had they seen her shoe? The pad she sat on? Worried she'd been spotted, she leaned forward enough to bring the rest of the woodpile into view.

What Chey never expected was to be staring at Sander's back. She would have known his physique anywhere. The broad shoulders, narrow hips, warrior-like muscles beneath the lay of his sweatshirt. He wore a beanie over his head, covering his hair.

Just as she opened her mouth to call out, the man turned his head, bringing his profile into view.

Sander's name died on her lips. Chey stared in horror at the malformed cheek, eye and half of the forehead that made up the man's face. It wasn't Sander—yet it was. The jaw, the general shape of the face belonged to her fiance. A resemblance so strong that there could be no denying some sort of kinship. Not exact, this wasn't a twin. A brother? Cousin? Something. This man was of Ahtissari blood, Chey would have bet her life on it. Now that she could see pieces of hair sticking out the bottom disappearing under the collar, Chey saw it wasn't golden like Sander's, but black. Ink black. Like Mattias.

What the hell?

Too caught up in her shock, Chey didn't think to sit back. She stared, taking note that the man seemed to have decent motor function. It was impossible to tell if there was another sort of disability to go with the malformed face. He gathered an armful of firewood from the stack, muscles flexing under his clothing.

Again, from the back with his face turned away, Chey would have sworn she was staring at Sander. It was uncanny, the physical resemblance when the stranger's face wasn't in sight.

After loading up on firewood, the man toted it to one of the other doors and disappeared up a flight of stairs, closing the door behind him.

Releasing a pent up breath, Chey palmed her forehead. What had just happened? Who was he?

The wisp of smoke that had been so familiar outside came rushing back, tickling her memory. She needed to remember where she'd seen it before, or why it was so familiar. Then it hit her; the day she'd learned Sander was a Royal, when she'd photographed the family, she had seen a slither of smoke far into the East woods, trailing up past the tree tops. She recalled wondering what else might be in the East woods that made the family put that section off limits to visitors. To anyone.

Was this building the source of the smoke? Is this where she was now, in the East woods? Suffering disorientation from getting lost, Chey had no idea if this was North, West or East from where she'd started out this afternoon. She suspected this might be yet another Royal family secret, however, and sought to reason through the semantics while also rifling through the bag for her cell phone. Mattias might have texted while she was sleeping.

No messages. The GPS, as well, was still offline.

Great.

The time surprised her a little. *11:42 p.m.* She would have thought it was the middle of the night.

Knowing she would have trouble going back to sleep, Chey considered her options. Should she creep up onto the upper floors and attempt to get pictures of the man? She wanted answers about his identity. Mattias and Sander, if she could get in touch with them, would know immediately. Probably without pictures, too, but she thought it best to provide some on the off chance that they didn't know about his presence either.

It struck Chey in that moment that perhaps this might be another of the King and Queen's 'aces'. A secret buried and locked away in the East woods, though what it all meant, she couldn't be sure. She assessed the risks of exposing herself on the upper floors and what might happen if she was caught.

What she *should* do was stay put, rest and regain her energy for departure the following morning.

Shucking the strap from the duffel bag, she leaned it against the wall in the shadows, checked for her gun in the pocket of her coat and eased to a stand. Listening for movement, she crept toward the door to the stairwell and opened it.

The stone staircase wound upward, lit only by a few small lamps attached to the ceiling. Chey ascended before she could talk herself out of it, rising until she reached the landing outside another door that must lead onto the main floor of the building.

This was crazy. What the hell was she thinking?

Opening the door, Chey peered along a hallway that radiated warmth and the faint scent of apple pie. Seeing the coast was clear, she left the stairwell and closed the door behind her.

You're insane. Someone could walk around a corner any second.

The risk of discovery did not stop her from advancing through the corridor, sneaking on stealthy feet away from the safety of the basement. The tips of her fingers and nose tingled at the temperature change. It felt wonderful to chase some of the chill away, even temporarily.

Moving down the hall, she assessed the layout as best she could, discerning the front of the building from the back, and where she judged the sound of voices to be. The low drone of conversation floated to her from somewhere on her right.

Coming up on what appeared to be a library or a parlor of some type, Chey pressed her back against the wall. She still couldn't make out the exact words, but she *could* make out three distinct voices, all male.

From the left, behind her down a separate hall, the maudlin song of a violin drew Chey's attention. Backtracking, alert for movement or approaching footsteps, she retreated to the secondary corridor and closed in on the lilting melody. She recalled Sander telling her he played as well. What were the odds that a cousin or relative was adept with the same instrument? She had no doubt that's who the source of the music was.

Pausing at the archway leading into the room, Chey bolstered her resolve and her nerve. Bringing the phone from her pocket, she poked her head around the corner just enough to get a glimpse of the interior. She prayed the whole time that the occupant didn't notice her.

The man with a physique so like Sander stood with his back to the doorway. Facing a roaring fireplace, he played the violin with passion and skill, swaying lightly on his feet in time to the tempo. Other musical instruments—a baby grand piano, cello, guitar—sat around what was obviously a music room.

Right away, Chey lifted the phone and clicked a few photos. She needed to see the man's face, which upped the risk of being spotted, so that Mattias and Sander would understand just how striking the resemblance to Sander was. She glanced up and down the corridor, checking for people, before returning her attention to the violin player.

He adjusted his stance, half turning his body toward the doorway. Chey clicked off a few more pictures, homing in on the disfigured profile. Firelight traced the strong jaw, a high cheekbone, the prominent nose. It cut more shadows into the sloping parts, making the man seem a little more like a monster than not.

The music stopped abruptly when the player stilled his arm and snapped a look toward the doorway.

Chey leaned back with a gasp. Tucking the phone into her pocket, she retreated from the archway, looking for a place to hide.

He'd seen her. Or seen movement. Something. He was coming to investigate.

Ducking into the nearest open door, she flattened herself against the inside wall, thankful that whatever room she'd stepped into was utterly dark.

A potted plant helped obscure her from sight.

The shape of the man appeared

silhouetted in the doorway, as if he was looking in. Chey held her breath, panic making her heart race.

Damn. *Damn.* She shouldn't have been so brazen. What if he discovered her hiding and raised the alarm?

The silhouette lingered, hovering in the arch. Finally, it retreated, continuing the search in other rooms along the corridor.

Chey waited until she couldn't hear his footsteps before leaving her hiding place. At the arch, she peered into the hallway. No one in sight. Chey bolted from the room back toward the other hall, pressing against the wall at the corner. The man could be anywhere by now. She hoped he wasn't in the hall when she emerged, which she did a moment later.

The corridor was empty. Chey glanced behind her, hoping the opposite direction was as well. She saw nothing and no one.

Running as quietly as she could for the door to the basement, she opened it and rounded onto the landing, easing the door closed in her wake. She winced when it creaked. Hastening down the stairs, stung by the difference in the warmth up there compared to the cold down here, she fled to the shady alcove and plopped down onto the moving blanket.

With any luck, the man upstairs would get distracted by someone else and forget the flicker of movement he'd seen. She needed to remain indoors until dawn, so her choice of whether to stay in the building or go out into the snow wasn't really a choice at all.

She had to stay and hope she wasn't discovered if she wanted to live through the night.

Chapter Ten

It was still dark when Chey left the security of the basement a handful of hours later. Out in the open, she saw the snow had stopped falling, leaving about a half foot on the ground. Adjusting the strap of the duffel over her chest, she eyed the vacant yard and the cover of trees beyond. She needed to get to the wall and the gate. Anyone looking out the windows on an upper level would be able to see her until she was on the other side of the wall, a place she really wanted to be right then. Just as she stepped for the cover of the trees, she heard the distinct rumble of an engine to her right. It didn't come from the yard, but somewhere around the corner of the building. Maybe there was a garage just out of sight.

Chey weighed her options. Obviously, someone had started the car. Had they left it idling and went back inside, like many people did when the weather was so frigid? Or were they still sitting within, waiting while the heat blasted through the interior of the vehicle?

Access to a car, in her estimation, was worth the risk of being spotted. It would only work if the driver had gone back inside, however; Chey wasn't willing to engage in a brawl—which she would probably lose—or a gunfight to have it.

Changing direction, she crept along the back wall of the building, ducking below dark windows. At the corner, she peered around the side.

Several bay doors indicated the entire part of the structure here at the end was a garage. One had been rolled up and exhaust puffed out of a tailpipe on the idling vehicle. Creeping forward, cheeks stinging from the cold air, she peered inside the garage.

A dim light shined down from overhead, glinting off the white paint of a rugged looking SUV. The vehicle didn't look brand new, but neither was it old. The tires appeared suited for bad weather such as this.

Waiting against the wall, she sought the interior for a driver. The tint on the windows made it hard to tell if anyone was inside or not. Cursing silently, Chey debated giving up on the idea of stealing the vehicle and just going on foot out the same gate she came in.

Even if she did get the car, an alarm would be raised sooner or later. How far could she get before someone found and stopped her? Then again, she might put a lot more distance between herself and the building before anyone got another car up and running.

Clenching her teeth, she bolted around the corner, going low along the side of the SUV. She approached the passenger side and tried to use the side mirror to see a driver. All she needed was a glimpse of the seat.

Empty. The driver's seat was empty.

Not allowing herself time to second guess, she ran around the front, opened the door and hopped in. The driver was probably inside getting a mug of coffee for the road. Dumping her bag on the passenger seat, she reached for the gears. Putting the vehicle in reverse, she eased out of the garage as quietly and as slowly as she could. In her mind, the less engine revving right now, the better. Rolling forward, she aimed for the front where a driveway had already been cleared. Once she hit pavement, she gave the SUV a little more gas.

Ahead, the main gate protecting the structure stood open. Chey thanked her lucky stars the driver had done all this beforehand, making her theft a bit easier. Pulling onto the road, she sped up, yelping when the back end fishtailed before the tires caught. Straightening out, hunched over the wheel from tension and stress, she drove away as fast as she dared. No other buildings dotted the slightly hilly terrain to the right. On her left, a broad meadow separated the structure from another length of forest that connected with the rest far back in the distance. It was a remote area, that much was obvious.

She took the first turn heading South that she came to, checking the rear view mirror often for a tail.

Someone had to have found the missing car by now.

Chey hit several lengths of road that had not been cleared, making passage difficult. The SUV handled it well enough as long as she went slow. She took a turn, and another, and another, until she felt marginally better that a tail wouldn't be able to find her. That didn't mean the police wouldn't, should they get a glimpse of her in the distinctive white car.

She planned to ditch it before too long anyway. All she wanted to do was cut some of the distance to the shore down. Even a semi-busy city would work. Anywhere she could get lost in crowds was good. Checking the built in GPS often, she remained generally on course, taking whatever paths she came to that led her where she needed to go.

Just as dawn started to break over the horizon, Chey spotted two headlights in the rear view mirror. Cautioning herself against panic, she retained the same speed. It could be anyone on their way into town for work or whatever else. People in this country were used to driving in bad conditions; it didn't stop them from coming and going.

Not far ahead, she could see the shape of a city looming out of the twilight. She knew she wasn't at the shoreline yet, but this would be a good place to stop and possibly ditch the SUV. As soon as the sun was fully up, she would become a sitting duck. The car behind kept a respectable distance and didn't rush up on her bumper.

Chey entered the edge of the city as the vehicle veered off another direction at the first light, allowing Chey to breathe easier. Definitely not in pursuit, just a citizen on errands of their own.

Cruising along the avenue, Chey turned right at the next stop sign, looking for a place to pull in. All in all, the city looked to be smaller than it was large, with a few main streets interconnecting onto less busy thoroughfares.

Parking in front of a cafe, Chey shut the engine down and took stock of her situation. Most of the businesses on this street looked to be closed. Did she dare stick her head in one anyway, in case her face had been on TV? She didn't trust Aksel not to pull out all the stops to find her.

Yet she needed access to shelter where she could wait a few hours to see if Mattias contacted her again. She thought about shooting him a text, but decided she shouldn't in case someone had gotten their hands on that particular phone.

A small restaurant at the very end of the row beckoned. In the window, a green neon sign proclaimed them open.

Chey disembarked, leaving the keys in the ignition. Slinging her bag over her shoulder, she hit the sidewalk and made for the restaurant. If anyone appeared to recognize her, then she would simply flee on foot and find a new hiding place.

She could do this.

Entering the restaurant, she found it small, cozy and warm from a fireplace blazing along the back wall. A proprietor called out a greeting, which Chey returned in their native tongue. She'd picked up a few words here or there, enough to converse with the most basic sentiments.

Sinking into a booth, she rubbed her hands together before removing her gloves. Tucking them away, she ordered coffee and a rather large breakfast, watching for signs of recognition on the waiter's face the whole time. Seeing no spark, or narrowing of the man's eyes, she sat back to wait. In the meantime, she contemplated everything that had happened since leaving the cabin on the run. She debated the odds that Sander had come out on top with Aksel and they didn't look good. Considering no one had contacted her before now only added to the idea that something had gone terribly wrong. Chey debated how to leave the country if Mattias didn't text or call her in the next day or two. She had enough money to pay for rooms until then, and not much more.

Taking a flight out was asking to get caught by customs. She would have to sneak aboard a boat, maybe, on its way to a port in another country. Even then, if she got caught, how would she explain herself? It might land her in jail no matter what.

At least the others wouldn't outright kill her, as Aksel would.

Digging into her breakfast after the waiter dropped it off, Chey ruminated over her options, disappointed with each new idea that arose. They all led back to the same place in the end: she couldn't get out of Latvala without crossing paths with someone who would check her identity, and that was a problem.

After the meal, she slouched in the booth, hands cupped around a cup of coffee, her phone sitting next to her leg on the seat.

The jingle of bells on the door two hours after finishing her meal drew Chey's gaze to the side. A hand landed on her shoulder before she could catch a glimpse of the person's face, startling her bad enough that she thumped the mug on the table. Just about to fight back, she realized it was a staying touch.

"Ready to go?" Mattias asked,

cautioning her with a gaze that peered out from a hood drawn over his head. It completely obscured his features unless someone was right in front of him.

"Yes." Chey didn't waste a second leaving money on the table and gathering her things. Relief felt like a drug in her veins. She wasn't sure how he found her —GPS on the phone, most likely—and didn't care. Mattias was here, and he would make everything all right.

Exiting the restaurant, she followed him to a waiting black Hummer and climbed into the back. A guard drove and another sat in the passenger seat, dressed warm for the weather instead of their usual suits.

Setting her bag on the floor at her feet, Chey looked across the vehicle at Mattias. "What happened? Someone followed me into the woods when I ran from the house," she said.

"I know. I'll tell you about it on the way. Sander has been forced to leave Latvala. We're going to have to figure out how to reinstall him as Heir to the throne." Mattias's grim expression boded ill for the near future.

Chey said, "I may have found a clue that will help."

. . .

As the vehicle drove the roads away from the small town, Mattias, frowning, glanced across the car to Chey. "What do you mean?"

Half turning on the seat, she met Mattias's eyes. "This is going to sound crazy, but I have proof. Anyway, I got lost in the woods after I left the cabin. I'm not sure how far I ran, or in what direction. I suspect I wound up in the East woods, however."

Mattias's frown turned into a scowl. "Why do you say that?"

"Because of what I found there. Tell me —have you or Sander ever explored that area?"

"No. What did you find?" He shifted in his seat, curiosity mingling with wariness on his features.

"Late in the evening, when I knew I needed to find shelter before it got darker and colder, I stumbled upon a building. It's surrounded by a wall, but I managed to get in the back gate and break into an outer basement door. While I was huddling down there, I fell asleep. The next thing I knew, someone was in the basement with me." She paused to lick her lips, then continued. "I opened my eyes, and in the available light—which wasn't much—I thought I was looking at Sander's back. I was so convinced he'd found me that I even started to call out. Thank God I didn't, because it *wasn't* him."

Mattias's frown deepened. "So you think a man who shares a build like my brother is somehow a clue?"

"Yes, and when you see these, you will think so, too." Chey fished her phone out and called up the photos she'd taken.

Mattias eased the cell from her grip and muttered something under his breath in his own language.

A curse, as far as Chey could tell. Maybe an exclamation.

"See? The profile...there is no denying he resembles Sander. It's not just the build. The jaw, the shape of the face where it isn't deformed, it *could* be Sander except for the black hair." Chey glanced from the phone to Mattias.

"Yes. This is striking. I wonder, then, if this has to do with the King's recent cryptic remarks about being able to force Sander into exile." He thumbed through the photos, examining each with critical care.

"It could be. Those were taken when I sneaked upstairs at one point, into the building proper, and discovered that man playing violin."

Mattias gave Chey a chiding glance for the risk of entering the house proper. Her information seemed to surprise him. "Violin? You saw him playing?"

"Yes. Sander told me he plays, too, although I've never heard him yet. There are one or two photos that show the violin, when I wasn't zooming in."

"He does. Excellently, at that." Mattias looked down at the phone, thumb passing along the edge of the next picture. "What else did you glean?"

"Nothing too much more than that. He almost caught me, so I had to hide then escape back to the basement. I stole a car in the morning, before sunup, and made my way through the countryside to that little town you found me in." Chey didn't ask for the phone back. Not yet. She saw Mattias forward the photos, likely to his phone or a secret email account. Then he deleted them from her photo gallery.

"You are a wily creature. I knew you would escape from the cabin successfully." Mattias, approval in his eyes, handed the phone back.

Chey took it and slipped it into her pocket. "I did what I had to. It wasn't fun, and I'm pretty sure my hands and feet will never feel truly warm again, but it's a small price to pay. Thanks for the forewarning."

"You're welcome."

"So what do we do now?"

"I'm thinking. Can you find that place again?" he asked.

"Maybe. It was dark and all I wanted to do was get out of there. I can get you to the general area and we can narrow it down. I think you'll find it fairly easy because it's some sort of old building, probably an orphanage or old hospital type place. Does it sound familiar?"

"Not really. If it's something the King and Queen are keeping secret, the building might not be on any current maps, either. So we'll need you to guide us back." Mattias pocketed his phone and clasped his hands in his lap.

Outside, the snowy landscape slipped past the windows. Chey couldn't tell where they were going or what their destination was. Maybe she wouldn't be able to find the building after all. She wasn't reassured to hear it might not be on a map somewhere.

Twisting in the seat, she glanced behind her, already fretting about directions.

"We'll find it, don't worry. Even if I have to take to the air and circle, then I'll do that. For now, we need to figure out who this person is," Mattias said.

"How will you do that?" she asked when she sat straight in her seat once more.

"I'm not sure," he admitted. "Just showing up and demanding information won't be met with good results."

"Why not? You're in line to the throne, a Royal, they wouldn't dare refuse you, would they?"

"They might have more guards there than you saw, or they might contact the King and tell him we're there. I cannot guess what might happen if Aksel thinks we're on to another of his secrets." Mattias, looking thoughtful, stared out the window.

Chey watched his profile rather than the landscape. "And see, I think the element of surprise is best. Just show up outside with as many guards as are loyal to you, and barge your way in. Talk to this man for yourself. He might not know anything, but *someone* there surely will. I mean, if the resemblance is this strong for us, then there is no way the staff there overlooked it."

"Probably not. I hesitate to storm the castle, as it were, until I know we won't be overwhelmed."

"What about secret documents? Do you think the King and Queen kept any?"

Mattias glanced back at Chey with a wry, humorless smile on his mouth. "What do you think?"

"Yes, I guess you're right. They probably burned it all if it ever existed in the first place. Could the man be a cousin? An uncle?"

"I can't be sure. Somehow I doubt it. The extreme precaution to hide him makes me think it's closer than that."

"A brother? Could it be another child like Sander, born of the King and another woman?" Chey asked.

"Let's discuss it inside. We're here." Mattias gestured to a large manor of stone nestled into the landscape.

Chey, distracted for the last several miles, didn't see any other homes in the near vicinity. The driver used a remote to open a gate that slid back on its rails. Pulling in, they cruised along a teardrop shaped driveway and stopped before a broad set of stairs.

"Another Royal holding?" Chey asked as she snagged the strap to her bag and got out.

"One of mine, actually." Mattias set a gentlemanly hand low on Chey's back to escort her up the steps and inside after a guard opened the doors.

This home was smaller than the castles, more cozy and inviting. It was still large by regular standards, with soaring ceilings, stained glass over some of the windows, and decorative, medieval looking archways leading into other halls.

Mattias guided Chey straight into a large sitting room with an array of plush, expensive chairs and couches. A fire was already blazing in the hearth and a middle aged woman dressed similar to Sander's staff on Pallan island entered a few moments later with servings of tea on a tray.

Shucking her coat and bag, Chey whispered gratitude for the tea, accepted a mug, and slouched down onto one of the couches. The long trek through snow and the broken night of sleep were catching up to her. Exhaustion threatened to sidetrack her attention.

Maybe the hot drink would help. She took a sip.

Accepting a mug of his own, Mattias chose to pace instead of sit.

"If it is a brother, and he has emotional or mental issues, he would be unfit to rule," Mattias said after several silent minutes.

"Then they wouldn't be able to use him as a weapon. Do you think he's an illegitimate child?" Chey asked.

"They might if they never planned to expose him and only use his presence as a threat to force Dare into exile. It means *someone* else has to know who can back up the claim. One of the higher advisers or something like that." Mattias paused near a window and brought the cup to his mouth for a drink.

"If you go public with it--"

"We cannot risk that. Not until we know for sure who he is and where he fits in the grand scheme of things. To do so might risk Dare's position for good. Right now, no one knows about his birth mother. He *could* come back and take the throne."

"Or *you* could just step in and become King when it's time. Sander can live something of a more normal life." Chey knew even as she said it that Sander wasn't cut out for anything but leader of Latvala. It was everything to him.

"He will be unhappy for the rest of his life if that happens. Never mind *I* believe he should have the throne instead of me. He's always had an edge I don't." Mattias took another drink.

"That doesn't sound like it's hard for you to admit. You're content with being his right hand, so to speak, aren't you?"

He smiled without looking away from the window. "Yes. It is a role I am well suited to, and he knows without doubt he can trust me. Paavo? There is a question whether he would not subvert to underhanded dealings. Dare and I are the way forward for Latvala and we both understand it on a base level."

"So what are you thinking? A surprise approach isn't the way, there are no documents to fall back on, and asking around the higher members close to the King and Queen might tip someone off who was never supposed to know there is another Ahtissari floating around Latvala." Chey tipped her temple into her palm, inwardly cursing her tiredness.

"I think this man must be an older brother. Dare mentioned Aksel said the

Queen 'had no choice' but to accept Sander as her own. What if *she* gave birth to the other boy around the same time as Dare, but they realized immediately there was a problem and Aksel covered by forcing her to accept his bastard instead?" Mattias glanced away from the window to Chey.

She sat forward as Mattias presented the idea. For some reason, it sounded like the most logical thing she'd heard yet. "It's so twisted, yet it makes perfect sense."

"It does. I would like to present this to Dare and see what his reaction is. If he thinks we're on the right track."

"Except he's on his way to Barbados and we're not. Won't someone inform the King if you go after him? It might look suspicious," she said.

"I don't need to go after him. We'll set up a secure feed and have a web chat as soon as everyone can arrange it. I would prefer to do this in person, but leaving here to fly all the way to Barbados is a waste of time. I have no doubt we can establish a connection that the King's spies are not aware of." Mattias finished his tea.

"Even better. Can I sit in with you? I'd

like to see him if that's all right." Chey took her time with her drink, relieved they wouldn't have to jet off across the world once more. She missed Sander and wanted to be near him, but not at the cost of risking someone's life or alerting the King that something was up.

"Of course. Excuse me for a few minutes while I get this set up. Feel free to choose a room upstairs to make your own." Mattias paused to touch her shoulder on his way out of the parlor.

"Thanks, I think I will. Wake me when you're ready." Chey lingered over the tea for another fifteen minutes before gathering her bag to head upstairs.

A short nap would do her good.

Chapter Eleven

The first thing Chey noticed about Sander was how annoyed he looked. His image flickered on the computer screen through the video chat program, a whole head and shoulders shot with a glimpse of what appeared to be a plain white wall in the background. A tee shirt of blue covered his chest, lacking a logo or any other identifying marks. Hair loose around his face, he stared into the webcam with evident irritation.

"All right, can you hear us?" Mattias asked Sander.

Evening had settled over Latvala between Chey's nap and their video conference, the late afternoon light bleeding away to full black beyond the window panes.

"I can see and hear you fine. That we're having to take these measures tells me you must have found something pretty damn strange," Sander said, then added, "Good to see you, Chey."

"Hi babe. Strange doesn't begin to cover it." Chey wished they were in the same room instead of thousands of miles away from each other. Hearing his voice and seeing his image on the screen made her long for his scent and his touch. Reaching out, she traced her fingertips over his image.

On the screen, he smiled, as if he knew what she was doing.

"Chey came across a building in the East woods while she was on the run--"

"I thought I told you never to go into the East woods?" Sander said to Chey. He frowned his apparent disapproval.

"Don't interrupt, brother. Let me get this all out. She came across a building, sitting separate from others. While she was there, she saw a man who bears a striking resemblance to you. We have pictures. Where he differs from you is some kind of deformity on his face, perhaps even in his brain. We're not sure. The resemblance is too coincidental to be denied." Mattias held up his phone with the image on it.

"It was an accident I wound up there. I got lost. Anyway, the man looked just like you. I told Mattias that for a second or two, I thought it *was* you," Chey said.

Sander sat forward on his end, squinting at the screen. It took a moment for his expression to show recognition and surprise. It became more obvious when Mattias scrolled through several of the photos, including the one of the man playing violin.

"I'll be damned," Sander said.

"Yes. Exactly. Chey and I have been conjecturing what might be going on, considering everything you've told us and what seems logical. My best guess is that Helina was pregnant around the same time as your mother, and when Aksel realized Helina's child might be compromised mentally, had you brought to take his place. It answers the question of *why* Helina was forced to accept you, and why the East woods were always off limits to everyone." Mattias lowered the phone and powered it off. He sat back in his chair and reached for a drink.

"It can't be a distant cousin or something of that nature?" Sander asked. He sounded disturbed and wary.

"Why take those extremes to hide his presence? If he was just a cousin, the secrecy shouldn't be at the level it is. What, then, would cause them to hide this man away? You said Aksel seemed certain he could remove you from the throne, and the only possible way now, after all this, is if he caught you committing treason or if you had an older brother that out ranked you. I'm putting my money on the older brother theory," Mattias said. "It's the most logical."

"I haven't committed treason. These charges would be devastating if they were true—and if they came to light. We need a way to prove it. Aksel told me Helina faked her pregnancy up until my birth, but it sure does fit into your scheme better if she was actually carrying and had the child close to when I was born. The problem is that if the man is not her child but another bastard," Sander snarled the word. "It will be for nothing. I will still not regain the throne, it will fall to you regardless."

"What if you could get a DNA sample from the man, and from Helina? I think you can use hair, which wouldn't be that hard to obtain," Chey said.

"Hair? I thought blood?" Sander said. He appeared to consider the idea.

"I'm not sure. Fifteen minutes on the internet and I'll have all the information you need." Chey knew she could find the answers fast.

"And just how do you propose we get the sample from the man?" Mattias said. "I could figure a way to get one from Helina without a problem. But I bet the guards will raise an alarm, either outwardly or discreetly, if we drive up and ask for a blood sample from someone who is not supposed to exist."

"I know the back way into the building. We go in at night--"

"No," Sander said, cutting Chey off. His voice took a stern turn. On the computer screen, he stared straight into the lens with a look that brooked no argument.

Chey scowled at Sander's expression. "I'm capable."

"No."

"You can't just tell me *no* and think--"

"Yes I can. I just did. Mattias, she is not allowed anywhere near that place," Sander said.

"I'll make sure she doesn't go back," Mattias said in his calm, reassuring tone.

Chey's jaw went slack. She glanced from Mattias to the screen, then leaned forward to glare right into the web camera. That way, Sander got the full effect of her discontent.

"I've been in that basement and up and down those back stairs. Not just that, but along two main corridors of the bottom floor. I know best how to get in and how to get out without raising the alarm," she countered, struggling to keep the edge of anger out of her words.

"No." Sander sat back in his chair like the King he was supposed to become, and crossed his arms over his chest.

Chey got her face out of the web camera and sank back into her chair. Scowling. When she glanced at Mattias, he had one hand over his mouth in the way people did when they were trying to control either laughter or a smile.

"It's not funny, Mattias. Don't egg him on."

"I'm not laughing." Mattias flashed his palms in the traditional sign of surrender.

Chey could tell by the look the brothers exchanged that they both wouldn't listen to a word she said in defense of her ability to get the sample.

Flat out angry, she got up from the chair and left the room, banging the door to the office closed in her wake.

. . .

Sander watched as Chey swirled out of Mattias's office and regretted her fury, but not his decision to deny her. All he needed was to be this far away and not be able to help should she fall into the wrong hands at the wrong time. Sending her on DNA collecting missions was not high on his list of risks to take at the moment.

"She's right though, Mattias. If we could get a sample, we would have irrefutable proof that this man is her son and that they've kept him hidden away all these years. Just the threat of exposure to the world should make the King and Queen back off from these ideas of exile and control," Sander said.

"What if it backfires, and they embrace it? Attempt to come at it from the angle of compassion?" Mattias asked.

"I don't think there is anything about their duplicity in replacing one damaged Heir for another, then lying about it all this time, that will go over well with the public. That's the kind of uproar Aksel won't want to deal with. He knows it will damage his credibility with the people and I think he'll back down," Sander replied.

Mattias's expression waned thoughtful. "Latvala is not a country rocked by many scandals. We saw the affect of the Valentina situation recently, which spread as fast as wildfire. This would strike closer to the hearts of the citizens and I fear one traumatic event after another could put the Ahtissari rule into question."

"It would only do so if the news actually went public. We'll be using the threat instead of the reality against Aksel and Helina, and I still believe they will back off rather than press the issue for exactly the reason you just stated. Aksel might be taking more risks than he can handle, but I do not think for a second he would put the entire throne and our bloodline at stake." Sander laced his hands behind his head, plotting his next move.

"You could be right. Perhaps it is the way we present it to them, with all our ducks in a row and no other secrets they can use to retaliate."

"They've got more secrets than Valentina's got lying hairs in her head," Sander said, muttering. "Trying to outguess whether they've got something else up their sleeve is impossible until we're on the back side of this thing. We'll take precautions either way, brother."

"Good." Mattias paused as if contemplating something else. He said,

"You want me to arrange for a sample to be collected from Helina, then?"

"Yes. Do what you need to. The sooner we make that connection, the better," Sander said.

"What about the man? I'm still thinking over ways to get in there without alerting the security."

"Leave that to me."

"You're half a world away," Mattias pointed out.

"I have those loyal to me, you know that. They will get the job done in my place."

"I suspect they will," Mattias finally said. "What of Chey?"

"Just keep her out of Aksel's hands. I don't trust that he won't move against her if he can find her."

"Done. When will we be in contact again?"

"Soon. I'll get my hands on a phone they can't trace. Good luck with the sample," Sander said.

"You as well. Call me with an update." Mattias clicked out of the video chat.

Sander tapped a button, shutting down the application. He closed the laptop and leaned back in his chair, turning his mind to the task of DNA extraction.

Later, there would be time to soothe Chey's ruffled feathers.

Chapter Twelve

While Mattias and Sander patted each other on the back and basked in their male superiority, Chey marched through the large house in search of another computer. Muttering about stubborn fiances the entire way, she came across a pretty library with bookshelves lining the walls and high beams that criss-crossed over the ceiling.

On the heavy mahogany desk, a laptop sat waiting for use.

"Perfect." Stalking over, she sank down into the chair and opened the computer. She didn't especially care that she hadn't asked permission or that she might be using Mattias's private laptop for her research.

In less than five minutes she got it fired up and hooked into a search engine, and from there it was a matter of seconds before results started popping up left and right.

"Oh look here. You *can* use hair

samples—but I would need to get the root along with the hair shaft. So it won't be as easy as gathering hair off a brush or something." Undaunted by the extra step she would need to take, Chey scrolled down to the other options.

"Saliva. I hadn't thought of that." She frowned, thinking over the problems she might encounter collecting it. That meant getting *inside* someone's mouth and that wasn't appealing in the least. She imagined sneaking into the strange man's room with a cotton swab, peeling back his lip, and running the swab along the underside while he was asleep.

After which he would probably wake up, furious, and pound her into the ground with his fist.

"The hair sample would be easier. That's just tweezers and a pluck. Still risky, but less invasive, I think, than trying the swab." She perused the rest of the article after glancing at the library doors. No one lurked out in the hallway.

"Okay, not just one hair, either, but at least five or six samples are recommended in case the root isn't attached to the first one. About sixty-or-so-percent success rate matching DNA that way. Not a fantastic percentage. The saliva is higher." Chey considered it. Blood was out of the question. Or was it? Was there a huge difference between a pluck and a needle prick? She might be able to pierce a calloused toe or finger or some other less sensitive spot whereas no matter where she plucked six hairs, the recipient of her torture would feel it. If she plucked five or six hairs at the *same* time, they would definitely notice.

Either way, she had the information she needed. In less than fifteen minutes, too. Chey closed out the search engine, shut down the laptop, and vacated the library.

No one had seen her come or go.

She stopped by the kitchen, empty of people now that dinner was past, and collected a sealable baggie. Retreating to the bedroom she'd chosen as 'hers' upstairs, she raided the bathroom connected to it for cotton swabs, tweezers, a bandage with gauze in case she got overzealous with her pricking (or in case she suffered an unexpected bloody nose), and a needle she liberated from a small sewing kit.

What she needed now was something small and lightweight to carry all the collection items in. She rooted through a few cupboards and found nothing suitable.

In the bedroom, she searched the nightstands. Nothing there, either.

Crouching in front of the dresser, she went through every drawer. In the bottom one, behind a few generic sweaters and folded knit scarves, she found a black fanny pack. Chey arched a brow, brought it up to eye level, and cringed at the bright yellow happy face plastered on the front beneath the zipper.

"These things went out of style in the eighties," she said, muttering under her breath. It would keep her hands free, however, and wouldn't burden her if she needed to move fast.

Three minutes later, she had everything stored inside the compartment. Chey wrapped the pack around her waist to test the clasp, and found she had to let out an inch in the strap to make it fit. More walks and salads were in order, apparently.

Taking the pack off, she stuffed it into the top drawer of the dresser until she was ready to use it. Decorative letterhead and pen in the nightstand that she'd seen while searching for the pack drew her attention next. Removing both from the nightstand, she flopped onto the bed and by the single light of the bedside lamp, spilled her thoughts over the paper.

I know what you're thinking. DON'T DO IT! But I'm going to. I'm going in. It shouldn't be too hard to infiltrate the building now that I've already been inside. Here are the problems I see that might arise: 1. Someone found the busted basement door and boarded it shut good enough to prevent a zombie invasion. 2. Someone boarded the door -and- posted a sentinel outside in the yard. 3. They added attack dogs to monitor the perimeter. 4. Someone welded the outer gate closed. 5. Man Who Might Be Sander's Brother is a light sleeper and takes offense to someone plucking/sticking/pricking him for his DNA. 6. Man Who Might Be Sander's Brother is faster than I am. 7. Said Man has no compunction about squashing fleeing woman like a noisome fly. 8. Everyone in the house exists in a high state of paranoia and moved MWMBSB to another location, making breaking and entering irrelevant. 9. Someone installed security cameras, saving me from the problem of the welded gate, attack dogs, the sentinel and boarded door when a sniper picks me off from a high tower. 10. I never find the building to begin with, because I didn't stop to take directions when I escaped the first time, and wind up stranded in the hinterlands with no gas, food or water.

In all seriousness, most of these scenarios could be plausible since my last visit, sans sarcasm. I should probably take a few extra things, like a screwdriver, flashlight and something sharp enough to defend myself if necessary.

I'm annoyed that Sander wouldn't even listen to reason. He just said 'No', as if he thinks that word has ever meant anything to me in my life. No in Chey's world often means Yes. He hasn't learned that about me yet, I guess. But he will. It makes sense to send in someone who knows the layout at least a little. Doesn't it? I can be quiet when I need to be. I've navigated the house in the shadows and won't need a flashlight—at least on the bottom floor—to guide me. That counts for something.

Besides all that, I want to help. I want to see Sander reinstalled as heir and one day take the throne. I owe Aksel a bit of payback and this would be a great way to *do that.*

Yes, I realize returning to the building is dangerous. I know I need to be cautious. A part of me thrives at the adrenaline I'm feeling though. Maybe this kind of lifestyle really is up my alley. The intrigue, mystery, adventure. Because it -has- been an adventure. Two months ago I would have hotly denied I wanted any part of all this.

Now, all I can think about is how I'm going to steal (borrow) the SUV in the garage and get the DNA sample.

Sander, if things go bad and they find this note after the fact—don't be mad I went. I have to go my own way sometimes. Trust I took every precaution I could and remember that I love you.

A series of knocks at the bedroom door startled Chey into dropping the pen. Scrambling, she stuffed the paper into the nightstand drawer, picked up the pen off the floor, and set it on top. Thinking it had to be Mattias, she crossed to the door and swung it open.

Mattias leaned against the frame, one knee bent in casual repose.

"What?" Chey asked. She hoped she hadn't left anything telling visible in the room behind her.

"I wanted to check on you, make sure you weren't seething after the conversation with Sander. He's only doing what the thinks is best for you."

Chey arched a brow. Her skin prickled with mild irritation. "Firstly, I'm not a child. Secondly, he should have at least listened to what I had to say. I'm perfectly capable of deciding what's *best* for me all by myself."

"That may be the case, but he can't deal with the rest of this and worry you're out getting yourself in trouble at the same time. You know?" Mattias scrutinized her face.

"He doesn't need to worry. I'm just going to go to bed and see if there are new developments in the morning." She exhaled as if put upon. It wasn't far from the truth. A small part of her hated lying to Mattias, though, and she struggled not to let her deception show in her eyes. Mattias had been good to her through everything. He might construe this as an abuse of trust and never confide in her again.

Mattias tongued the edge of his teeth while he regarded her. He glanced at his watch, then straightened out of his lean.

"Very well. Get some decent rest. I'll see you in the morning."

Chey detected a hint of wariness in his tone. Thankful he didn't press the issue, she inclined her head. "You too. See you in the morning."

Closing the door when he departed, Chey leaned against it. With any luck, she would have the DNA in tow come daybreak.

. . .

At exactly eleven o'clock, Chey stuck her head into the hallway. Small lights attached to the walls provided dim illumination. Seeing no one, she exited her room, the fanny pack in place beneath a new coat she'd found in the closet. Designed for winter weather, the thick, heavy jacket was just what she needed for the trip. Heading downstairs, she made the main level and paused aside the banister, listening for voices or movement.

She knew there were several guards and a few other staff members on the premises. What Chey *didn't* know, was if there was an alarm system that might flash bright red lights and scream warnings if she tried to leave the house. Peering toward the front door did her no good. Two potted plants with broad fronds blocked part of each wall where an alarm system might be mounted.

Veering away from the foyer, she aimed for the dining room and kitchen where she thought doors to the garage might be located. The garage was on this side of the house, so it made sense access should be here, too.

She found what she was looking for in an extra room off the kitchen. One whole side was shelves, the other contained a small sink, a few cupboards and a door. Next to the door was a row of pegs from which several keys dangled. Choosing a ring with a definite logo on the chain, she exited into the cold garage and closed the door behind her.

So far, so good. No alarms went off.

Matching the logo to the vehicle, she approached with a glance at the three other cars parked on either side. All three were SUV types made for questionable weather, and none appeared to have blinking lights of alarm systems on the dash.

Using the key, she let herself inside the one she would be using. This is where the whole plan got tricky. She needed to get the garage door up and the engine started without alerting the entire house. At least until she was on the road and able to put some distance between herself and the rest.

Pressing the button on the remote hanging off the visor, she jammed the key into the ignition as the bay door rolled up. In reality, Chey knew it wasn't as loud as it seemed. Cringing at the rumble, she started the engine and began backing out immediately. Slowly, so she didn't clip the garage door on the way.

Once more, she expected sirens and flashing lights.

Nothing.

Just the growl of the engine and the garage door easing to a stop.

Chey backed all the way to the gate, using the second remote on the visor to open it. Whipping onto the street, relieved to see it plowed of snow, she threw the SUV into gear and glanced at the house.

A light inside the foyer snapped on, visible through the front windows of the manor.

"Crap." She picked up speed, turning on the headlights, determined to get lost before they could find her. Engaging the

GPS, she drove away from Mattias's holding using every short cut and side street she could. Generally, she went in the same direction as the town where Mattias picked her up to begin with.

That was her starting point. It was where she knew she needed to get her bearings and begin backtracking toward her destination.

To her great relief, Chey saw no flash of pursuing headlights in the rear view mirror. It appeared as if her break was a success.

. . .

She made good time on the sparsely traveled roads, checking the onboard GPS every now and then. Darkness made defining her bearings harder, but not impossible. Certain houses with many windows—or a few—along with odd shaped Inns and other businesses helped guide her where she needed to go.

When she drove into the small town where Mattias found her at the restaurant, the real hunt began. One road at a time, Chey backtracked through the countryside, taking it slow. This was where her attention to detail would really matter most. The moon cast its pale glow over the scenery, highlighting peaked roofs, broad meadows and a glimpse of a snaking river that Chey didn't remember seeing on her first pass.

Strange.

Had she already taken a wrong turn? Or had she not been paying close enough attention at the particular moment she'd passed it? She decided she'd missed the river in favor of three houses that she *did* remember on the opposite side of the road. All three had tiny blue lights rimming the eaves, as if the owners lived in perpetual Christmasland, refusing to take them down no matter what season it was.

She was on the right track so far.

Forty minutes later, Chey brought the SUV to a halt in the middle of the road. Forest stretched to the right, a pasture to the left. Nothing for the last ten minutes had looked familiar. If she was honest, nothing had looked familiar for the last *fifteen.*

An offshoot road intersecting with this one some miles back had caused Chey a bit of heartache. She didn't recall coming in from that direction. Yet this didn't feel right, either, and she decided to rely on instinct instead of sight. Turning around, she headed back to that smaller road. Once she was on it, she started scanning the roadsides for a landmark. Anything would do. There were no houses out here, which was both a blessing and a curse; it told her she was in the right area, at least, because Sander's brother—if that's truly who the man was—lived in the middle of nowhere.

A few minutes later, when doubt began to surface again and fear niggled at her that she might be lost, Chey spied a five way stop ahead.

"Yes! I remember that for sure." Driving up to it, Chey put the SUV in park, engine idling, and leaned forward to stare out the windshield. This was an unmistakeable landmark. She was in the right place, on the right road.

The only problem now was that she couldn't remember if she'd driven straight through, or had come in at one of the slight, angling roads. Chey hadn't bothered to look for road signs, and even if she had, there were none to be seen. No names, no other identifying marks to denote one path from another.

"Okay, just think. Did you drive straight through, or did you veer off?"

Imagining herself back in the driver's seat coming from the other direction, Chey attempted to figure out whether she turned or not.

Putting the SUV in gear, she went straight through the intersection. To the best she could recall, Chey thought she hadn't swerved from the stop sign. At least she had a new starting point to work from if this road proved a dead end.

Marking the mileage, she decided she'd give this one ten miles, then she would turn back.

Just before she hit five miles, another road cut away to the right. Chey eased the car to a stop. In the distance, through a sparse stand of trees on the other side of a long meadow, she could *just* make out lights. The dark mass behind what she assumed was a structure suggested forest.

"Bingo. Gotcha." She cut the headlights. Turning down the smaller road, Chey inched forward, looking for a good place to pull off. She didn't want to park too far from the building, nor too close. If she needed a quick getaway, she didn't want to run a half mile to reach the vehicle.

Judging she was about a quarter mile

away, she pulled onto the shoulder, shut the engine off, and opened her door. She left the keys in the ignition. Climbing to the ground, she eased the door closed and broke into a jog. Ahead, the trees clustered together near the wall surrounding the building, providing extra cover when she cut overland from the road. Shoes crunching through the snow, Chey paced herself, breath coming in white puffs past her lips. It was rough going where the snow covered fist sized rocks that tripped her up when she stepped on them instead of over them.

Reaching the trees, she ducked into the canopy and followed the line around toward the back of the property. This was the point she began hoping no one had found the broken basement door. If so, she imagined it would set off a chain reaction much like she'd written for her journal.

Slowing to a walk, she paced herself. It wouldn't be a good idea to use all her energy this early.

Following the trees to the back, she set her sights on the big bramble bush and the iron gate. Cutting into the open, obscured from the lower level by the wall, she jogged toward the gate, wary of dogs, guards and anything else that might suddenly jump out at her from the gloom.

To her surprise, she found the gate as she had the last time, latched but not locked. Opening it a fraction, she checked the flat ground between the wall and the building. No dogs. At least none in sight. No sentinel, either. Steadying her breathing, she slipped inside, closed the gate, and crouched to run the rest of the way to the basement stairs. Slinking down those, careful not to slip on ice, she came upon the door.

She saw the crack between the door itself and the frame, suggesting it was sitting just as it was when she'd closed it last. The latch wouldn't fasten thanks to splintered wood, meaning the door would remain open a couple inches until someone fixed it.

Entering just enough to get a good look at the basement, she discerned no one was down there gathering wood or anything else. Closing the door as it had been, she stepped over to the wall and eased along the stone toward the stairway to the main level. Pausing at the base, she opened her coat and unzipped the fanny pack to allow for quicker, quieter access. She wouldn't know if she needed the tweezers or needle until she saw whether the man was awake or how many clothes he had on.

Creeping up the stairs, she came to the landing and opened the door.

This was it. There was no changing her mind now.

As before, the lower level remained dimly lit. Chey could see both directions down the hall. No guards lurked at either end, or anyone else for that matter, making it easier for Chey to skulk through the shadows, up the staircase leading to the second floor, and along another main hall with many doors opening off into private bedrooms.

Feeling exposed, she sought a dark, empty room that allowed her to get out of the hallway where anyone might see her. The man could be anywhere. Chey had counted no less than eight doors she would have to search behind in order to track him down. She didn't want to consider what the odds were that someone would still be awake this late and catch her at her game.

Determined to continue, she plotted her course and exited the bedroom, choosing the door directly across from the room she hid in. Not giving herself time to think, she grasped the knob and went in. Stealth was imperative. Meager light from the hall slanted into the bedroom, highlighting several things at once: a pretty bed against the far wall, fluffy stuffed animals lined up on a decidedly feminine dresser and a girly lampshade with little sparkly crystals dangling off the edge. The shape of a slim body could be seen under the covers, a blonde swath of hair spilling across a pillow.

Chey took in all those minute details in a heartbeat. Backing out of the room, she eased the door closed and moved to the next. No one needed to tell her that was not the place she would find who she sought.

The next room also had feminine trappings, and the one after that. Chey stifled frustration while at the same time thanking her lucky stars that all the occupants had been asleep. Entering the fourth room, Chey peered into the gloom. Right away she discerned the masculine furniture and color scheme. While it appeared to be a well situated space, the décor was nothing befitting a Royal, abandoned or not. Unlike the others, the bed proved to be empty.

Chey wondered if this was the

brother's room. If so, where was he? She had not heard the strains of a violin, so the likelihood of him playing in the music room was slim. The longer she stood there, the more Chey believed a teenage boy lived here rather than a grown man. It had that feel to it.

Backing out, she closed the door and went to the next, bracing herself before swinging it open. A startled gasp greeted Chey immediately. From the bed, a woman flipped over on the mattress and angrily broke into the language of Latvala, gesturing 'get out' with one hand.

This is it. You've done it now, Chey girl. She's going to call the guards and you're going to wind up behind bars. Even while the mantra ran through her mind, Chey retreated, closing the door. She stood there, right there, while pinpricks of shock raced along her arms and legs. Crap. Although she'd known this would happen eventually, and prepared herself for coming face to face with someone who wasn't the man she needed, it was still a bigger surprise than she thought it would be.

It occurred to Chey that the woman, who did not call out for guards or chase her into the hall, probably hadn't been able to see Chey very well. Backlit by light, all that woman had made out was Chey's silhouette. Perhaps she thought it was one of the other girls, someone coming in to play a prank or bother her.

Chey looked up and down the hall. She knew she needed to move. Unfreeze her feet. This was a bad time to blank.

Galvanized into motion, she hit the following door, the last in this row on this side of the hall. She went in a little too fast, albeit quiet, and scanned the space while her mind raced.

Straddling a chair backwards, a man sat near his window, the glow of the moon bathing his disfigured features. Arms laced across the back of the seat, he stared pensively out the panes, spine relaxed into a slight curve, feet on the ground. He was fully clothed, from a flannel over a tee-shirt to heavy tread boots.

The split second glimpse of the man in repose vanished when he popped up straight and looked at the door. At *her.* Chey knew this was the man she needed. Struck again by just how much he resembled Sander, she had no time to dwell on it before the man frowned and clipped out a word in his native tongue.

Questioning her, no doubt, over why she'd just barged in his room with no knock, no warning.

Chey hadn't expected to find him fully coherent and alert. Panic made it hard to think. Rushing him would end up badly for her, she knew that without being told. He would overpower her in a second. Just like Sander. Chey was no physical match for this man.

He cut another word out, sitting up even straighter.

You're lingering too long! Think, think, think! Do something! Make a plan. Figure it out.

While she ranted at herself, the man pushed up out of the chair.

That was all it took. Chey pivoted and ran down the hallway, looking ahead to the dark doorway on her right where she'd hidden the first time. If she could duck in there, maybe he would run by, give up searching eventually, and she could sneak back when he went to sleep —eventually—and get her sample.

He was quick. Too quick. Chey felt him closing the distance and gave up on the idea of hiding. She hit the stairs and went down as fast as she dared. Panting terrified breaths, she didn't give up on a plan, was too determined to get answers for Sander. There had to be a way to salvage the situation.

At least the man hadn't called out for guards.

Hitting the first floor at a run, she veered down the hallway toward the door to the basement. She felt fingers graze her shoulder and almost screamed.

He was *right* behind her. She wouldn't make it to the basement without him catching her. Darting to the stairwell, she wrenched the door open. He grasped her elbow with another curt word on his tongue.

Chey wrenched free, grappling with him, nearly losing her footing as she went down the basement stairs.

And then she *did* lose her footing, balance going askew as she flew forward, hands out to brace her fall.

No one had to tell her this was going to be a hard, devastating landing.

Chapter Thirteen

The steel band of an arm caught her around the ribs and prevented Chey from taking a header to the cement floor. Surprised at the almost gentle way he handled her, she regained her feet with his help, bumbled down the final steps and turned around when he released her.

This close, she could see the sunken eye socket, the caved in part of his forehead. His cheek on that side also looked a little funny, though his mouth was fine, as was his jaw and chin on both sides.

Regardless of all that, she still had the impression that it was Sander bearing down on her instead of a strange man.

He cut another few curt words into the air, appearing puzzled.

Chey couldn't believe he wasn't calling down guards or attacking her for trespassing. *Get the sample! Get pieces of hair, or prick his arm and gather the blood!*

"I'm not here to hurt anyone, I promise, I just--" Chey's explanation died when the man darted a look past her shoulder. His prominent eye gleamed, narrowed.

Someone was behind her.

Chey knew it because her sixth sense had also kicked in, sending chills over her skin and the hair up on the back of her neck. She yelped when a pair of strong arms wrapped around her.

"You're in more trouble than you can even imagine," Sander said at her ear. Then he broke into his mother tongue, addressing the stranger.

Gasping, Chey looked back and up. Sander's distinct scent swamped her even as the familiar shape of his body imprinted itself on her back. She glanced between the men, easing in Sander's arms until she stood on her own merit.

"I thought you were in Barbados!" Chey couldn't believe Sander was standing there in the basement with her. Had he been lying about his location the whole time? He gave her a brief, withering look that sent hackles of anger up in place of the chills. Any other time, Chey would have lit into him.

Face to face, there was no denying

these men were related. They stared at each other while the stranger returned a calm, somewhat bemused sounding reply to Sander.

"Do you speak English?" Sander asked.

"Yes," the man replied. His accent was heavier than Sander's, voice raspy and low.

Chey tugged at the hem of her jacket while attempting to calm the frantic pace of her heart.

"I am Sander--"

"I know who you are," the man said. "I am called Laur."

"Good, Laur. Then you must realize we are somehow related," Sander said, extending his hand.

The stranger clasped it and shook, still staring hard at Sander's face. "I have known a long while, even though they try to hide it from me."

Sander shook and released. "Yes, they have hidden it from...everyone. This is Chey—who is *not* supposed to be here."

Chey tightened her lips and glared at Sander a moment before turning a tentative smile on Laur. "Sorry about all this skulking around. I believed it necessary."

Laur extended a hand to shake with

her as well. He seemed so much like a gentle giant, capable of doing mass damage if you rubbed him the wrong way.

"Chey," he said. "I take no offense."

Chey shook his hand. "Laur. You might have if I'd had time to pluck some hairs out of your head or pricked you to take a blood sample."

At least she was honest. Chey felt Sander's ire grow by leaps and bounds. She refused to look at him.

"For what reason?" Laur asked.

"We don't have a lot of time. To make a long story short—we would like to find out if you are Queen Helina and King Aksel's son. Their *real* firstborn. For that, we need a hair or blood sample--"

"Or saliva. That would be easiest," Chey interjected. She sensed Sander boring a look into the side of her head, and she returned a haughty, irritated glare of her own.

The gleam of his blue eyes promised retribution.

"I am willing," Laur said, inadvertently interrupting the stare down.

"Thank you," Sander said, returning his attention to his likely brother. "Once we find out for certain and deal with other problems arising from all this, perhaps you would do me the honor of visiting my house for a longer, less clandestine conversation."

"I have everything we need." Chey fished out the swabs and the baggie.

"I would be pleased, and I will say nothing of your visit here this evening," Laur replied.

Chey was struck by how cultured he seemed despite everything else. She extended two swabs. "Just take each one and smear the tip along the underside of your lip."

"Thank you," Sander said. "Discretion is imperative for *everyone's* safety."

Chey knew without being told that Sander was gently warning Laur that he could be in danger as well. If the King and Queen thought news would get out over Laur's birthright, would they take steps to eliminate him? She shuddered at the thought.

Laur took the swabs from her fingers and followed her directions exactly. Chey opened the baggie for Laur to drop the swabs in. Once he did, she sealed the baggie, rolled it up around the swabs, and stuck it back into the fanny pack.

This entire ordeal was turning out much different than Chey expected.

"I understand." The gravity in Laur's reply suggested he understood what Sander said, and also what Sander did not say.

"Excellent. As much as I would like to stay, I know there are guards here. We must be away before the alarm is raised," Sander said, hooking his fingers under the crook of Chey's elbow. "I look forward to the next time, Laur."

"As I. Should the guards rise, I will distract them," he said, following Sander and Chey to the busted basement door. He touched the splintered edge and glanced at Chey.

She gave him a contrite little smile that vanished the second Sander 'escorted' her outside.

The men traded a few more words in their own tongue. Then Sander hustled her by the elbow to the outer wall, through the iron gate and away from the building. They went low and fast, coming upon Mattias and another two guards waiting in the trees.

Well. That was just fabulous. The whole lot of them were in on it. Chey withheld any blistering diatribe while they jogged overland in the direction of the parked SUV. A cramp developed low in her stomach halfway there, but she refused to stop or even pause. Hell would have to freeze over before she would show one ounce of weakness.

She wasn't surprised to see another SUV from Mattias's house parked behind the one she'd borrowed. It inflamed her further to know they must have realized she would make an attempt and simply followed her here or however it was they found her. She opened the back door when Sander reached to do the same and climbed in without his help. Just before the door closed, she heard him snarl a low noise of discontent and frustration.

Good. Now he knew how she felt.

A few minutes later, with guards driving both SUVs, they were on the road back to Mattias's.

. . .

"What *were* you thinking?" Sander thundered the second they entered the house through the side garage door.

Chey's mouth opened in disbelief that he didn't wait for Mattias and the guards to properly disperse—which they did immediately following the bellow—before shouting at her.

"Why did you *lie?* How dare you--"

"Yet, it was all right for you to lie to Mattias?" Sander made quotation marks with his fingers in lieu of trying to mimic her voice. "I'm tired, I think I'll go up to bed." He dropped the finger quotes. "Was that not what you said? Which was a lie, when you were planning to leave all along."

Furious, Chey yanked off her coat and the blasted fanny pack. Mattias had possession of the swabs in preparation for having them sent to a lab for testing. She tossed her things onto an extra chair sitting against a wall as they stormed through the house. "You should have taken me more seriously, then! I'm not completely helpless--"

"And yet had Laur not been the man he is, or had I not been there to back you up, you would have been in a world of hurt!" Sander rounded on her in the foyer, before they ever reached the stairs.

Chey, fists at her sides, glared at him. "Stop interrupting me! You were supposed to be in Barbados. *Exiled.* Yet here you are, magically back in Latvala."

"I *was* in Barbados. Then I boarded a private plane for Latvala because I had no intentions of living under house arrest while my father wreaks havoc here. When we had our little video conference, I was already more than halfway home." He towered over her, blue eyes glinting with fury.

"You could have said something! Maybe I wouldn't have rushed out to try and help *you*," she said, jabbing a finger into his chest, "get your blood samples or hair roots or whatever else."

"What matters is that you completely disobeyed me--"

"Don't talk to me about obeying. I'm not a dog," she hissed. "All you had to do was tell me you were almost home and I wouldn't have gone out there."

"Yes you would. You would have done the exact same thing. Using my return is a cheap excuse," he growled. "When I tell you not to do something, it's for a damn good reason!"

Seething, Chey got on her tiptoes. It was the only way she could go nose to nose with him, though it still wouldn't have worked if he didn't have his head bent down like that. "You don't know what I would or wouldn't have done. Even something more along the lines of, *I really don't want you to go, Chey,* would have had a much bigger impact on me than your imperious 'No.'"

"I disagree," he said in a silky tone. "I think you would have gone no matter what. Any argument I made, or pleas, would have fallen on deaf ears. 'No' was just the more expedient way to express my feelings about you taking off by yourself on some hair brained mission that could have gotten you killed!"

By the end, the silkiness had given away to a sandpaper rasp. He reached inside his pocket and pulled out her journal entry from upstairs. The one she'd stuffed into the nightstand after Mattias knocked on her door.

"You're impossible. I had it under control!" Which was a blatant lie. She *would* have been in big trouble had Laur not spared her a nasty fall, and if he would have called for guards. Thankfully, he hadn't. Sight of her journal paper caused her blood pressure to skyrocket.

Sander snarled at the obvious lie. "You're pushing it, Chey."

"What are you going to do. Put me over your knee? I'm not five! And I'm back, and safe, which is more than I can say for your lies--"

"It wasn't a lie. You never asked me where I was. Besides that, it was safer for me to keep my whereabouts just then as close to the vest as I could. I *am* technically in exile. They need to believe I'm there, not here, until we clear this mess up. The next time I tell you not to go somewhere, listen to me!" He shoved the folded paper back into his pocket without offering it to her.

Their mouths were so close she could have kissed him. Right then, she wanted to sock him in the nose. Pivoting on a heel, she marched to the stairs and trotted up them.

"That's perfect," he said to her back. "Walk away before the conversation's finished."

"Oh, it's finished Mister! It was finished--" Chey lost steam when Sander stalked through an archway into some other part of the house. Furious all over again that he cut her biting retort off, she made the second floor landing, headed to her room, and slammed the door closed behind her hard enough to rattle windows in their frames.

· · ·

The man is completely infuriating! How dare him tell me 'No', then read me the

214

riot act the second we get home. If Sander Ahtissari thinks for one minute that I'm the type of woman to simper and swoon, he's got another think coming. Yes, I might have been in a spot of trouble when he found me, but honestly, I think Laur would have let me take the samples or the swabs if I'd explained, meaning I would have gotten out of there unscathed (let's not talk about my stumble down the staircase, where Laur saved me from falling) and had everything we needed from Laur's end for the tests.

I never expected Laur to be so genteel and kind. Who knew? But sometimes that's why you take risks. It would have worked out in the end.

Back to Sander—that man is on my List. I'm angry enough to spit nails.

Chey wadded the paper up and threw it against the far wall. Scowling, she tossed the pen on the nightstand and pressed the heels of her hands against her brow. An hour after the end of the argument with Sander, Chey knew all thoughts of sleep for the rest of the night were out of the question. It was three-something in the morning, when the house and the night were still and silent.

Her mind raced over the events that led her here. She couldn't find that much blame in what she'd done. Not enough to cause the blow up between her and Sander.

What annoyed her more than anything was that she kept listening for him in the hallway beyond the door. Wondering if he was going to show up, tail between his legs, apology in his eyes.

She snorted at herself. Sander would never tuck his tail over anything. He might apologize, but he would never compromise his masculinity by creeping around, begging for mercy.

No, this little stand off was going to last much longer than a night. *She* certainly wasn't about to grovel and plead. Where was the sample from Helina? Did anyone have a hair root or a saliva swab?

She thought not.

Indignant, she rubbed a hand over her stomach, wishing the icky feeling would leave. She couldn't pinpoint exactly what didn't feel good. It wasn't quite nausea, not quite a cramp. Or a little of both? She didn't know. It made her more irritable than she already was.

Sliding down deeper into the covers,

she tucked her hands beneath her head and stared at the far wall.

It was going to be a long night.

Chapter Fourteen

The tension in Mattias's home knew no bounds. For two days, Sander and Chey collectively seethed, alternating between dirty looks and silent treatments. She took her meals when she knew he wouldn't be anywhere near the kitchen or the dining room table and avoided parlors or sitting rooms if she knew he was in there brooding.

It didn't help that she felt increasingly worse. Chey began to worry by evening of the second day when the nausea plagued her to the point she had to spend three hours curled over the toilet in her private bathroom.

This was the wrong time for the flu.

The sound of a knock penetrated the haze but she felt too horrible to get up and answer it. Sander could glare at the door all night for all she cared.

A few moments later, Mattias appeared in the bathroom doorway.

"What's wrong?" he asked immediately,

frowning.

"I don't feel good, obviously. I think I've got the flu." She lolled her head to the side, glanced at him, then stared toward the wall once more. "If you're here to plead his case—"

"I came to tell you we successfully retrieved a hair sample, a few of them actually, from Helina. Both hers and Laur's are on their way to a lab for testing." Mattias crossed to a cupboard and pulled out a folded, fluffy washcloth. Taking it to the sink, he ran it under the water, wrung it out, then walked it over to press against her forehead.

The caring gesture reminded Chey so much of what her mother might have done that tears stung the back of her eyes. Mattias patted her brow, the back of her neck, and her hairline.

"This is very un-Princely of you," she said, voice thick with emotion. What was wrong with her?

"On the contrary, I think it's very Princely of me." He set his other hand between her shoulder blades. "Better?"

"A little bit. Thanks." Chey accepted his help with grudging appreciation. It wasn't Mattias's fault she and Sander were on the outs. "How long will it take to get the results?"

"You're welcome. A few days at the most. We should know something more definitive by then." He took the washcloth away from her skin and set it on the counter.

"Then what?" she asked, cutting a look away from the wall to Mattias.

"We're discussing options. What I also came to tell you is that Laur is sneaking out and coming here for a couple hours. Not until later of course, when his house is mostly asleep."

Chey sat up, hair tousled, and frowned at Mattias. "Sneaking out? Is that wise? What if someone discovers him missing?"

"They'll think he went into the woods. I doubt they'll notice him gone though for the little while he'll be here." Mattias squeezed her shoulder, pressed to a stand, and paused near the doorway.

"Thanks for letting me know. I'll come down when he arrives." Chey hoped she felt well enough by then.

"Good. I'll knock on your door to let you know." He smiled, then exited the way he came.

Chey sniffed and crawled up off the floor. Closing the toilet lid, she picked up the washcloth on her way into the bedroom. Sliding onto the bed, she rolled onto her back and laid the cloth across her forehead.

If she wanted to see Laur, it would mean being in the same room as Sander. The thought upset her—and made her long for Sander's presence. Just now, feeling as crappy as she did, all she wanted was his warmth and scent. He had a way of embracing her that chased all her ills away.

"Don't get weak, Chey. It's just the flu." She chided herself not to wimp out and get soft on Sander. He owed her an apology and that was that.

The next thing Chey knew, someone was touching her shoulder, shaking her awake.

Sitting up with a gasp, washcloth falling into her lap, she thrust a hand out to automatically ward off the shadow lurking at the side of the bed. Only then did she realize it was Mattias, dark gaze glinting in the low light.

"I wanted to tell you that he's here. Laur. Downstairs in the first parlor." He removed his hand from her shoulder. "How are you feeling?"

"Oh. Thanks." Chey plucked the damp cloth off her lap and set it on the nightstand. "I'm—I guess it's better. I'll be down in a few minutes."

"All right. We're taking him back at three," Mattias said before retreating. He closed the door quietly behind him when he left.

Chey squinted at the bedside clock. *1:15.*

She'd been asleep for hours.

Putting her feet on the floor, she realized the nausea wasn't as severe as it had been. Part of her wanted to slump right back into the sheets and sleep the rest of the night away. Instead, she changed into jeans. Or tried to change into jeans. She struggled with the button, which didn't want to close.

"Seriously?" she spat, angry that bloat prevented her from getting the button done. Peeling the denim down, refusing to lay on the bed and wriggle into them, she flipped the jeans onto the covers and sought velveteen lounge pants instead. A matching dove gray, zip up top went over a thinner white shirt beneath.

Better.

Pulling on socks and tennis shoes, she hit the bathroom last and attempted to make herself look less like a pale ghost and more like a human. It required a touch of blush, lip gloss and a streak of color on her eyelids.

Even then, she thought she looked peaked and tired.

"Of course you're tired, Chey. You spent the whole evening puking and it's now the middle of the night." Exasperated with herself, she departed her bedroom.

On the way down the hall toward the stairs, she braced herself in regard to Sander. She hadn't seen him since an accidental glimpse earlier this morning when they passed each other going and coming from the kitchen. Chey had steadfastly refused to acknowledge him.

He'd returned the favor, which had stung more than Chey wanted to admit.

At the archway to the main parlor, Chey was struck by the sight of Laur in more moderate light. He stood near the fireplace with a drink in hand, his deformity on vivid display. From one side, the left, one almost couldn't tell there was anything wrong. Not until he turned face on. Then the cavity and the depressed eye socket were impossible to miss.

He saw her standing there staring and lifted his glass her way in a silent toast.

Chey smiled, aware Sander sat perched on the arm of a sofa not far from his possible brother. "Hello, Laur. I'm very glad to see you could make it up for a visit."

"Good evening, Miss Chey. Thank you, I'm happy to have the company. Can I get you a drink?" he asked. It might not have been his house, but that didn't stop Laur from stepping up like a gentleman to offer.

"No thanks." On impulse, she crossed the room to kiss his cheek. His good cheek.

He bent his head and stooped his shoulders to make it possible.

Chey thought there was a little extra color under his skin when she leaned back. "Thanks again for saving me from a nasty fall on those stairs."

"Of course." He cleared his throat and smiled again.

Chey, impressed with his chivalry and gentle giant manner, touched his arm with warm affection before diverting to a plush chair. Sinking down into the confines, she got comfortable. Mattias stood somewhere beyond Sander, a tumbler of amber liquid in hand. He arched his brows when she glanced his way. All Chey did was give him a quick smile before returning her attention to their guest.

After all, that's why they were here.

"So you grew up in that place?" Sander asked, apparently resuming a line of questions.

Laur glanced at Sander and nodded. "My whole life. It's all I've known."

"And who are the other occupants?" Mattias asked.

"Others like me. Of my nature, I should say. One is a mute, one is severely disabled." Laur gave a few examples. He glanced down into his glass and gave it a swish.

"How many, would you say?" Sander asked.

"There are twelve of us. Most have been there since early childhood."

"But you're the oldest out of everyone, yes?" Mattias added.

"Yes," Laur said, inclining his head. "The youngest is eight."

Chey saw Mattias and Sander exchange a look. She thought they were wondering if all the occupants were of Royal blood. Not Helina's, per se, but maybe nieces, nephews or cousins. A repository for the Royal blooded who weren't up to snuff. The thought made Chey a little nauseous. They were still people, with thoughts and dreams and hopes like anyone else.

"Do any of them know where they come from, or do they arrive so young that the house is all they know?" Sander asked.

"They come as babies, usually," Laur said.

"Amazing," Mattias said. There was a note of discord in his voice, as if he too was dismayed at what he thought might be going on.

"But you're educated, and I see they followed tradition by encouraging English. Do you speak any other languages?" Sander asked. His expression waned serious and sober.

"Russian, German, Estonian and Hungarian," Laur said.

Chey almost fell out of her chair. How many was that total? Six? She supposed that's what came of being forced to live in the same place, in total seclusion. One learned many things to keep their mind occupied. She wondered if Sander and Mattias also spoke that many languages.

Sander inclined his head. "I hear you play the violin as well."

"Yes. It is my favorite among many."

"What others do you play?" Sander

asked. "I play the violin myself."

Laur's brow arched. "Yes? I play the piano, guitar and cello. Lately, the harp."

Chey felt completely out of her league. She spoke one language and played no instruments.

"We should play before you go," Sander said.

"It would be my pleasure," Laur replied.

"How did you come to believe you were related to Royalty?" Mattias asked.

"The television. Usually we are limited as to what we may see. One day, during a parade, I saw Prince Dare and suspected then."

"But you never asked your caretakers?" Mattias pressed.

"I did not think it prudent on my behalf," Laur said with an arch of his good brow.

"Probably wise," Sander said. He stood up off the arm of the chair and paced closer to the fireplace, where Laur lingered.

Chey, seeing them side by side, knew there was no way Laur wasn't directly related. The men were built almost identical and except for Laur's black hair, the facial features were eerily similar. It was mostly the jaw, a trait all but one Ahtissari brother shared. Chey recalled Gunnar's wasn't quite as well defined as the others.

"Did the King or Queen ever visit?" Sander asked, resting his elbow on the heavy mantle.

"Not to my knowledge," Laur replied. "We had few visitors barring new tutors or staff."

Sander's lips thinned. "Right. So I guess you're expected to live your life out there."

Laur inclined his head, as if it were a foregone conclusion, something he had already come to terms with.

"Let's play, shall we?" Sander said, diverting away from the fireplace with a sudden pivot.

"Absolutely." Laur finished the contents of his glass and set it aside on a side table.

"He's good. I hope you can keep up," Mattias teased Laur.

"You should be wondering if he can keep up with *me,*" Laur countered. He ducked his chin, as if such self proclamations were rare and embarrassing.

Chey smiled to herself watching Laur.

The brief glimpse of bashfulness was endearing. She couldn't believe how kind and easy going he was, considering what he was learning about his life. A cast aside because of his looks, Laur didn't seem angry to be overlooked or left alone from parents who ruled the country he lived in.

Not many people, she thought, would be so forgiving.

Cutting a sly glance across the room, Chey perused Sander's physique with a stark longing that surprised her. It wasn't just his body she missed, it was Sander himself. His teasing, the intensity, the way he made her feel special and unique.

He brought back two violins from a glass case and handed one to Laur. Sander, grinning at Laur's quip, added, "Put your money where your mouth is, brother."

Laur, startled at the familiarity, took the violin in his big hands and tucked the end under his chin. "Prepare to be one upped, pup."

Chey joined Mattias and Sander in laughter.

"Paganini?" Sander asked, mimicking the tuck, eyes on Laur.

"Twenty-fourth Caprice."

"Of course," Sander replied with a devilish grin.

Chey curled into the chair, taking the opportunity to enjoy the camaraderie and get her first look at Sander playing the violin. He looked dashing in black and white, the shirt thrown open at the throat. Tonight he'd left his hair loose instead of tied back, the golden strands brushing the tops of his broad shoulders.

Timing it precisely, the violins both sprang to life. The complicated finger work and fast pace of the piece presented many challenges, and the men met them all head on. Laur, intent and focused, regarded Sander as the parlor filled with the classical strains of a master. Sander, in turn, watched Laur like a hawk when he wasn't looking at the instrument.

Fascinated, Chey glanced from one to the other, lingering more on Sander than Laur. She hadn't forgotten their argument or her ire, but she also wouldn't pass up this experience for anything. Who knew when the men might get together to play again. More, once it was over, she would have to go back to ignoring Sander. It was becoming a burden to have this uncomfortable space between them.

Mattias did not waste the opportunity

to commemorate the occasion. He used his phone to snap several photos during the evening.

The violinists finished with a flourish and a laugh from Sander. Laur pointed his bow at the Prince and settled into a slower piece. There were obvious places their pacing was off from one another, or a sour note hit the air, always prompting a playful cringe or grin from either man.

After fifteen minutes, they set the instruments aside, poured more drinks, and settled in while Laur cycled through a round of his own questions. Chey joined in the conversation here or there, enjoying Laur's company more and more. She saw Sander and Mattias were as well. It did her heart good to see the men bonding.

Over too soon, Mattias regretfully mentioned it was time to get Laur back to the house. Laur and Sander clasped hands, then bumped chests in a half hug. Mattias did the same. Chey repeated her cheek kiss and accepted a one armed embrace from Laur in turn.

It seemed to Chey that a gaping hole was left in Laur's wake. The second he was out of the room, she noticed what an impact he might have on someone's life.

Right after that, she realized she was standing in the parlor alone with Sander. He stood somewhere behind her, out of sight. Should she confront him, attempt conversation? Wasn't it time to put all this behind them? All she wanted was an apology at this point.

Taking a fortifying breath, she turned around.

Sander leaned near the fireplace once more, elbow propped on the mantle. Watching her.

It was now or never.

. . .

"Look, Sander. This is ridiculous. We can't go on pretending the other doesn't exist--" Chey halted when Sander interrupted.

"Oh, I know you exist. The problem is, you still think you're right, and I don't, so until we come to some understanding about that, we're going to have this friction between us." At some point he'd poured himself a drink and lifted the glass to his mouth, pulling down a swallow. He watched her over the rim.

A shiver of fresh irritation slithered down Chey's spine. "No, the real problem is that you don't want to admit that I was more than capable of obtaining that sample on my own. I mean look how kind Laur is. All I would have had to do was ask at that point."

"How did you know that I wasn't planning something of my own?" he asked in a voice gone dark and silky. "What if--"

"But you didn't! You *didn't* plan anything..."

"*What if,*" he bellowed, cutting her off. "I had sent a team in there? They could have mistaken you for an adversary. You still fail to understand that there are forces beyond yourself here. It's not just Chey against the world. It's Chey and the Royal family, the covert operations I have at my command, and any number of other plans or personnel that could have flipped that situation on its ear."

"If you would have trusted me to begin with, we wouldn't even be having this conversation! You should have realized I could handle it--"

"Yes, yes, I saw how well you were handling it. On the run, scared half to death, wondering if he was going to squish you under his pinky because he *could* have, or something far worse, if

Laur was not the man he is." Sander thumped the glass down and stalked across the room. Heading for her.

Chey stiffened, making herself taller, though for what good it would do, she didn't know. The closer he got, the more she had to tilt her chin up to retain eye contact. "So that's it then. That's all. I'm in the wrong and you won't ever see it differently."

He stopped in front of her, staring down into her eyes. "You can't be doing this when you're my Queen, Chey. You run off like that on some hair brained 'mission'," his tone mocked the term, "and you'll wind up kidnapped for ransom or dead. So yes, you're in the wrong and come hell or high water, I'll make you realize it."

"Who said I would do that if I was Queen?" she shouted. She got no further. Sander intercepted the conversation. Hijacked was more like it.

"Because you're doing it now and you still don't see the danger you put yourself in. You're so intent on proving whatever you think you have to prove--"

"I did it because I thought I had the best shot at getting the sample!" Furious, Chey swung away from him and jogged out of the parlor. She went fast up the stairs, so fast she caught the toe of her shoe on the stair and stumbled. Recovering, she ascended to the second floor, marched to her room and closed the door behind her with both hands. The bang echoed like cannon shot through the house.

So much for reconciliation.

. . .

Sander stared at the parlor archway, listening to Chey stumble up the stairs. He had half a mind to go after her and finish their argument until they came to some sort of understanding. His temper was too precarious and he knew it. What drove his anger was her recklessness and, if he was honest with himself, his fear that he would come upon her someday face down in a ditch or in a backwater cabin strapped to a chair, dead, all because she'd rushed off to prove she could help. It made his blood run cold, the thought of his enemies—and he did have them—getting their hands on her.

The slamming door set his teeth on edge.

Stalking out of the parlor, he took the stairs by two, veering down another hall at the top. He kept a room here with changes of clothes and a few other personal items for the times he visited. Entering his domain, he gathered both phones, the folder on the nightstand, and the backpack sitting at the end of his bed.

The best way to keep his little hellion safe was to obliterate as many threats as he could. Currently, that was his own mother and father. The next steps in this deadly dance had a high potential to backfire and he needed all his concentration to pull off their plan.

Distractions like this could cost someone their life.

Giving the room a last glance to make sure he wasn't forgetting something important, Sander departed. Not just the room but the house itself, mouth set in a grim line of determination. He would have preferred to settle things first, to replace Chey's tears with smiles.

Time was not on their side, however, and with a snarl of discontent, he piled into an SUV, backed out of the garage, and drove away into the night.

Chapter Fifteen

Chey knew something was wrong the second she opened her eyes the following morning. Stomach in knots, nausea holding her in its vicious grip, she hugged the toilet and heaved for an hour. If this had been the flu, like she suspected the night before, she wouldn't have had that lull after the first round of vomiting. Would she? It didn't fit the pattern, at least in her mind. Whenever she'd suffered the flu before, there were all those other symptoms, too. Fever, aches and pains. She didn't have a fever, that was easy enough to discern, and her aches and pains were relegated to sickness this morning. Chey sat up straighter, startled. *Morning sickness.*

Gasping, she covered her lips with her fingers. Could it be?

Was she pregnant?

She cast back for the last time she'd gone through her monthly cycle. November. Had it really been that long ago? Shocked to her core, she wondered how she could have missed it in the ensuing months.

"Well, look at the chaos and the flying back and forth between countries. What did you expect?" she chided herself, talking out loud. Her voice echoed off the bathroom walls.

Pushing off the floor, she flushed the toilet and went to the sink. A long mirror ran the length of the equally long counter, bouncing her reflection back. She looked pale, cheeks more pronounced than usual, with dark circles under her eyes. Other clues were the tiredness she'd experienced lately and the fact that she couldn't do the button of her jeans yesterday.

"Oh my God, I'm pregnant." She stared at her reflection, letting the shock of it sink in.

Pregnant. How far along was she? Her stunned brain couldn't calculate the math.

What she *did* know was that they were in the first weeks of February, a far cry from November. She wasn't sure when exactly to start counting from. Maybe ten weeks along? Twelve?

She needed a pregnancy test to be

absolutely sure.

Brushing her teeth, she rinsed, splashed her face with cold water, then hopped in the shower. Too anxious to linger in the hot spray, she made a quick job of it. Changing into a pair of ash gray yoga pants and a thin ribbed sweater of white, she departed her room in search of Sander.

She couldn't wait to tell him she suspected she was carrying his child. Regardless of their argument and the tension between them, news of a baby was a joyous occasion. Their fight would melt away into nothingness, where it belonged.

Coming up empty on the upper floor, Chey descended to the main level. Mattias's voice coming from his office drew her that direction. Maybe he would know where Sander was.

Mattias ended his call when she appeared in the doorway. He smiled his welcome and gestured to one of the chairs opposite his desk. Dressed in black slacks and a midnight blue button down, he looked like he'd been up for hours.

"Good morning, Chey. You're looking better. Have a seat?" he said.

"Hi. Actually Mattias, I'm looking for

Sander. Do you know where he's gone to?" She rocked on the soles of her shoes. It was so hard not to confess what she thought might be happening.

His expression sobered as he perched on the edge of his desk. "He left last night, Chey, to get our plans underway. We're expecting the results today or tomorrow from the samples, and once we have them, things will get dangerous quickly."

All she heard was that Sander was gone. Gone. Without a word of goodbye. It hurt so much that she glanced at the floor to hide the sudden sheen of tears.

"I'm sorry," Mattias said with a wealth of compassion.

She teethed the inside of her lip. "It's all right. I suppose I shouldn't be surprised." Yet she was.

"It's a precarious time. If it makes you feel any better, I know it was difficult for him to go without talking to you first. Once this is over, this particular event, things will smooth out." He got up off the desk and strode closer to set a comforting hand on her shoulder.

"I'm sure." Chey wasn't sure at all. She wanted to believe they would work it out. They *had* to work it out. Confirmed hotheads, the both of them, and when they went at it, they *really* went at it. That didn't mean everything was over and done.

"Chey," he said, trying to get her attention.

She glanced up. Met his eyes.

"It'll be okay." He squeezed her shoulder with gentle pressure. "Sander might have a temper, but he's rational in the end and he's loyal to those he loves. Things will be fine, trust me."

Chey smiled and wished it didn't feel so shaky. She would never understand how Aksel and Helina, considering how they were, had raised such compassionate, caring children. "You're the best almost brother-in-law a girl could ever have. Thanks."

He laughed. "You're welcome."

"Mattias?" She maintained eye contact so he would know what came next was serious instead of frivolous.

"Yes?" he replied, a curious gleam in his gaze.

"Is there any way someone can drive me to the closest town? I need...well. I need a few things that I don't have with me." She made it sound of the feminine hygiene variety, which wasn't far from the

241

truth. "I'll make sure I disguise myself so no one recognizes me."

Mattias considered it, expending a few seconds in silence. "Yes, of course. I'm waiting for an important call, or I would take you myself. I'll have Olev drive you in."

"I appreciate it. How long do you think it'll take? I can't remember where the closest store is around here."

"Twenty minutes. Here." He released her, reached into his pocket, and withdrew a fold of money secured by a silver clip. Peeling off several bills, he extended them.

"Thanks, I forgot about money." Chey's money was sitting in a bank in another country and at Kallaster castle, inaccessible for now. She took the bills and folded them once more to fit in her palm. "I'll go change and meet Olev in the garage, all right?"

"Sounds good." He winked and pulled his cell phone out of his pocket after returning the money.

Chey swung away and headed back upstairs to her bedroom. Once there, she changed again, drawing on a pair of jeans that had fit her a bit loose to begin with. They were loose everywhere except the button, which now fit against her skin instead of the usual inch gap. She traded tennis shoes for warmer boots, a beanie that she pulled over her head and all her hair, and a pair of sunglasses that obscured a good portion of her face. A glance in the mirror proved she was all but unrecognizable.

Tucking the money into her front pocket, she descended the stairs and went straight to the garage, where Olev was already waiting in the SUV, engine idling with the bay door rolled up. Blonde, tall and broad, Olev wore dark clothes and a coat that hid the shoulder holster beneath.

Chey got into the front instead of the back.

"Miss Sinclair," he said in greeting. Once her door was closed, he reversed out of the garage and headed toward the main gate.

"Hi Olev." Buckling in, Chey tilted her head against the seat.

"Any particular place?" he asked as he got them on the road.

"Just somewhere that sells a good variety of things." She closed her eyes, caught between potential joy at the idea of being pregnant and sorrow that Sander was gone. Chey tried not to read too much into him leaving without seeking her out.

"Got it," Olev said. He sped along the streets, not too fast and not too slow, taking great care to avoid any ice patches or stranded cars.

Twenty minutes later, he pulled up outside a quaint looking store in a town with only one main street. All the shops faced the road with extra parking in the back. Snow lined the curbs from plows that had been running all night.

Olev shut the engine off, disembarked, and came around to open Chey's door.

"Thanks," she said after undoing the buckle. Olev helped her down by a hand while scanning the area with discreet swivels of his head. Professional and aware of the need to stay undercover, he pretended to be a doting boyfriend as he escorted her casually to the front door.

"I'll wait out here. If you need anything inside, raise your hand to flag me. I'll see it," he said near her ear.

Chey inclined her head, understanding he wanted to watch the road and sidewalks. "I will. Be right back."

Olev pulled out a cell phone and feigned a call while she went inside. The tall windows along the front of the store allowed him to mark her passage up and down the aisles.

Grateful for the escort and the knowledge she had someone there if she needed them, Chey still hoped he didn't pay attention to where exactly in the store she went. The interior was set up a lot like corner pharmacies back home, with one wall dedicated to prescriptions and the other aisles catering to a wide array of products ranging from toys for babies to stationary to first aid.

The smell was both clinical and floral thanks to a row of candles in jars on a rounder right inside the door.

Feeling conspicuous, Chey stopped near a section of make up and other cosmetics. She chose a few lip balms, a new hair brush and several hair bands that went into the basket hanging on her arm. Swinging around into the feminine hygiene section, she went on the hunt for her primary target: pregnancy tests. Finding them with ease, she then debated what kind to get.

It struck her then that she could be carrying the next King or Queen of Latvala. The knowledge made her hand shake. She chose a brand that looked easy to use and put three tests into the basket.

Chey wasn't taking any chances.

A few bottles of lotion followed the tests in with the rest of it before Chey headed to the counter. She traded hellos with the clerk in her halting use of their mother tongue. After paying and accepting her change, she scooped the bag off the counter, bid her goodbyes, and headed to the door.

Olev saw her coming and had it open by the time she got there.

"Find what you need?" he asked, ending his phone call.

"I did, thanks." Chey felt confident Olev hadn't pinpointed what products in particular she'd been after.

Once in the SUV, Olev wasted no time getting them back on the road for home.

Distracted by the possible pregnancy and the upcoming test, she stared out the window. Low music poured out the speakers while heat kept the temperature comfortable.

Before she knew it, they were pulling into the garage at the house.

"I appreciate you taking the time to drive me, Olev," she said, climbing down from the car.

"Of course, Miss Sinclair. Anytime." He shut the engine off and followed her into the house.

Chey cut away for the stairs with her bag in tow.

Time to find out whether or not there was a baby on the way.

. . .

Two minutes was a lifetime. Chey paced in the bedroom while the test sat on the counter in the bathroom. She glanced at the nightstand clock and exhaled frustration that the digital read out wasn't what she wanted it to be. Could two minutes really last this long? She had half a mind to run in there to see if there was any early indication. One pink line, negative. Two pink lines, positive. Maybe she would be able to tell already.

One more glance at the clock.

Now it was time.

Chey walked into the bathroom, wishing Sander were here to experience this with her. She couldn't wait another second to know, didn't want to drink or eat or do anything that might harm the baby.

Approaching the counter, she held her breath. Stopping before the skinny stick, she glanced down.

Two pink lines. Two *very* pink lines.

"Oh my God, oh my God!" Chey covered her mouth over a gasp of shock. It didn't matter that she'd mostly deduced she was pregnant. This made it *real.* She was going to have a baby. Cupping her hands low over her stomach, she let the reality of it sink in. Again, she realized this child's role in life would be so much different than she ever imagined a baby of hers would be. She didn't know if girls ascended the throne like boys did, but she would find out soon enough.

What would Sander say? It pained her that they were at such odds. She wanted to fix things between them before she told him. Wanted all the warmth and affection in place of the tension and silence.

Just to be on the safe side, she went through all the motions again and took a second test. In case there was a glitch, she wanted to see if she got the same result twice.

She did. Two pink lines popped right up. This time, she stood there and watched, tears stinging her eyes. Two tests couldn't be wrong.

Gathering up the evidence, she crushed the boxes and wrapped them in tissue before discarding, so the staff wouldn't see. The tests themselves she hid inside her make up case beneath a lift out section.

Exiting the bathroom, she started for the nightstand and her phone. Halfway there, she came to a halt. Should she tell Mattias? She felt it was important that someone know besides her. Yet she hated for anyone to know before Sander. What if it slipped out and he overheard someone else talking?

No, it was better to get Sander back here as soon as possible so they could talk and she could find a way to tell him.

While she debated, someone knocked at her bedroom door.

Maybe Sander had returned.

Crossing the room, she swung the door open. Olev stood there, grim faced.

"Prince Mattias requires your presence in the main parlor. It's urgent," Olev said.

"What's wrong?" Chey stepped out after him and followed Olev to the stairs, trotting down to the first floor. She held the banister the whole way, cautious about an accidental stumble.

"I'll let him explain," Olev said. He

indicated the parlor in question and swiveled away for the foyer where another guard waited.

Chey glanced after Olev, then entered the parlor. Mattias paced in front of the blazing fireplace with a phone to his ear. Speaking in his native tongue, the words fell rapid and brusque from his lips. When he caught sight of her, his gaze lingered. He held up a finger in a *one moment* gesture.

Taking up a lean against the arm of the couch, she wondered what in the world was going on.

Hanging up, Mattias pushed the phone into the pocket of his coat. "Thanks for coming down, Chey. I'm afraid we have a problem."

"What is it? Nothing happened to Sander, did it?" Her blood ran cold at the thought.

"Laur contacted me an hour ago, stating he thinks the guards in the house are onto him. He overheard them talking over whether to call the King to tell him what they've discovered."

"Onto him? You mean they know he left the house or something? But you said they'd probably think he just went into the woods," she said, fretful that something might happen to Laur.

"He's not positive exactly what they know or don't know, but they're suspicious enough to consider contacting my father," Mattias said. "I've called Sander back to the house."

"I'm not sure I understand the urgency," Chey admitted. "Once you get the results back, then you can work to free Laur and the others, yes?"

"I fear if the King thinks Laur has communicated with the outside world, he'll give the order for the guards to clean the house." Mattias's mouth pressed into a tight, displeased line.

"Clean the house?" Chey wasn't following.

"Kill them all."

Chapter Sixteen

"He can't do that!" Indignant, furious, Chey paced around the edge of the sofa. "Why would he? What would he gain?"

"Using Laur in passing to privately threaten Dare into exile is one thing. Having Laur presented to the outside world, exposing what he and Helina have done, is another. Right now, Aksel thinks Dare is confined to Barbados. Once he realizes—and he will, sooner or later—that Dare is unaccounted for, he'll take whatever steps he deems necessary to protect himself. That includes obliterating an entire house full of 'defective' people should he even suspect for a moment that Dare has discovered Laur's whereabouts. More than that—the truth behind it." Mattias snarled over the word 'defective' and paced counter to Chey, clearly agitated.

Chey rubbed her brow with her fingertips. The thought of anything happening to Laur, that sweet, gentle giant, made Chey sick. He deserved better than that. Better than being confined to a single residence his entire life.

"So you think the guards might realize Laur went somewhere, rather than just wandering the woods?" Chey asked, glancing at Mattias.

"If someone saw him go out, they might have had a guard follow discreetly and hide in the trees. If that guard saw headlights from our SUV in the distance, where we picked Laur up, then their suspicions would be raised. It's even possible that someone heard you three in the basement. What if a guard followed Laur down and listened in where you couldn't see him? There are any number of scenarios." Mattias muttered a curse. "We should have been more careful."

"I think you were very careful. How could you have known?" Chey hadn't seen nor heard any guards the night she went skulking through the house—but then she'd been upstairs with the residents, not hitting up every room on the first floor. It was possible a guard happened to be in the right place at the right time to see Laur rush through the door to the basement stairs and followed to see what his hurry was.

As Mattias said, it could be any number of things.

"It was important to find out what Laur knew and didn't know, but at what cost?" Mattias said.

"I'm not sure. What are you and Sander going to do?" Chey understood Mattias and Sander's desire to make the connection with Laur, no matter the risk. One never knew when the King might uproot the people living in the home, making it difficult to initiate contact again. And Mattias was right. They had needed the information Laur possessed.

"Laur using a house phone to call was risky. He must really be feeling out of sorts. I can tell you what we *won't* do. We won't sit back and allow Aksel to have them all taken out at his convenience. I've called in more security, but they won't be here for another hour and a half at the soonest. That means we might have to take most of the guards here with us." Mattias glanced across the room and met her eyes. "We'll leave two behind, which isn't as many as I would like."

"I'll be fine, don't worry, Mattias. I promise I won't leave the house or anything." Chey had to protect the baby above all things. Running off into the night, into possible danger wasn't high on her list of things to do.

Not anymore.

She realized then that she'd put the baby in jeopardy by going back to get the sample. A dozen *what if* scenarios ran through her mind, all of them more horrible than the last.

"I know you won't, Chey. I worry more about leaving you and the staff here without adequate protection."

"No one even knows we're here, right? We'll be okay. It's you and Sander and the others that need to take care." Chey understood the men had to take action. She wished it didn't make her so nervous.

"My staff will keep our confidences. Even so, it doesn't mean Aksel or his security won't figure out what's going on. Especially if they heard Sander in the basement. This holding is the closest to where Laur is staying, which makes it an automatic target." Mattias ran a hand through his sleek black hair.

"Then arm the staff. They know how to shoot, don't they? At least they'll be able to defend themselves."

"That is a very good idea, actually. The ones who have experience should be an asset, just in case. And what of you,

Chey? Will you want a weapon once more?" Mattias asked, indirectly referencing the gun he'd insisted she have at the cabin.

"I'd rather be armed than not in the event people show up here to do us harm." Chey *would* shoot an unwelcome intruder if it meant life or death. The brief lessons Mattias had given her before had not been forgotten.

Mattias inclined his head as if he approved, then raised his voice in his own language, speaking to those not in the room with them.

Chey guessed he was passing orders to the guards to arm everyone else. Crossing her arms over her chest, she paced, wishing Sander would walk through the door. If the brothers were even thinking of going to pull Laur and the others out of that house, she wanted to take Sander aside and tell him about the baby. She felt it was imperative that he know.

Out in the foyer, Chey heard the guards gather, then disperse. Just then, Mattias's phone went off. He silenced his orders and answered with a curt greeting.

Chey glanced out the curtained window at the road beyond the surrounding iron fence. No SUV, no headlights closing in on Mattias's manor. Not yet.

"Chey," Mattias said, ending his call. He was on the move, crossing the room to gather her elbow in his hand. With gentle insistence, he guided her out of the parlor. "That was Sander. He doesn't want to take a chance with Laur and the others. I'm going to rendezvous with him not far from the home and we'll shut the whole operation down. For now, I need you to come with me."

Chey fell into step with Mattias, climbing the stairs to the second floor. "What do you want me to do?"

"I'll show you. Two guards are staying here and the rest of the staff with training have been armed. It provides an extra layer of protection on the off chance someone has figured out we're onto the situation. Unfortunately, there were no handguns remaining to give you." He escorted her to her bedroom, walked in without preamble, and guided her to a section of wall where crown molding had been used to create dividing lines and frames.

"If the others are more experienced, then that's where the weapons needed to go. I don't mind," she said, eyeballing the wall with a skeptical look. She couldn't figure out what they were doing here.

"Only a handful of people know this exists. If, *if* you need a place to hide, then come up here and get yourself into the corridor. You press right here, exactly." Mattias released her elbow to depress a specific spot over the cream colored molding.

To Chey's shock, a panel moved outward with a whisper of sound. It created a narrow doorway that Mattias stepped into. Chey followed, emerging into a long corridor that ran either direction away from her bedroom. A hidden passageway lit by small lights attached to the walls.

"Where does this lead?" she asked. The corridor was clean and neat, despite its lack of adornment or furniture.

"At both ends, it leads down. Keep going if you feel the passageway has been breached. You will come upon a wine cellar at the last door. There is an underground tunnel behind the south wine rack. Just move it aside, it will roll easier than you think it might. Move it and follow the path. It will lead you to another set of stairs that empty on the other side of the far wall behind this house. From there, lose yourself in the trees." He met her eyes in the gloom. "*Only* if you must. Yes? If there is no other alternative. This is an extreme precaution that you won't need to use, I'm sure, but it's better to be safe than sorry, as they say."

Chey memorized the route. She took it all very seriously given her condition, and once again, wondered if she should confide in Mattias. "I'll remember. It's good to know there's a way out."

"Excellent. I must go." He led her back into her bedroom and showed her how to ease the panel shut. When he was done, it just looked like any other part of the wall.

"Mattias," Chey said, glancing from the hidden doorway to his face.

"Yes?" He paused, expectant.

"...be safe. Please tell Sander I said the same." It was time to forget the argument and the strife between them. Although she meant to tell Mattias about the baby, Chey decided to wait and tell Sander to his face.

He searched her eyes, then inclined his head. "I will."

Chey watched Mattias retreat, closing the door behind him.

She paced the bedroom, praying her decision not to tell Mattias wouldn't come back to haunt her.

. . .

Sander glanced across the front seat of the Hummer when Mattias climbed in the passenger side. "Did you prepare Chey?"

Mattias closed his door. "I showed her the hidden passageway and explained how to get off the property if she has to. Are we ready?"

Sander spoke above the idling engine. "How many men did you leave behind?"

Mattias pinned an impatient look on Sander. "Two. They're the best of the best, Sander. They won't let anyone get to her without forfeiting their life first. I think she'll be fine."

A muscle flexed in Sander's jaw. He disliked leaving Chey without more protection than that. "All right. Yes, we're ready. We've got eight plus you and I to make a raid. I think we should bust through the gate and storm the front instead of sneaking overland to come in the back. If they're suspicious at all, they've got more lookouts than before. They might pick us off one by one if we're out in the open."

"I agree. Laur sounded mildly distressed by what he'd overheard. Surprise is our best option. Go in with the lights off, keep us invisible as long as possible." Mattias, dressed in camouflage fatigues like Sander, double checked the weapons attached to the holsters on his shoulders and belt.

A guard jogged up to Sander's window. He tapped with a knuckle.

Sander rolled the window down. "What is it? We're about to move out."

"Your Highness, the King has just made a public statement."

"What did he say?"

"He confirmed you've gone into exile of your own accord, and that in Latvala's best interest, *Paavo* will ascend the throne." The guard looked uncomfortable imparting the news.

"Paavo?" Sander spat a curse and glanced at Mattias even as his brother glanced at him.

"He knows," Mattias said, speaking of the King. "He knows we've discovered Laur and the others and he's taking action."

"That's what I thought." Sander cut a look back to the guard. "Our plans haven't changed. Tell the others we're departing."

"Yes Sir." The guard jogged back to the short line of Hummers idling behind Sander's vehicle.

"Aksel skipped over you because he knows you're involved," Sander said, putting the Hummer into gear. Leaving the headlights off, he pulled onto the road, using moonlight to guide him. They were a handful of miles away from the building, too far for anyone to see them under cover of night.

"I believe you're right. But to go public with it..." Mattias exhaled a sound of frustration. "He must know you're not in Barbados any longer, either."

"My main concern is getting Laur and the others safely away. We'll worry about my exile and Paavo later." Sander picked up speed, noting the other vehicles were keeping pace at the rear.

"Did you have luck with the generals?" Mattias asked.

"I approached the three I felt most comfortable with. Ones I knew would give their allegiance to me and back me if I attempt to take the throne." Sander picked up speed, glancing at the GPS to double check the upcoming turns.

"Three is a good start. That is a substantial amount of leverage on your part. What did they say about your exile?" Mattias asked, staring ahead out the window.

"I explained that I was all but forced to leave Latvala and had no plans to remain in exile. They're going to make discreet inquiries down the ranks and see where we stand. I can't wrest the throne away from Aksel without the military behind me." Even then, Sander knew, it would be a tenuous, precarious task. He had to play his cards just right against the King or he could lose everything.

"I can't believe it's come to this," Mattias said, removing a gun from its holster as Sander took another turn. He checked the safety and held the weapon along his thigh.

"I can't either, Mattias. I never thought I'd see the day we had to unseat our own father," Sander said, voice gone grim with the reality of their situation.

"He's made his bed, brother. And made choices that threaten the welfare of our country. I think the people will understand we did what we had to."

"Let's hope so. All right, we're close," Sander said.

Mattias reached over to unbuckle his seat belt.

Sander did the same. He wanted to be able to move fast when it mattered.

He slowed for the final turn then picked up speed. Faster, faster, until the speedometer read sixty. Both hands on the wheel, he braced for impact as the entrance came up on their right.

As he cut the wheel hard toward the gate, he realized too late that the thing had been blown off its hinges. Someone had already rammed it. Sitting lopsided against the posts it sat between, the damaged gate was not now an obstacle.

Cursing under his breath, he sped toward the stairs. Stomping the brakes, Sander put the Hummer in park, opened his door and hit the ground running. Taking the steps in two great leaps, Mattias right on his heels, he timed his approach to the front doors so he had room to lever a foot up to kick them in. An obnoxious *bang* echoed through the foyer as he and Mattias, followed by several guards, rushed inside. More guards followed as the other Hummer screeched to a halt on the drive.

Low and fast, with his weapon at eye level, Sander moved room to room, sweeping each as he entered. He knew Mattias and half the guards had split off back in the foyer as planned, covering more ground in short order.

Several lights were on, most were off. It made for rough going where the drapes had been drawn tight, allowing little illumination in through the windows.

"Anything?" Sander shouted. He had a bad feeling in his gut. A really bad feeling.

"Nothing," Mattias replied.

Sander turned toward three of the guards on his flank. "Check the basement. Report if you find anything."

Three guards cut away and disappeared around an archway.

Other guards called down from upstairs a few moments later. "All clear!"

Sander stalked out into the foyer just as Mattias strode out of a library. He met his brother's eyes.

"They're gone," Mattias said. "The whole house is empty."

"He got to them before we could." Sander snarled a curse in his mother tongue. As the guards came down the stairs from the second floor, Sander said, "Any evidence?"

"Your Highness, it looks as if it was a fast evacuation. Clothes are still on hangers and in drawers, beds unmade."

"They can't be that far. Where would they have taken them, Mattias? What vacant building is close? He wouldn't risk bringing them to the main seat," Sander said. The uneasy feeling turned into something more sinister. He felt as if he was overlooking something.

"There isn't anything that I know of in the East woods. Nothing sitting empty. There are several buildings to the south he might use," Mattias said.

He stepped closer to his brother. It pissed Sander off to think his father was one step ahead of them. "I don't like it, Mattias. What if Aksel sent men to your place while evacuating this one?"

"I was thinking the same. We should return there immediately, secure Chey, and then figure our next step." Mattias was moving as he finished speaking.

Sander left the building at a run. "Someone get on the phone and call the guards at Mattias's holding. Tell them they might have visitors."

Chapter Seventeen

In the upstairs bathroom, Chey sat on the edge of the jacuzzi tub and tried to get her stomach to calm down. The toilet was close by, just in case she failed to control the churning nausea that had her in its grip. She wasn't sure what to make of this evening sickness—wasn't it supposed to happen in the morning? Thinking back, she remembered several mornings when she *had* felt nauseous, a fleeting hour of feeling icky before it passed.

Taking a deep breath, she stood up. Cool air would help. Descending to the main floor, she swung toward the kitchen and the back door that would allow her to stick her head out into the chill evening. Passing through the large dining room, she saw headlights from the street glint off the walls and a few metal sculptures.

Mattias had only been gone twenty minutes, if that. He and the other guards shouldn't be returning this fast. Maybe it was Sander, a thought that kicked her heart into an immediate, quicker rhythm. Pivoting on her foot, distracted from the nausea by the idea of seeing Sander, she went to the window to peer through a crack, still too wary of the circumstances to simply assume it was him.

Blinded by headlights, she squinted past the pane though no details of the vehicle, much less the driver, presented themselves.

"Miss Sinclair! Get back from the window." One of the guards appeared at her side in seconds, curling a gentle but firm grip to guide her deeper into the house.

"That might be Sander..."

"It's not Sander. Nor is it Mattias," the other guard said. He'd drawn his weapon, the muzzle aimed at the ceiling with his arm cocked against his side.

"What? Then who?" Chey, remembering Mattias's concerns and warnings, didn't appreciate the trickle of fear the unknown brought with it.

"We're not sure yet," Olev said. "I think you should take her upstairs--"

The crack of the intercom interrupted Olev. Static cut through the voice that rattled into the foyer via the device.

It was the mother tongue, a language

Chey didn't understand.

The guard at her elbow began guiding her toward the stairs. "Go up, Miss Sinclair? Please stay in your room until we figure out what's going on."

"All right." Chey didn't need to be asked twice. She was halfway up when the voice came through without the static.

Laur's voice. Speaking quick and urgent.

Chey didn't need to understand the language to recognize fear. "That's Laur! Let him in." She descended to the foyer, wondering who had driven the man here.

"Miss Sinclair, he might not be alone," Olev said, shooting her a pointed look.

Chey, caught between the desire to stay and find out about Laur or head upstairs, lingered on the bottom step. Indecisive. The other guard, Henri, pushed the button on the intercom to let Laur through the gate.

"Come get me if he's alone, please," Chey said. It was the only way she felt all right about departing if the man needed help.

"We'll let you know," Olev said.

Chey hastened upstairs and down the hall to her room. Closing the door, she engaged the lock. Pacing back and forth, she sorted through scenarios in her mind about what might have happened. Regardless, although Laur sounded upset, at least he was alive. Where were Sander and Mattias? Maybe they would arrive right behind Laur.

A flash of light across her windows alerted Chey to another vehicle at the gate. She couldn't see straight on from her bedroom's vantage point. The gleam of black she glimpsed with her cheek pressed against the cold pane sent a thrill through her.

Sander. Bolting for the door, she exited into the hall and made for the stairs. The rollicking pitch of her stomach would just have to wait, she decided. She wanted to get Sander alone if everything was all right and tell him the news.

At the top of the staircase, she saw Laur with Olev and Henri. The men were speaking in their own tongue, rapid words that fell over one another. They were so intent, none of them saw her. She hurried down to the foyer.

"What's going on? Is that Sander and Mattias coming in behind yo--" Chey's words faded as the doorknob turned and the top lock snapped over. There was something sinister about the methodical precision with which the person on the other side used to gain entry. Her subconscious understood the danger before Chey had time to process what it meant. She crouched even as Olev herded her and Laur out of the foyer, gesturing to Henri with his gun hand.

Henri snapped off the lights and took up a shooter's stance right there in the archway between the foyer and dining room.

What frightened Chey more than anything was the *silence* of it all. One moment the men had been talking in hectic sentences, the next, darkness enveloped the house and everything went still and quiet.

Behind her, she heard the deadly *thwip thwip* of a silencer. Heart in her throat, Chey ducked into the kitchen, Laur at her side. For a big man, he moved with more stealth than Chey would have given him credit for. Olev guided them toward a long, skinny hallway on the other side of a row of cabinets. It ran the length of the house, with windows on one side, and a wall on the other.

Olev pushed them into a shallow, recessed area and twisted back toward the way they came, gun up. He fired within seconds, two successive pulls of the trigger. The silencer on the end of his weapon muted the sound.

She heard two thumps down the hall and guessed he'd just taken out two of the intruders. Did that mean Henri was dead? What about the other employees? She didn't know where they were or what they were doing.

Cautioning herself against all out panic, Chey waited with Laur hovering at her back. Shoulder pressed against the recessed wall, she glanced along it to see if there was a door leading either up or down. Nothing. No door, just a hutch with collectibles and a few potted plants.

From somewhere deeper in the immense house, Chey heard a gun that didn't have a silencer on it pop off two rounds. Intuition told her it was one of the household staff. There probably hadn't been time to fit everyone's piece with more hardware.

Laur set a hand on her shoulder, as if he wanted to reassure or calm her. Chey touched his fingers with her own. Hers trembled while his were steady. Olev continued to glance both ways down the hall, features stone-like and intent.

Finally, after what felt like an eternity to Chey, he gestured them into the corridor.

She was afraid to expose herself. Olev could only cover one direction at a time, leaving another shooter several seconds to get a shot off. The hallway was narrow, too, without many places to hide. A potted plant or a decorative half table wasn't going to save them.

Darting out anyway at Olev's insistent gesture, she hugged the wall and went as quick as she could the way he motioned. Ten steps later, she saw what he was aiming for; a set of back stairs, for use by house staff, wound upward to the second floor. If she could reach her room, she could duck into the hidden passageway and at least get out of sight of anymore shooters.

Making a dash for it, she was three feet from the entrance when a shadow at the other end of the hallway snapped her gaze there. A shooter, bringing his weapon up.

Three feet suddenly seemed like a mile. A mile where every step felt as if she was wading through a vat of honey, slowing down her momentum. Laur brushed past her shoulder, putting himself between her and the shooter. The contact sent her into the safety of the stairwell.

A moment later, Laur slumped to a knee.

"No!" Chey, on her way up, paused to look back. Laur fell forward, landing face down in an ungainly heap. "*No!*"

Olev appeared like an angel of mercy, shooting down the hallway over Laur's body.

Choking on a sob, torn between the desire to rush down and help Laur or dash upstairs to her bedroom and possible safety, she expended several precious seconds, indecisive. Leaving Laur to die in the narrow hall made her sick—but how would she feel if the shooter caught up to her and took her out as well?

She had a child to think about. An innocent baby who couldn't protect itself. *She* needed to be that person, to prioritize in a critical moment when her mind told her one thing and her heart told her another.

Turning, she ran up the stairs, tears streaming down her cheeks. At the small landing she encountered a door and opened it without thinking to go slow, check for danger on the other side. Swinging the door wide, she found herself at the very end of the hallway her bedroom sat off of.

Around the corner at the other end, coming from the direction of the main stairs leading to the foyer, another shadow emerged. Moving low and fast.

Chey had no time to go forward. Not another step. A scream ripped from her throat, deafening in the silence, as she backtracked to the smaller stairway. Olev bolted upward from the bottom, ready to defend her. Something knocked the door aside behind her, closing in quicker than she could escape. Then a strong arm clamped over her shoulder and across the front of her body, tugging her back against the solid bulwark of his.

Before she could scream, she heard Sander's voice near her ear.

"Stand down, Olev. It's me. Mattias and the others are behind me and also below."

"Prince Dare," Olev said, lowering his weapon. Tension all but crackled from the security guard. It eased as recognition set in.

Chey wilted with relief. Bringing her hands up, she clutched Sander's trapping arm and sank into the warm strength of his chest. Her heart was hammering so hard she thought it might pop from the pressure.

"Shhh," Sander whispered. Then, to Olev, "I've got her. Go down and meet the others. Warn any employees that we're here so we don't have any accidental shootings."

"Yes Prince Dare." Olev retreated, pausing at the bottom of the stairway to kneel next to the fallen Laur. He felt for a pulse.

"Oh no, *no,*" Chey said when she saw Laur. She heard Sander pull in a surprised breath. "He was trying to save me. Push me out of the way," she whispered.

A moment later they were both rushing down, Sander with an arm still around her, keeping her close.

Olev glanced up, apology in his eyes. "I'm sorry, Sir. He's gone."

. . .

Chey rocked on her knees, hands over her mouth, while Sander turned Laur over. Moonlight from the windows in the corridor spilled across Laur's face, making a deeper shadow along the deformed side. Sander sought a pulse despite that Olev already checked. His movements were gentle but concise, fingertips pressing against Laur's throat.

Elsewhere in the house, she heard 'clear' ring out several times. It was a distant reassurance that whatever hitmen had intruded were subdued—or dead.

Mattias rushed down the corridor, holstering his weapon. Coming to a knee, he touched either side of Laur's head as if the man were precious and glanced at Sander, something desperate in his dark eyes.

Sander sat back on his haunches, fists on his thighs. He shook his head. Laur was, as Olev said, gone.

Broken-hearted, Chey covered her face and cried for the loss. At the same time, fury boiled her blood that Aksel and Helina could be this cruel. To sacrifice their child in the name of the throne.

Mattias cursed under his breath.

Sander, still and silent, stared first down at Laur, then up at the ceiling.

Chey didn't know if he would shout or punch things or what he might do in the thrall of grief. She'd never seen him out of his element in this way before. That he was hurting couldn't be missed. Pain glinted in his eyes, sagged his shoulders.

In the end, he didn't shout *or* punch holes in the wall. He reached out with a hand and smoothed it over Laur's temple and into his hair. A kind, tender gesture that indicated just how torn up he was inside, even if he collected himself and refused to show it outside. He took a deep breath, glanced at Mattias for a lingering, telling moment, then rose to his feet and stepped over Laur's legs to ease Chey up off the ground.

"Come on. Let's get you upstairs. Are you hurt?" he asked.

She leaned on him, letting Sander bear the brunt of her weight. "I'm *furious,*" she replied through her misery. "Not hurt, no."

"I know. Here..." Sander paused to scoop her into his arms, groom-style. "Mattias, have someone take Laur to a trusted mortuary and put no less than five guards on him."

"I will," Mattias said, pushing to his feet, expression grim.

"Let me know as soon as the others are located." Sander ascended the small staircase, carrying Chey as if she weighed no more than a feather.

"When is it going to end? When will all the danger and the attempts on people's lives stop? He didn't deserve to die," Chey said, teeth chattering over the words. She had hit her limit with death and threats.

"As soon as I can make it," Sander said. "And no, he didn't deserve to die."

He carried her into her bedroom and used his boot to knock the door shut. Ferrying her to the bed, he laid her down and hovered over her, searching her eyes.

Chey smeared tears off her cheeks, unable to quell her shaking or her upset over Laur. While Sander searched her eyes, she searched his, chest hitching with a small hiccup. "What will happen now? Will Aksel and Helina just be allowed to get away with this atrocity? They can't. You *have* to do something, Sander."

"I plan to. Trust me when I say they won't get away unscathed." He sat on the edge of the bed, weapons tucked into the holsters on his shoulders and around one thigh.

Chey had never seen him quite that armed, nor dressed in what appeared to be fatigues. Her fingers trailed over the arm he braced on the other side of her body, effectively trapping her in place.

"Why aren't you angry? How can you not be fed up with it all? I don't understand," she said, letting her thoughts spill into the open. When she'd had enough, she *really* had enough. The lingering effects of fear made her temper shorter than usual.

"I *am* angry. Don't mistake my control for indifference. Flipping out in front of the men will do no one any good, least of all me. But trust that vengeance will be mine." He spoke with solemn assurance, never breaking eye contact.

"I wish it made me feel better. I mean, it does, but it doesn't. You know?" Chey smeared another tear angrily off her cheek. "I'm tired of them. Both of them. Tired of worrying about whether I need to look over my shoulder because they've decided to get rid of me, or whether they'll finally back off and leave me—leave *us*—alone."

"You'll never stop having to look over your shoulder, not completely. That's an unfortunate fact that comes with this life. But we can reduce the threat considerably now that we know where it's coming from, and because I think Mattias and I have collected enough evidence to force his hand." He gathered her fingers into his, smearing the remnants of her tear off her skin with his thumb.

"Is that what you're going to do? What does that mean, exactly?" she asked, needing it spelled out for her.

"It means, if I ever want to be King, I'm going to have to go public with it all. He made an announcement earlier this evening about my exile, so now I'm forced to act on my own behalf. He's afraid I'll do exactly what I've set out to: remove him from power. This was a preemptive strike on his part."

"Removing him from power is great, but will that make him stop trying to get rid of me? He can still hire people, can't he?"

"He can, yes. I will make it much harder on him to be able to get at you, though. Or any of us for that matter."

There was something about the look on Sander's face and in his voice that triggered concern in Chey. It wasn't quite calculating or cunning, yet she knew there was more to it he wasn't saying. Would he and Mattias take *permanent* action? Was Sander set to become just like his father out of necessity? Killing people because it suited him, or made his life easier? The questions ran rampant through her mind. What was more, would she care?

Yes. Yes, she would care. She didn't want to believe Sander, or Mattias for that matter, would stoop to such levels. They needed to rise above killing for killing's sake, throne or no throne.

She knew it wasn't that easy even as she thought it. An entire country was at stake. The rise and fall of an empire rested squarely on the decisions Sander was about to make. Either he and Mattias would best the King and Queen, beat them at their own game, or fall prey to some unseen ace Aksel had up his sleeve. Chey thought he should be well out of aces by now.

"How?" she asked, hoping she was wrong thinking Sander might stoop to murder.

He cocked his head, holding her gaze. "Why do you have that look on your face?"

"What look?" Chey resisted the urge to cringe. Sander knew her too well.

"*That* look. Like you're suddenly wary of me." He arched a brow.

"I'm not wary of you. I just--" she paused to collect her thoughts. Her body felt heavy and strange now that the adrenaline rush was wearing off.

"You're worried I'm going to do to him

what he did to Laur," Sander said.

"Not worried. It did cross my mind, though," she confessed. She wondered if it would drive another, new wedge between them. If he would be offended— or if he would confirm he was a man of his father's making.

"I am many things, Chey, but a cold blooded killer is not one of them. No, I will not send a hunting party, or an assassin, to kill my parents. I have a much more mundane idea in mind. Like exposing them for what they've done and what they are, then banishing them to the mountains or even to another holding elsewhere, as he did to me, so that his reach to people that matter is harder."

"You're not mad I wondered, are you? Because that's one part of you I don't know. You *could* have been a man like that."

He shook his head. "No, I'm not mad. You have the right to know if I'm the same man that way. After all, he *did* raise me. It's not in my blood to end people's lives unless it's in self defense or a situation like tonight, when others need to be defended."

"Okay." She exhaled in relief.

"I want you to gather all your things

here. I'm going to have you flown back to Pallan island where I know you'll be safer. All right? Mattias and I need to work this out, so I'll be staying here for the time being." He cupped her jaw and leaned down to brush a kiss across her mouth.

Chey started to say a thing. The kiss cut her off. She kissed him once more before he leaned away and finished her thought. "I want to stay here. Maybe not in Mattias's house, but close by. Isn't there somewhere—what about that place in the woods? Or not, because they already knew I'd been there?"

"Yes, I wouldn't feel safe leaving you there." He didn't deny her out of hand. Instead, he grew quiet, appearing to think about her request.

Chey wondered if this was the time to tell him about the baby. It felt wrong after Laur though, so she remained mute on the subject for now. As anxious as she was for him to know, she also wanted the occasion to be somewhat happy instead of riding on the coattails of grief.

Sander was quiet so long she worried something was wrong. She reached up to smooth the frown that had developed on his brow. "What is it?"

"I'm deciding whether—yes. Actually,

give me fifteen minutes to talk to Mattias, all right?" He caught her hand and brought it to his mouth.

"Sure, of course. I'll be here. You won't leave the house, will you?" Chey didn't want to be further than a few yards from Sander at any time in the immediate future.

"No, I won't. And if I do, you'll be coming with me." He kissed her temple and rose off the bed. "I'll be right back."

Chey watched him cross the room to the door. He winked before stepping out.

Slumping back into the pillows, she rested an arm over her brow and closed her eyes against the horrible image of Laur lying dead at the bottom of the stairs. She agonized over all the things he would never get to experience, all the things he would never get to do with his brothers. What a waste of a good life, of a good soul.

Whatever Sander was planning, Chey hoped it ripped Aksel and Helina out of their privileged existence and made things much less pleasant for the duration.

It was far better than they deserved.

Chapter Eighteen

Sander closed Chey's door and stood in the hall, hands on his hips, head bent. He allowed himself thirty seconds to center the righteous fury and indignation Laur's death brought. Thirty seconds to calm his pulse, to latch onto the idea that had sprouted while talking to Chey. Otherwise, he might make a wrong move in this chess game gone wild.

It wasn't just his temper he sought to control, but the intense grief he felt over Laur's death. He wasn't the type of man to give in to tears or openly express too much sorrow. It was his way to let it eat him up inside and present a calmer facade to the world. Too aware of an opportunity lost, of a life cut far too short, he reined in his desire for immediate bloodshed and siphoned all that energy into a plan so that nothing like it would ever happen again.

His argument with Chey seemed trivial in the aftermath of all this. Even though he knew it wasn't, not when it put her in jeopardy, he couldn't find it in himself to deny her wish to be close or to hang onto an old grudge when there were more productive things to do.

He struck out for the stairs leading to the main floor in search for Mattias, sure he already knew where to find him.

As he suspected, Mattias was staring out a window at the evening in the parlor, a drink in hand, open bottle at his elbow. Mattias suffered in the same way he did, he knew, and said nothing at first while he walked over to pour himself a tumbler full of liquor. Sander swigged half of it down, hissing at the afterburn.

"Seriously, brother. How have I allowed my own parents to manipulate me so? I should have dumped Viia the second I knew I could never marry her. I should have done—and said—many things I did not." Mattias was the first to break the silence.

"We all have our regrets. What we need to do now is make sure we reduce the likelihood of having them in the future. Our little plan? We need to expand it," Sander said, taking another drink. He stared out the same window as guards moved discreetly around the house and the grounds, securing the property against any possible second attack.

"What do you mean, expand it?" Mattias said, glancing sideways at Sander.

"I think we should have Aksel and Helina detained." Sander met Mattias's eyes. His brother's jaw went slack and he looked at Sander as if he'd grown another head. Any other time, it might have been amusing. Right now, Sander could find little to be amused over.

"You want to arrest the King and Queen? Sander, have you lost your mind?" Mattias asked, incredulous.

"Detained, not arrested. There's a difference."

"On what grounds? You have to have a reason to detain the King, you realize?"

"Of course I realize," Sander said with a dark scowl. "Abuse of power. First for forcing me into exile, and second for the murder of his own firstborn in an attempt to hide the truth from the public. If that's not abuse of power, I don't know what is."

Mattias had another drink, still watching Sander. "Will the military acquiesce? You have the ear of three Generals, but what of the men?"

"They will do whatever their

288

commanders tell them to do, I suspect. As long as there is good reason. I'll have to go to the head council members and inform them of my intent. The problem there is timing. If I go too early, before Aksel is detained, then one of them will tip him off and he'll have me killed. It needs to be timed exactly, and I need your support to do it all." Sander held his brother's eyes. He didn't doubt Mattias would rise to the occasion. It was why they were as close as they were.

"You have my support. As ever. And I agree—timing is critical. I fear public backlash, however. If you do not also have their support, all of this will come to nothing. They will restore Aksel, you will be exiled by force this time, probably stripped of your rank and everything else, and forbidden to ever return," Mattias said.

"It will be up to them to decide. There is nothing more I can do than present my case as it is, and leave it up to the citizens. If it comes to that, then I'll accept my exile and that will be that." It left a bitter taste in Sander's mouth to think of Aksel winning this hand in their game of war.

"Say Aksel and Helina are detained,

and you are granted ascension, do you plan to follow through? You have not changed your mind because of who your mother is, have you?"

Sander looked out the window. Mattias knew him well, indeed. It was a question that haunted him, as Aksel knew it would. He was not rightful heir, not according to law nor decree. Removing Aksel and Helina as an obstacle would have allowed him to ascend *if* he did not confess to the public his true birthright. *If* his conscious would let him. He was a man bound by honor his whole life—should he keep this secret, it would forever change that.

"Sander?" Mattias said, pressing the issue.

"The only way I can do it and not suffer guilt for the rest of my days is to also announce who I really am," he said.

Mattias fell to silence. The sound of the bottle came again, followed by a splash of liquor.

Sander held his tumbler out; Mattias filled it.

"You take a great many risks, brother," Mattias said into the quiet.

"Doesn't it take many risks to become great?" Sander asked.

Mattias had no answer.

"Tomorrow, just before dawn. I'll order the Generals to detain the King and Queen while I call an emergency meeting with the council. I'd like to refrain from a public announcement for a few days so we can locate the other members of that household and bury the dead," Sander said. He would not be rushed through his goodbyes to a possible brother he barely got to know. Sibling or not, Laur's life tale was a sad one. He thought the man—and any others—deserved to be respectably laid to rest.

. . .

Chey stood under the hot steam of a shower like the burn might rid her of the horrific images regarding Laur's death. Unable to rest after Sander's departure, she'd retreated here to stand under the spray, arms crossed over her front with her hands hooked onto her shoulders. Chin tucked, she mourned in private the events of the night.

When would the upheaval end? Or at least tread onto common ground? She wished desperately for quieter, less dreadful times. Walks on the half moon bay, exploring the mountain on Pallan island, traveling to different countries at Sander's side—that's what she wanted.

A shadow looming outside the curtain startled a gasp out of Chey. It was only Sander, peeling back the barrier to step under the spray with her. He was golden and glorious, all sinew and honed strength, the clothing shed somewhere along the way. She decided she must have looked downtrodden and melancholy; he drew her against him and cradled her head with his hand, exhaling a sound of quiet frustration. The water sluiced over them both, creating rivulets that snaked over contours and into the hollows, making their hair stick to their skin.

"Tomorrow before dawn," he said at a low decibel that vied with the hiss of the shower head, "I intend on detaining the King and the Queen. Several respected Generals have pledged their allegiance to me, and I will put their honor and trust to the test. I'll claim abuse of power as my reason to the council in the hope they do not attempt to over ride me."

Shock made Chey stiffen in his arms. Cheek against his chest, sensing he was not done, she remained quiet.

"The King and Queen will remain under guard for several days while we lay Laur—and any others—to rest. Then, I'll take the entire scandal public, explaining my reasons and my plans. I'm going to confess I am not the true heir to the throne at that time and allow the council and the people to have their say."

Stunned, unsure what to say, Chey smoothed her palms along either side of his spine. The implications were immediately clear: Sander was taking an enormous risk and stood a good chance of losing his right to rule the country. A right she wasn't sure he had any longer, if he went public with the news. Tilting her head back, she sought his eyes.

His were troubled, filled with shadows and concern.

"Are you absolutely sure that's what you want to do? Confess Helina is not your true mother?" Chey asked. "As much as I would love to be selfish and have more of you to myself for the rest of our lives—I realize that you were born to be King. Your heart lies in leading and protecting the people of Latvala, and I don't think you will ever truly be happy if you cannot do so."

"If I keep the ruse, then I will not be

happy, either. Guilt will eat at me and make me miserable. I know this about myself, at least. It's better if I'm open and honest, something I have always tried to be with everyone. Sure, some things can never be shared, that's a given. But this...this is simply too big, too encompassing, to brush under a rug," he said.

"What are the odds of you still taking the throne?"

"Honestly? Slim to none. I like to hope for the best, but it's because the worst case scenario is difficult for me to contemplate. The people might forgive me for detaining the King and Queen, though I imagine they will chose to have the rightful heir seated as King when all is said and done." He looked over her head, staring at the shower wall.

"What will happen if Mattias takes over?" she asked. "Will you lose Kallaster castle?"

"It's a good bet Mattias will break tradition and leave the holding to me. It'll be his choice, after all, and he's not bound by any legal law that says he *has* to take it to become King. It's just been the way of it for so long."

"So you won't be exiled, then?"

"The people can't exile me. Only the King or the high council if the offense is bad enough. Being born not of the Queen is no fault of mine, so it's likely they'll allow me to remain in Latvala and live my life out here as a Prince. Unless they deem it necessary to strip me of that title as well. If they do, then I'll have to forfeit all my holdings as well as everything else." He settled his whiskered chin against the side of her temple.

"What does Mattias think you should do?"

"What my heart tells me to. Though he would be supportive of me keeping the bastard secret because he thinks I should be King. At least this nonsense with Paavo taking control is over." He made a gruff, annoyed sound in the back of his throat.

"He wouldn't do a good job?" she asked, running her hands up to make circles over his shoulder blades.

"My younger brother is an honorable man, but his politics and personal ambition get in the way of what *should* be done. He would make many bad choices for Latvala. Aksel is blind to it, or perhaps condones some of it, seeing that he has allowed certain Officials from other countries to sway his thinking about our military involvement in skirmishes we have no business being anywhere near."

Chey considered the complications of being Royalty. If it wasn't interpersonal strife, it was politics.

"Hypothetically, if your military *was* to engage in skirmishes, would you actually be fighting?" Chey moved her head back far enough to see his eyes.

Sander glanced down, gliding his hands low to settle on the back of her hips. "We're all trained for battle. Yes, I would be fighting."

"But you can't all go. What if the worst happens and you're all killed? Won't the throne fall to some second or third cousin?" Chey failed to keep a frown from building on her brow.

"We wouldn't all fight at the same time. The council frowns on the heir actually going onto the front lines, though they have no final say. It's my nature to fight alongside my countrymen. My choice to give up the throne if I die."

"I'm glad you won't be sending people into situations unless it's really necessary, then." She refused to think more about him going to war. Several of her friends had relatives serving in the forces, and she remembered well the anxious wait for news of their loved ones.

"It's nothing you need to worry about right now, if that eases you any." He pressed a kiss between her eyes.

Chey had the urge, once again, to confide about their baby. They weren't quite as raw as they were a couple hours ago. The timing wasn't perfect—and then she wondered if it would ever be. The situation with Aksel could take another turn, and another, landing them in a precarious position.

"Let's get cleaned up, all right? You washing my hair will take my mind off all that other stuff." Chey knew her smile didn't convey the ease he was trying to give her.

Sander echoed her smile, which looked strangely sober and somewhat maudlin. He reached for the shampoo and got down to business.

While he put his hands in her hair, she tried to figure out the best way to tell him he was going to be a father.

Chapter Nineteen

Dressed in lounge pants and a thin tee shirt of yellow, Chey toweled her hair dry before the mirror. Sander, in just a pair of black pajama pants, stood next to her, hip against the counter, shaving off his whiskers.

She kept glancing at him, undecided whether to just blurt her news out or leave a note on his pillow or what.

Without looking at her, he said, "You're staring."

"I'm your fiance, I'm allowed to stare."

"You should try my face sometime. Do you even know what color eyes I have?"

"Of course I do. They're green." She knew very well they were blue.

He paused, dumbstruck, and sought her eyes through the reflection.

She quirked her lips and arched a brow. Clearly, her expression said, *gotcha.* It lacked the verve and animation of their usual banter.

Sander's features waned wry. His eyes

lidded and he snorted before resuming his shaving.

Chey set the towel down on the counter, over her make up box. Recalling she'd put the pregnancy tests inside earlier, an epiphany hit about how to tell him about their child.

Taking the towel over to a drying rack, she draped it over a rung and returned. Her fingers snapped the clasp to the kit open. Just as she was about to lift the lid, someone knocked at the bedroom door.

Chey bit back a curse. Maybe whoever it was would go away quick. "I'll get it. You finish removing the sandpaper from your face."

On her way past, she pinched his hip.

"You *like* the way it feels when I rub it on your--"

"*Sander.*" She refused to laugh. Her heart wasn't in it, despite that a flicker of amusement raced through her.

Opening the bedroom door, she found Mattias there, fully dressed. She wasn't sure whether to be alarmed by the look in his eyes or not. A look she couldn't exactly read. Was it bad news? Good news?

"You both come down to the parlor as soon as you can," he said.

Sander appeared at the archway to the bathroom, rubbing his now smooth skin with a small towel. "What is it?"

"Just come down," Mattias said, features enigmatic and impossible to figure out. He disappeared down the hall.

Chey closed the door and glanced at Sander, bemused. "What was that about?"

"I don't know. Let me put a shirt on and we'll find out." Rather than intrigued, Sander looked disturbed. He retreated into the bathroom and the walk in closet. Moments later he emerged in a long sleeved shirt of steel gray. Foregoing shoes, he escorted her out of the room.

"If it was an emergency, he would have said, right?" Barefoot herself, Chey padded alongside, putting thoughts of baby confessions aside for now. There was still time when they got back before bed.

"No telling with him. Let's hope not."

They descended to the first floor and went straight to the parlor. Several guards stood with Mattias around the television. Images of what looked to be a mass gathering scrolled across the screen. People bundled in heavy coats, scarves and caps carried handmade signs. Others held candles. Many chanted and called out.

Chey couldn't tell where it was, if it was a riot or a demonstration or something more serious. Although she had picked up several words in the native language, she couldn't read one word of it.

"What's going on?" she asked. Around her, a few guards commented in their own tongue, which helped Chey not at all.

"I'll be damned," Sander said. He stood right in front of the television, crossing his arms over his chest.

"What? What is it?" she asked again, annoyed that everyone in the room understood but her.

"The people," Mattias said. He flanked Sander to the left.

"What people? From here? Why are there so many and where are they?" she asked.

"They're coming out in droves in support of Sander. Aksel made that announcement earlier, remember? That he'd been exiled? The people of Latvala are expressing their displeasure at it and also their demand to see him reinstalled as heir," Mattias replied.

Chey glanced from the screen to

Sander. All she could see was part of his profile. An intent look had taken hold of his features. "They're not angry because they think you exiled yourself, then?"

"Apparently not. Maybe the people realize Dare wouldn't voluntarily do that," Mattias said.

Another guard who had been in the foyer entered the parlor, cell phone in hand. "It's not just at the family seat. It's all over. Kalev, the smaller towns and villages. Not hundreds but thousands."

Sander tongued the underside of his teeth. A calculating gleam made his blue eyes bluer. He pivoted away from the television, determination writ in every line of his body.

"Sander, what are you doing?" Chey asked, following him with her eyes.

"Getting dressed." He glanced at the guards. "Prepare to leave within fifteen minutes."

"Yes sir," the guards said, spinning away to do as asked.

Chey marched after Sander. "Leaving? Just where do you think you're going?"

He stopped at the bottom stair and turned only his head to the side to bring her into view. "Kalev. Come on. You're coming with me."

Chey's mouth fell open. "You can't be serious. What are you going to do in Kalev? After everything that happened tonight? It's too dangerous."

He didn't argue. Twisting his shoulders around, he plucked her up off the floor and carried her groom-style up the stairs. He took the last few in pairs, as if he wasn't carrying anything in his arms at all.

"Sander!"

"You ask too many questions. Get dressed. You're coming with me," he repeated, heading into the bedroom.

"You're impossible." Chey shut her protests off lest he change his mind and leave her behind once more.

. . .

The trio of Hummers arrived in Kalev just past eleven o'clock in the evening. Moonlight gleamed off snow piled at the sides of the street and rooftops covered in it. Nervous at being exposed so soon after the shooting at Mattias's house, she watched as the nearly empty streets became less empty the closer they got to the main part of town. They knew from the news reports that the biggest gathering in Kalev was in front of a municipal building; the closest they were able to park was three avenues over. Crowds made it impossible to drive any closer.

Once a few citizens noticed the Hummers, and what it meant, word spread like wildfire.

Sander, fearless in the face of such support, exited the Hummer with Chey in tow. He kept her close, a long coat of black covering black jeans and an iron gray sweater beneath. She chose a navy coat with cream piping on the collar and cuffs and wool slacks that would keep her legs warm in the cold. Mattias flanked her on the left side.

They walked straight into the fringe of the gathered, Sander shaking hands and greeting people one at a time. He was a force all his own, confident and brazen and prepared to stay out as long as it took to garner as much support as he could.

What shocked Chey more than anything was the reception *she* received. The citizens remembered her, oh yes they did, and her welcome came with warm smiles, fond touches to her hands or arms, and now and then a frigid cheek kiss.

While Chey fretted they would be attacked by rogue assassins cut loose by Aksel once the King saw what they were doing, she didn't back down from the challenge of making her presence known among the natives. More and more people flocked to the avenue where Sander paused to speak to several reporters. Hundreds upon hundreds chanted their support as he explained he was not in exile after all. Boldly, he told the people to expect much more news in the coming days, alluding to a big announcement that he refused to discuss beforehand, no matter how much the reporters badgered him.

During a lull in well wishers, Chey had the opportunity to watch Sander, back lit by citizens armed with candles and signs, reveling in the natural leadership and dominance he displayed. This was no shrinking Prince; here was a man back to fight for what was his, for what he believed in, even though he gave no hard details.

Pride swelled in her breast for his easy charisma and eloquence in the aftermath of Laur's death. He went all out, promising details and information as well as his word that he would not leave the country again.

The people wanted Sander, not Mattias or Paavo, as heir to the throne.

Four hours later, the crowds still strong and defiant, Sander made his goodbyes alongside Chey. The group departed, Hummers forging a slow path along the middle of the street while people cheered and waved their signs.

Slumping into the seat once they were away from the scene, Chey rubbed her forehead with gloved fingers. Her nose was frozen, as well as her cheeks, skin stinging as the driver turned up the heat.

"I think it went very well," Mattias said from the front seat.

"So do I. With any luck, word will spread. By morning, I hope to have thousands more behind me," Sander replied. He seemed to hum with left over adrenaline.

"Do you think your father will try to preempt you?" Chey asked.

"He might try, but he can no way know what I plan to do. He'll never expect to be detained." Sander pushed up the sleeve of his coat and glanced at his watch. "In less than two hours, in fact, if all goes as it should."

"Is this going to force you to move up making an announcement?" Chey asked. Sander had wanted to wait. Now she wasn't so sure waiting was a good idea. He had the support of people in the street, a growing movement that might go stale if he disappeared for another two or three days.

"Yes. I'll have to do it not long after we detain the King and Queen. Waiting would mean losing all the momentum the people have so graciously given me," Sander said.

In the front seat, Mattias inclined his head, agreeing. "I'll arrange it so we'll be able to have the funeral in private anyway. When we get a lull in the activity, that's when we'll do it."

A pall fell over the group that lasted until they arrived at Mattias's home. Chey, torn between emotions, accepted Sander's help down out of the Hummer after the driver parked in the garage. She was cold to the bone, exhausted, and starting to feel a little nauseous again. The adrenaline of seeing and interacting with large crowds, not to mention the niggle of fear that assassins might suddenly appear around any corner, fizzled like water drops on a hot griddle.

Inside, she noted the arrival of more guards. They stood sentry at every entrance and exit as well as at the base of the stairs and the archway to the halls.

She knew the bodies of the dead or wounded had been removed while they were gone. Small comfort.

Upstairs in the bedroom, Chey peeled out of the heavy coat, the gloves and the boots. She had just draped the coat over a rack by the door when Sander touched her shoulder. Turning, she glanced at his eyes.

"What?" Then she realized he wasn't removing his clothes.

"I'm heading to the castle. I'll be with the Generals when they detain the King and Queen," he said. "Mattias will begin the meeting with the council in my stead until I get there."

"But...you didn't say you were leaving. Did you just decide this now?" Chey fought to keep her dismay in check.

"I hadn't planned on it. Right now, I feel it's best to be involved on all fronts. There are more than enough guards here to protect you this time. You're safe. Once we have any and all dissenters contained, I'll send for you. So gather what you need to, all right?" he said, cupping her jaw in his hand.

The chill from outdoors hadn't dissipated. Chey shivered. "If that's what you think is best. I--"

"I do. This is the hardest part, the most dangerous. We'll be past it, with any luck, before lunch time rolls around. Then it'll be dealing with fallout, the media, things like that," he said, bending to brush a kiss against her mouth.

Chey, interrupted from blurting news about the baby, kissed him twice more. "There's--"

He covered her lips with a finger. "I have to go. Rain check, okay?" Sander kissed her forehead then stepped around her to the door. "You have my number. If *anything* goes wrong, or you need me, call."

Exasperated, all she could do was watch as he let himself out. Too tired to care about missed opportunities, she shed her damp clothes, pulled on yoga pants and a sleep shirt, then fell into bed.

If tomorrow—or later today—was going to go anything like she thought, she needed at least *some* sleep to cope.

Chapter Twenty

"You ready for this?" Mattias asked.

Sander stared out the window of the limousine. Just landed in the helicopter, they were on their way to the castle, prepared to rendezvous with the three generals and enough troops to overpower the guards. He tugged on the edge of his leather glove. They had made a stop over between leaving Mattias's to change into much more austere clothing. Suits, polished shoes, clean, long coats.

"As ready as I'll ever be. I can't believe it's come to this," he repeated. The dividing window was up between the front and the back, protecting his conversation with his brother.

"I can't either, to be honest," Mattias replied. "I wish it felt less like a coup than not."

"Yeah, same here. That's exactly what I was thinking. He brought it on himself though." Sander had no sympathy for the King or the Queen. Not after Laur.

"He did." Mattias's phone went off in his pocket. He pulled it out and answered. "Yes?" His expression remained neutral for two seconds, then shifted into something more keen.

Sander regarded him rather than the snowy landscape. His brows arched when Mattias made eye contact.

"Yes, thank you. Keep the contents secure." He hung up. "Positive. The DNA tests were a match. Laur *was* our brother."

A muscle flexed in Sander's jaw. He kept tight control over his temper. Now wasn't the time to lose it. "We were not wrong, then. It solidifies the decisions we've made here, as far as I'm concerned."

"Yes, it does."

"Here are the troops." Sander saw the gleam of moonlight on a cluster of military grade vehicles in the road ahead. He counted no less than twenty carrying troops and three Hummers containing the generals themselves. All lights were off, engines silent. They were too far from the castle as yet to be detected by spotters in the towers.

Mattias twisted a look out the window.

The limousine pulled to a stop in the

other lane. Sander said, "Good luck with the council. Keep them occupied until I get there."

"I've got it covered. Take care." Mattias spared a thin smile.

Sander exited the limousine when the driver stepped back to open the door. Already, all three Generals stood outside on the ground in full military regalia. They saluted Sander, then extended their hands to shake. Sander went through the motions with crisp efficiency.

"General Masing, Rummo, Vaser. Good to see you all. Everyone still on board with our plan?" He assumed so considering they were blocking the north bound route leading to the castle. Sander didn't like to assume, however. He wanted verbal confirmation.

Masing inclined his head. He was in his early sixties with hair gone mostly silver. Sharp-eyed, the General was Sander's main ally.

"Everyone stands in the same place as when we spoke last," the General said, obviously speaking for the rest as well as himself.

"Excellent. Once the lead vehicle gets to the guardhouse, the men will need to get out fast and secure the guards. We need control of the gate at all costs."

General Masing inclined his head. "All right."

"Once we're inside, I want the special teams to go forward first and detain the King and Queen. I don't know if his guard will open fire or not, but I suspect they might. Your men are all prepared for that possibility?" Sander asked, looking between the Generals.

"Each and every one. They were selected for their loyalty to you," Masing said.

"Good. Once the King and Queen are detained, I want them confined to their personal bedchambers. The King in his, the Queen in hers. We'll deal with everything else from there," Sander said.

"We reminded the troops just before we left to separate the King and Queen," Masing said.

Satisfied that everyone was on the same page, Sander pushed his sleeve back to check the time. Dawn was fast approaching. If they wanted the element of surprise and darkness to help disguise their movements, they needed to get moving.

"Then let's get on with it," he said.

Masing, with a gesture to his vehicle,

said, "I have your seat in my car here, Your Highness."

Sander glanced at the limousine a final time before climbing into the Hummer. Masing closed the door behind him.

Collectively, engines roared to life. Headlights remained off.

The limousine cruised forward ahead of the rest, picking up speed. One by one, the Hummer and other vehicles followed.

Faster, and faster, prepared to literally storm the castle.

. . .

The guards at the gatehouse were not prepared for the assault. Guns in their face, they relinquished control of the gate, hands in the air, weapons stripped from their person.

Sander caught glimpses of it as the gate opened and they sped through, rushing toward the entrance. Although armed, he did not draw his own weapon. Teams of men trained in this kind of exercise swarmed from the cars before they came to a complete stop. He climbed out as shouts and warnings were subdued before any shots rang into the cold morning.

Taking the stairs, he ascended while more guards poured down from the upper levels, contained by the troops who were better prepared and had surprise on their side. By the time he made it to the private floor of the Royal rooms, his brothers and sister were in the hall in their sleepwear and robes, furious and demanding answers.

Answers he was not yet prepared to give.

Rounding into another hall, he strode toward the King's chamber, appeased to see Aksel's men subdued and his own standing in their place. Stepping into the King's private domain, Sander caught sight of his father immediately.

Aksel, red faced, eyes gleaming with anger, sat in a plush chair while troops took phones out of the room, as well as televisions, and even Aksel's personal cell phone.

"What is the meaning of this!" Aksel demanded when he saw Sander.

"Your son is dead—but then that was your plan the second you realized Mattias and I had discovered who he was. Pity I could not save him. He was a man worth saving." Sander tempered the fury that tried to creep into the syllables. Faced with his father, he found it more difficult than he imagined. He talked over Aksel's bluster and shouting.

"I am hereby detaining you for abuse of power. You *and* the Queen," Sander said.

"You cannot--"

"You will remain detained until my meetings with the council are over, and until I have explained your cruel streak to the people of Latvala." Never raising his voice, Sander continued speaking past the King's curses and threats. "When I am through, you will no longer be King. It may take several days for the council to think over all the information I am about to give them, and a few more days beyond that for the people to decide where their loyalty lies. Since it is unlikely I will be taking the throne, they will back Mattias instead of Paavo, for even they know without being told he is the natural leader behind me."

Startled into momentarily silence, Aksel broke it with a question. "So you will remain in exile, then? Self imposed?"

"No. I intend to tell the people *why* you forced me into exile, and the truth of my mother. Should they grant me the throne anyway, it will be me taking your place," he said.

"The council will never allow it. Not when they know. What are you thinking! To announce that to the world--"

"Yet you did not hesitate to announce my exile in my stead when it suited your needs," Sander said, cutting Aksel off. "This suits *my* needs. It satisfies my honor, of which you know nothing about. I will accept what the people and the council decide for my fate."

"The laws of this country won't allow it, that's what. To be branded a bastard is far better than you deserve," Aksel said, a vein throbbing in his forehead, cheeks ruddy with anger.

Sander realized with sudden insight that he was feeding the beast. Dangling fresh meat outside the bars of an animal's cage. He also realized that he didn't care to hear Aksel's limp excuses and thin threats. This man was a King past his prime, a man grasping, drowning, fighting to keep what he thought was his. Sander cared not to hear Aksel gloat over Laur's birth or death, did not want to be present while his father attempted to spin some story or another that was likely another lie.

Turning on a heel, he left the room. Aksel's vehement diatribe faded the further he walked, until he could no longer hear it. Refusing to consider pandering to Helina in any way, shape or form, Sander stalked the hallway en route for the stairs. His brothers and sister had disappeared into their rooms, dressing he knew, to descend to the lower floors to find out what was happening.

They could sit in on his council meeting and learn with the rest.

Taking his phone from his pocket, he made a call.

"Olev. Have Chey brought to the main castle at noon. I want an escort of no less than eight for her. Do not stop for anyone."

Chapter Twenty-One

Chey opened her eyes to the glow of the sun streaming through the cracks of the curtains. Squinting, she sat up in bed, rumpled and disoriented. What day was it? The events of the prior evening blitzed across her memory, reminding her why she felt so weak and drained. The attack on the manor, Laur's death, the late night visit to Kalev. So much turmoil.

On the heels of that, she remembered Sander returning to the castle to have Aksel and Helina detained. Pushing the covers back, she shuffled out of bed. Heading into the bathroom for a quick bit of personal business, she took a turn at the sink after that to wash her hands and brush her teeth. Combing her hair into loose waves, she secured half of it back with a simple barrette and traded night clothes for a business suit in navy with white accents. Once or twice, she suffered a bout of dizziness so strong she had to shoot a hand out to balance against the

319

sink or the wall.

Gathering what few belongings she owned, she stuffed them into a bag, preparing to leave whenever Sander called for her.

The knock at her door came just as she added her make up kit to the small pile. On a whim, she fished the pregnancy tests out and put them in a zippered side pocket of a purse. She didn't want to be separated from the evidence, not while Sander remained unaware of her status.

"Coming," she called, hurrying to the door. Olev, sober faced and serious, waited on the other side.

"Miss Sinclair, Prince Dare has requested we take you to the family seat. Are you ready?" He glanced over her attire with a quick sweep.

"Yes, all my things are on the bed." Chey knew it was useless to try and carry any of it herself. The guards would ease it from her fingers with gentle smiles and carry it for her regardless. She glanced at the digital clock on the nightstand to see it was straight up noon. Cringing inwardly at how long she'd slept, she stepped aside so one of the guards in the hall with Olev could enter to retrieve her things.

"Any news about what's going on?" she asked as they descended to the main level.

"Nothing yet, Miss Sinclair. We haven't heard back from Prince Dare or Prince Mattias since early this morning," Olev said.

Curiosity warred with worry while they piled into the cars. Distantly, she noted many of the guards were accompanying them on the trip. Sander was taking no chances, and for that she was grateful.

The drive was not overly long, yet it felt an eternity to Chey. All the small towns they passed along the way had groups of citizens in the streets, smaller pockets of support for Sander, some carrying signs and others simply adding their presence to make a statement. It pleased her to know they loved Sander so. As he loved them. She knew it was a large part of the reason he meant to confess his birth status, risking it all to retain his honor. He might hate not leading his country should the council and courts go against him, but at least his conscious would be clear.

Ambivalent about her return to Ahtissari castle, Chey regarded the imposing structure as it loomed up out of the snowy landscape sometime later. Sunlight glinted off the white covered turrets and winked off hundreds of window panes. The roads in and out, of course, had been freshly plowed for easy access. What was different this time, were the clusters of military looking vehicles parked at the turn in the road for the gate, and at the gate itself. Guards lurked in pairs and trios, armed to the teeth.

Passing through the gate with no trouble, the vehicle cruised up toward the broad front steps where yet more military awaited. Olev helped her to the ground while another man retrieved her luggage.

"Thanks," Chey said, releasing Olev's hand. She glanced up at the facade of the castle, pensive and thoughtful. Her first month here had been fraught with danger, discovery and startling insight, both about the Royal family and herself. There were personal demons to conquer before she could ever feel comfortable about living under this roof. She needed to accept that there would always be situations out of her control, that plots and secrets and forbidden knowledge was a way of life in this world.

Just as she crossed the threshold, she realized this was an inadvert changing of the guard, as it were. Aksel and his old ways of rule stood no chance against Sander and Mattias.

Chey paused three steps inside the immense foyer, struck by an epiphany. Her child would one day enter these doors as King—or Queen. They would stand right here, looking at the same vaulted ceiling, the same set of sweeping stairs. The ghosts of the past and all their figurative skeletons couldn't change the fact that she and Sander would shape and mold the next figurehead according to their beliefs and personal standards. She understood then the importance of her role, not just as Sander's wife, but as a mother. All her experience, compassion, honesty and loyalty played a part in the kind of person who next became King or Queen.

If Sander retains rule, she reminded herself. *If.*

"Miss Sinclair? Is everything all right?" Olev asked, brow pinched with a frown.

She glanced away from the castle interior and curved a small smile. "Yes. I'm sorry. Lead on."

Olev escorted her through the grand hallways to a heavily guarded sitting room on the main floor. The palest peach covered the walls, with ivory crown molding outlining the seams and the ceiling. Rich fabric covered plush chairs adjacent to a large fireplace while sofas, divans and side tables cordoned the room into sections. It had the feel of money and power and extreme luxury.

"Prince Dare asked that you wait here. He will join you shortly. Can I get you anything to drink or eat, Miss?" Olev asked.

Chey set her purse on a table near one of the chairs close to the roaring fireplace. "Water, please. Thanks."

"Absolutely. One moment." He stepped out into the hall while a guard closed the door.

Heat from the flames made for a toasty atmosphere, the scent of pine and cinnamon subtle but pleasing on the senses. She approached the carved mantle and perused the many photos lined up there, stalling over several with Sander posing next to his parents or siblings. Even as a younger boy she could see the distance between him and his father. Oh, he had pride by the bucket; true affection, the kind that kept children coming back year after year to see their parents for all manner of celebration, was missing. Even when Sander stood right next to Aksel, an enormous metaphoric gap remained.

She was not displeased to see it. Chey wouldn't ever be able to deal raising a child to be anything like Aksel. Sander was an entirely different breed of man.

"Did you have any trouble on the drive up?" Sander asked from the doorway.

Chey twitched a look across the room, surprised at his quiet entrance. He wore a different suit, one cut so fine and elegant that it took her breath away. Dove gray silk, a black brocade vest, and crisp white shirt outlined his shoulders and tapered over his lean hips. A white silk tie added to the austere effect. He'd tied his hair back into a low tail, jaw still clear of whiskers. Recalling late that Sander had asked a question, she shook her head.

"No, none at all. How did it go with the council?"

Olev returned with her water. He passed it off to Sander who murmured his thanks, then closed the door in Olev's wake. With slow steps, Sander walked the glass across the room. He handed it off, expression sober and hard to read.

"After hearing everything Mattias and I had to say, despite the hard evidence of the DNA tests, they have decided the rule of law cannot be overthrown like the King was, and that I will not be allowed to ascend the throne. Mattias, not Paavo, will be announced official heir."

Chey accepted the water, watching his eyes. She didn't put the glass to her lips and a moment later, gasping at the news, was glad she had not. Even though she'd known all along the council might vote this way, it was shocking to hear the words come out of Sander's mouth.

"But why not? I mean, I know, I know, your mother was another woman--"

"Yes, she was. We took a saliva swipe from me as well and sent it along with Laur's. Helina definitely did not give birth to me, which, in the eyes of the court and the land, makes me a bastard, unfit to be King." He slid his hands into the pockets of his slacks, the hem of his suit coat caught on his wrists.

Shocked, Chey searched Sander's face for clues on how he *really* felt. She couldn't decide if it was resignation or acceptance or something more maudlin that lurked in the blue of his eyes. "I just don't know what to say. Honestly, I thought for sure you would be the one. I can't believe, even with all the support of the people, they won't bend the rule this once."

"If you bend or break a rule like this, then you have to start breaking them all. I understand their position, that they're bound by covenant and law." He glanced down at his shoes, then back to her face. "It was close. They argued it for three hours straight, and I do mean argued. Many feel I should take the crown regardless. The diehard lawmen, though, they won the day."

"And there's nothing else you can do? Nothing else you can say?" she asked, dismayed to the point she didn't want to drink the water now. But she did, in small sips, in case he spouted something unexpected and made her choke.

"I spent an hour pleading my case. There isn't anything else *to* say." He looked at the pictures on the mantel, mouth quirking at a corner.

"So what happens now? Do you just...ride off into the sunset and lead a normal life? Will you be stripped of the title of Prince, have all your holdings revert back to the crown?" Chey asked. She set the glass down on a small end table and rested her hands on his hips, careful not to wrinkle the suit.

"They're deciding the semantics as we speak. Mattias is still in there, furious, fighting to at least have Kallaster castle remain mine. I don't ever think I've seen him that mad," Sander said with a faint tick of his lips. He looped his arms low around her, staring down into her eyes.

"I'm so sorry. I really am. You fought so hard. What will the people think? What will they say when they find out? You had so much support last night." Chey remembered the hundreds upon hundreds clogging the streets. Not just last night but this morning as word spread deeper into the countryside.

"I imagine they'll accept it as they know they must. As of last night, they still didn't know I'm a bastard." He said the word with a wealth of distaste. "Once they realize, I think it will take the wind from their sails. The people know as well as we do that a bastard cannot ascend the throne. After all, this was part of the reason I had my 'marriage' annulled to Valentina. What a hypocrite it makes me if I don't accept what law the council passes down considering how vehement I was in my desire not to put someone else's blood on Latvala's throne. So it's come full circle, and the people will love

Mattias as their new King as much as they would have loved me."

"It's awful. I can't help it. Even I, a veritable stranger here, know you're the best one for the job." Chey got on her tiptoes to kiss his chin. "But it doesn't matter to me what you are or aren't, as long as you're mine."

Lifting his hands, he cupped each side of her jaw. Cradling her face like she was precious. He spoke low, resonant. "I know. I also know how much you hate not wearing your ring, so get and wear it. I'm going to make the announcement some time today."

Chey searched his eyes. "Are you going to tell them about the baby, too?"

On his way to kissing her mouth, he paused. His eyes narrowed, features sharpening with intent. "*What?*"

"I *said,*" she whispered, emphasizing the word, "are you also going to tell them we're having a baby?"

Chapter Twenty-Two

Chey muffled a laugh when he suddenly picked her up, lifting her off her feet, and twirled her in a gentle circle. Then he kissed her like a man deprived of affection for years instead of hours. She saw instant joy replace all those other emotions he'd carried into the room. For this moment, at least, he allowed himself to revel in the news she had to give.

"How long have you known?" he asked, refusing to set her down.

"Only yesterday. I kept trying to tell you, but...too many things happened." Chey wouldn't ruin this moment with mention of the attack at Mattias's home.

"Unbelievable. Are you certain?"

"Yes. I took two tests to make sure. Plus, there are other signs. Ones I completely missed with all the traveling back and forth and everything. I'm definitely pregnant." Chey hoped the prospect of fatherhood would offset some of the disappointment she knew he was feeling about the loss of his Kingdom. It meant their child would never take the throne or rule after Sander, as she'd thought.

Sander's eyes gleamed, bluer than blue. "That's excellent news. I want to step up the wedding then, make it sooner than later. Is that all right with you?"

"Yes, it's fine with me. We can make it a small affair, since I doubt many in your family will want to attend anyway." Chey was under no illusion about that.

"We'll figure all that out later. How far along are you?" he asked, after kissing her again.

Chey licked the taste of him off her lips. "I'm not positive. Ten to twelve weeks, I think. I'll need to go to the doctor soon."

"You'll have everything you need the second I'm done with these announcements. I have a news conference scheduled within the next two hours, and my family is waiting in another room to find out the details from this morning. Come with me," he said, letting her slide to the ground.

"All right." Chey couldn't hide from Natalia forever. Might as well get the showdown over with, so they could all get on with their lives.

Sander squeezed her before capturing her hand.

As he led her through the room, Chey picked up her purse from the table and followed at his side. During the short walk, she mentally prepared herself, promising she wouldn't allow Natalia to get her too riled up.

Up two flights of stairs, on the level where the Royals lived, Sander guided her to a set of carved double doors. He opened one, led her inside, and closed it behind them. Ten times the opulent splendor of the one below, the Royal sitting room consisted of lavish furniture, gilt accents and oil paintings in elaborate frames of their ancestors.

Paavo, with his black hair and green eyes, paced with clear agitation near the ornate fireplace, hands in the pockets of his slacks. Everything about him was neat as a pin: the tuck of his snowy button down, the knot of his royal blue tie, the crease along the pant leg. Even his hair, combed carefully back away from his face, had been styled to perfection.

Aurora, his betrothed, perched on the edge of a plush chair, hands folded demurely over one another on her lap. She was the picture of elegance and poise.

Gunnar, the youngest, the brother who most closely resembled Sander with his fair coloring, brooded on a lounger, one foot resting across the opposite knee. He had a tumbler in one hand filled with amber liquid. Krislin, his wife, sat nearby, darting worried looks between the others.

Natalia paced the room like a lioness on the hunt, obviously drunk, hurling what must have been curse words at Mattias's head.

Chey only understood it was offensive by the stark look of disapproval on Mattias's face.

"Oh, we're *finally* graced with his presence," Natalia spat when she spotted Sander and Chey. "And he brought his little bitch with him. This is just *perfect.*"

Paavo diverted course and headed straight for Sander. "Mattias will tell us nothing. What the devil is going on?"

"Why are father and mother being detained? Is this a coup, Dare? Have you lost your mind?" Gunnar asked, pushing off the lounger. Although he had a drink in hand, Gunnar was in full possession of himself.

Sander slowed to a stop at the head of the room, hand wrapped around Chey's. "Calm yourselves. I'm going to give you an abbreviated version of the whole. You can pick my bones clean for details later." He paused to glare at Natalia. "Mind your tongue, sister, or I'll have you locked and secured in your room, as well."

Natalia snarled. Aurora gasped.

"So it's true, then? You had them detained?" Paavo said. His skin picked up a ruddy hue, as if he was containing a mountain of anger.

"I did. You see, he sent a team to murder your eldest brother, the *true* heir to the throne. I'm sad to announce Aksel succeeded in that quest," Sander said.

Gasps of shock circled the room. Paavo and Gunnar talked over each other, crowding closer to Sander, demanding answers.

"You're lying! There is no elder brother, we would have known!" Paavo shouted.

"Dare, what is this you say? Why, then, were we not informed?" Gunnar asked.

Sander edged in front of Chey, blocking her with his body when his brothers grew too close. A blatant warning that they come no closer.

334

"Listen and learn, and stop interrupting." Sander, who sounded on the edge of irritation himself, continued. "Aksel and Helina were pregnant at the same time as my mother, who is *not* Helina. Aksel and Helina will not admit that's the case. They keep insisting she faked her pregnancy for me, so that she could graciously take her husband's bastard child in as her own."

Sander snorted to show what he thought of that notion.

The entire room went silent and still. Even Natalia, wearing a shocked expression, stalled out by the side of a sofa.

"Laur Ahtissari, their firstborn, a boy child terribly disfigured, was sent off to a place in the East woods," Sander paused to let that sink in, "where he was raised—imprisoned, more like—for the rest of his life. My guess is that when he was born, they decided he could never rule not only because of his disfigurement, but because they didn't know whether his brain had also been compromised. Honestly, I'm surprised they didn't kill him then."

Chey glanced at Mattias when he began moving from person to person, showing them images from his phone.

Images of Sander and Laur the night he visited Mattias's house. The recognition on each face, from the brothers to the women, proved there was no disputing the familial resemblance.

"Chey, by accident when the King's men came after her, discovered Laur's existence. We obtained DNA samples and also some from Helina to prove he was her child. The tests were a positive match. I submitted mine as well at the same time, and there is no doubt the Queen is not my mother. In that, at least, the King told the truth." Sander squeezed Chey's hand.

She squeezed his in turn, letting him know she was fine. It was difficult to watch each child roll through the wave of emotions that came with each new revelation. Shock, belief, resignation. That the brothers were distressed over the circumstances could not be denied. Gunnar especially looked beside himself.

"Mattias and I went to rescue Laur—and others like him—from the building last evening. But Laur had escaped first, fleeing to Mattias's country holding where he was gunned down in cold blood, all to keep the people of Latvala from knowing what the King and Queen had done.

Because I believe Aksel has abused his power as King, I had him detained. After a long meeting this morning with the council, they have decided Mattias will ascend in Aksel's wake instead of me."

Silence hit the room next. The only sound came from the fireplace, where a log cracked, throwing red hot embers against the grate.

Mattias, the only person in the room beside Chey not surprised by the news, pushed his phone back into his pocket. "You'll need to leave for the public announcement shortly," he reminded Sander.

Finally, with a voice that shook with disbelieving anger, Paavo said, "I find it suspicious that father leaves the throne to me, and suddenly, Mattias is named the successor after a clandestine meeting *you* arranged, Dare."

Sander narrowed his eyes, as did Mattias. It was Sander who replied first. "Did you not hear a thing I just said? Your beloved King *murdered* his own child."

"He was no brother I ever knew!" Paavo declared, moving from an even tone to a shout.

Chey twitched with surprise.

"Are you so desperate to lead, then, that killing innocents mean nothing to you?" Sander asked, his voice gone silky, edged with something dark.

"Of course it means something to me. I, however, did not have the luxury of ever meeting this Laur, so you'll forgive me if my attention turns to the living. Namely the millions of people counting on this family to rule," Paavo said, features reddening with indignation.

"Mattias is the natural next in line anyway. The only reason you were named is because Aksel knew Mattias had deceived him in the end and was aligned with me. He used you as he's used the rest of us, Paavo. Your place in the natural order of things puts you far out of the running for position of King, a position, I might add, that you are not ready for." Sander stared Paavo down.

"And you keep speaking as if you have any place in the order at all any longer, *half* brother," Paavo said. He stepped around Sander for the door, forgetting Aurora on the couch.

Aurora rose, fingers over her lips, a nervous look in her eyes. She followed Paavo from the room, easing the door closed behind her.

Chey felt Sander stiffen beside her at the callous, cruel taunt Paavo delivered.

"He has never dealt with this kind of stress well, you know that," Gunnar said when Paavo was gone, speaking almost too quiet to hear.

"Yes, but it does not excuse him, Gunnar."

"Maybe not. Our family is coming apart at the seams," he said after another moment. Gunnar returned to offer his hand down to Krislin, who clasped onto it and stood from her seat. Gunnar paused shoulder to shoulder with Sander, facing the other direction, and left a final comment near his ear. "No matter what, you'll always be Dare Ahtissari, brother of my blood, fit to be King."

Sander clapped Gunnar on the back of the shoulder.

After that, Gunnar led his wife out of the sitting room.

Natalia, unusually silent throughout, started laughing. She laughed and laughed, until it reached a hysterical pitch.

Chey cringed inwardly, expecting Natalia to throw a vase or some other hard object to kick off yet another tantrum.

"Natalia," Mattias finally said, cutting through the woman's giddy, drunken giggles.

"This is just...too rich. A dead brother I never knew existed, *another* brother who turns out not to be worthy to even live in the castle nor have access to the monies and titles due the rest of us, and the little woman who thought she would be Queen. What an impossible tale." She buried another laugh into her palm.

Mattias shot Sander an impatient, annoyed glance, closed the distance to his sister, and escorted her firmly by the elbow toward the door.

"Good luck with your speech, Dare. They're expecting you in the front in eight minutes," Mattias said. Then he was gone, Natalia in tow.

"I need a drink," Sander said half under his breath. He released Chey's hand and approached a side bar where he poured himself two fingers of scotch.

Chey wasn't sure what to make of it all. She expected Natalia's vehemence, but not Paavo's. "I think they all need to process what just happened."

"Don't we all," Sander said, tossing back a swallow. He hissed, pacing her way. "Would you like something? More water?"

"No thanks. I'll get something after you speak. Where are you doing the announcement?" she asked, aware that time was ticking off the proverbial clock.

"I chose the Monument of Kings. It's an outdoor display of statues depicting the lineage of my ruling ancestors."

"Oh, the one in the park, the life sized replicas?" she asked, recalling photographing it with Mattias.

"No, this is a more formal representation. Come on, we better get going." He finished off his drink, set the tumbler on a table, and sought her hand to lead her from the sitting room.

Chey held onto his hand tighter than usual, dreading the event to come.

. . .

The Monument of Kings turned out to be a square shaped dais sitting on a field of grass. Currently, the ground was buried under a half foot of snow. Lined along the back of the dais were white statues of once reigning Kings. Tall and imposing, they stared out with sightless eyes at a swath of land stretching away toward the shore. The platform, white stone as well, looked well suited for public announcements.

What struck Chey more than anything was the amount of people surrounding it on all sides. From five streets away in Kalev, they began encountering the masses. Sander's limousine cruised along the avenue, fronted by a Hummer full of troops as well as more behind. People packed the sidewalks, balconies of double and triple storied buildings, and crammed into businesses to await Sander's arrival.

More troops kept the streets clear, politely barring anyone from blocking the road to the Monument.

Chey glanced at Sander often, aching inside for the official end to his right to the throne. She knew it was hard on him, harder than anyone might expect. He bore the responsibility with his usual stoic reserve, jaw set in a hard line.

She looked down at her hand, his ring sitting prominent on her finger. Relieved to be wearing it again, she admired the cut and sparkle, wondering what his brothers and sister would think when they found out. Sander hadn't had time to tell them in the impromptu meeting.

At the venue, she disembarked with Sander, hand caught in his, surprised all over again at the sheer amount of people filling the grounds of the Monument. The statues towered above the platform by at least fifteen feet, the detail exquisite.

Chey returned greetings and well wishes, using several of the few words in the Latvala language she knew. The simple ones were easy: Hello, Thank you, Please, Good afternoon, and others. She accepted flowers from several women who appeared quite happy to see her at Sander's side. It brought the sting of tears to Chey's eyes, the kindness of the people.

Sander was gracious in his interactions, pausing often, using quiet words to express one sentiment or another.

After a twenty minute delay, Sander guided her up the steps to the platform. By then she had an armful of different flowers, hair tousled by an errant wind. Sander, unruffled by the crowds or the weather, released her hand after a roar swept through the throng and lifted it high. He stepped up to a microphone and stared out at the sea of faces, features taking on a grim cast.

Chey's heart ached. She stood to his left a few feet from his elbow, giving him room.

When he began, the crowds hushed, creating a vacuum of silence. Chey shivered beneath the coat she'd donned over the suit. Sander's voice echoed into the day, sun shining down from a startling blue sky. It wasn't long before the crowd gasped and began to whisper, reacting to the news Sander had to give.

Aware of the many photographers and cameramen, Chey schooled her features, careful not to show too much emotion one way or another. A ripple of shock replaced the gasps, and then a surge of shouting Chey didn't understand. The people looked unhappy at whatever Sander had just said. A few women started to cry, something Chey hadn't expected. Were they upset Aksel and Helina were detained? Would this whole thing backfire on Sander, making him an enemy of the people he cherished so much?

A few of the men looked angst ridden and angry. Some had their fists in the air, others rattled off insistent phrases in the mother tongue.

Chey knew exactly when he announced their engagement; a roar lifted into the day and thousands of eyes swiveled her way. She lifted the bouquet of flowers, gifts from many in the crowd, and saluted them. Chey wasn't sure it was the right thing to do, but the people cheered harder, louder. Nestling the flowers in the crook of her arm, she met Sander's eyes across the few feet that separated them.

He wore pride mixed with affection in his gaze, masking the pain she knew must be there as well.

Turning back to the microphone, he finished his speech, lifting a hand, this time in farewell.

Choked up, Chey touched the tips of her fingers to her forehead, trying to cover the rush of emotion from cameras.

With a sudden surge, the crowd flooded up the stairs onto the platform. For a moment, Chey was so startled she almost ran the other way. It would have been impossible; the throng surrounded them from all sides, packing in as if they were overflowing the stage of a popular rockstar.

Once the initial surprise passed, Chey discovered she wasn't afraid to be among them. These people were not her enemies. Many had tears on their cheeks, some were openly begging Sander—who was attempting to make his way to her—to take over as King. The citizens pleaded in ways that made Chey's heart ache even more. It was wrenching to see them so supportive of someone the council would not allow on the throne.

For three hours, she remained at Sander's side while he shook hands, accepted condolences, and attempted to assure the people Mattias would be a solid ruler in his wake. Finally, the troops eased into a circle around them, making it possible to leave the platform and head through the crowds toward the waiting limousine. She stopped every time Sander did, which was often, to speak with those who hadn't been able to reach the platform.

In the limousine once more, she slumped into the seat, laying the flowers and ribbons across her lap. The floral scent permeated the interior.

Overwhelmed, Chey didn't know what to say.

It appeared Sander was at a loss as well. He stared out the window, one hand twined with hers, as the driver took them away from the Monument.

One sign in particular, held by a pedestrian alongside the route, brought tears to Chey's eyes. It read: *We love you. Be our King.*

Chapter Twenty-Three

Kallaster castle never seemed more like home. For the rest of that day and the next, Chey settled into a routine that didn't demand much in the way of energy or emotional investment. Sander paced more than he lounged, staring out the windows at the sea. He brooded in silence, coming to terms with the new hand life had dealt him. When he took calls, they were from Mattias only. Everyone who wanted a piece of the former heir had to go through his brother. They took their meals in his suite, secluded from everyone but immediate staff, preferring to ensconce themselves in private thoughts that they sometimes shared with each other.

Sometimes.

Chey didn't push him, and didn't push herself. She wanted the down time as much as he wanted to be performing duties as King. In the end, she thought it might help settle Sander's mind to be away from the constant turmoil of court and the rest of his family. Part of their retreat had to do from learning the fate of the rest of Laur's household: only three of the eleven remaining had been found alive. Sander took the news hard. Chey mourned the loss with tears of frustration, attempting to console herself with the idea that Aksel and Helina's murdering spree was over.

This morning, their plans were different. Chey slipped a small pearl earring through her lobe, watching in the bathroom mirror although her eyes had gone distant, mind elsewhere. Coming back to herself, she perused the strict black slacks and matching fitted coat. It was a somber outfit for a somber occasion.

Exiting into the main bedroom, she glimpsed Sander straightening a cuff on his own suit of black. He wore it as well as he wore anything else, the color complimenting his golden hair and skin. Solemn and silent, he slid his arms through his sleeves and plucked her long coat off a peg, holding it open for her.

"Thanks." Sliding her arms through, she adjusted the collar and gave the suit jacket beneath a gentle tug to straighten out a wrinkle.

"You're welcome. Have everything you want to take?" he asked.

"Yes. I'm not taking a purse. Don't see the need. I'll put my phone in my coat pocket." Which she did right after she mentioned it.

Sander escorted her out, steps brisk, eyes hidden behind a pair of glasses he put on at the last second. Chey had a pair as well, which she slipped into place as they descended to the main floor.

From there it was a matter of a car ride, then a hop from the island to the mainland in the helicopter, and another trip in a long limousine. The day was as solemn as Chey felt, with an overcast sky and the threat of more snow later in the evening. Driving through the Latvala countryside, she watched the terrain fly by, aware Sander did the same beside her on the seat.

The limousine turned down a final road, a desolate area with no homes or other structures in sight. Trees crowded closer to the asphalt, then fell away as they arrived at an iron gate. A tall fence stretched in two directions, obviously to protect the cemetery sitting within its confines. Small and compact, a guardhouse stood sentinel at the entrance, manned by a guard in military dress.

Once inside the gate, the limousine cruised along a well cared for road, circling to the right when a fork emerged. He followed it into a pretty area with trees sparsely dotting the ground. She thought it strange there were no headstones in sight yet.

That rectified itself moments later, when a row of crypts overlooking a sprawling lake came into view. Other statues and headstones, some more ancient than others, flanked the path on the opposite side. The limousine stopped at a separate parking area beyond the immediate burial ground. Other cars had arrived before them, along with a hearse. Two other limousines sat on the far side of the lot, windows up.

Chey accepted Sander's hand when they climbed out. He closed the door himself, rather than wait for the driver. Striking out for a cobbled walkway, he guided her toward the site of the headstones rather than toward the crypts.

Some of the engravings depicted names and dates that stretched back centuries.

"Why are some of these here, and crypts over there?" Chey whispered.

"Only the Kings are buried in crypts. Wives and other children go here," he replied.

"Is this not open to the public?"

"No. That's what the other monuments are for. These would become defaced or raided by tourists if we allowed anyone in."

"Why just tourists? You wouldn't worry about that with regular citizens?" she asked.

He glanced her way. "I'm sure a few might risk it, but on the whole, we're a suspicious lot about disturbing the dead. Most people wouldn't dare even touch a headstone, much less dig up a body for whatever jewels might be on it."

"I see." She found that interesting. "So you'll be buried here someday, then?" Even if he was a bastard, he was still of the blood.

"No. I'll be put somewhere else. Maybe Pallan island, overlooking the ocean. What do you think? Would you prefer a private place just for us and our kids there?"

Chey didn't want to think about her own death, yet. She touched her stomach, letting her hand fall away a moment later. "I guess? I don't know. I haven't given it a lot of thought. I'm too busy living."

"We'll talk about it later, but I think it's a viable option. I like the island quite a lot."

"I do, too," she said. Ahead, Chey saw a cluster of people standing near a freshly dug grave. Her heart seized in her chest, a pang of sorrow making it hard to swallow past the knot in her throat.

Mattias, resplendent in black, stood on a royal blue length of material lined with only a handful of chairs. To Chey's surprise, Gunnar and his wife were there, along with a matronly woman she didn't recognize.

"The woman took care of Laur when he was a baby. She acted as his mother and expressed a deep desire to be here today," Sander said.

"You're not afraid she's a spy or something?" Chey asked. It wasn't beyond the realm of possibility in her mind.

"Mattias says he believed her when she explained she was just the caretaker. And she admitted she knew, later on, that he must have been of royal blood. By then she loved him like a son, so we thought it would be cruel to deny her this simple thing."

Chey squeezed Sander's hand. "That's nice of you. She looks grief stricken."

The woman, in a plain black wool coat, with her silver hair caught back by a matching band, didn't appear wealthy or as if she had any other agenda but to mourn. Her face, pale and lined with wrinkles, wore a mask of dire remorse and sorrow.

"The guards cut her, the cook, the butler and a few others loose when they took the rest of the siblings on the run. It's not just Laur she's mourning today," Sander said.

Mattias glanced over when they arrived graveside and inclined his head.

A man of the cloth stood speaking with two other individuals nearby. He ended his conversation and approached.

When Sander greeted Gunnar and Krislin, Chey did likewise, surprised to see both not only acknowledge her, but greet her with what appeared to be genuine warmth.

Taking a seat next to Sander, she settled her hands in her lap.

The small ceremony was harder to bear than Chey thought it might be. All she could think of was the waste of a perfectly good life, the gentle giant who'd spared her falling down the stairs and took a chance to come visit relatives even if it might cost his life. What brought the flood of tears to the surface was the violin. Encased in a small glass case, the two men standing not far retrieved it from somewhere beyond the seats and placed it atop the coffin. A gift from his brothers Sander and Mattias, the priest intoned, should Laur have the urge to play again.

No one had to tell her it was the same violin Laur had used the night of his clandestine meeting.

After the brief ceremony, Chey stood at Sander's elbow while he and Mattias took turns explaining to the curious Gunnar what his half brother had been like. They paused to say goodbyes to the old woman, and eventually, once the priest was gone and the coffin was ready to sink into the earth, bade Laur a final farewell.

Chey touched the wood of the coffin before letting Sander lead her to the parking lot and the waiting limousines. Ready to depart and head back to Pallan island, Chey kissed Mattias's cheek and spent a moment with Gunnar and Krislin, who looked sincerely distressed at the events.

Mattias, fishing his phone from his pocket with an impatient exhale, stepped away from the group with an apology, promising to be brief.

In the middle of agreeing to meet Gunnar and his wife for luncheon the following week, Mattias returned, expression as serious as Chey had ever seen it. She braced herself for bad news, clutching Sander's arm with a fresh onslaught of worry. Fearful the council had decided to arrest Sander, or banish him from the lands, or some other horrible fate, she watched Mattias meet his brother's eyes as he drew abreast of the group. He wasted no time getting to the point.

"We need to return to the castle immediately. The King is dead."

. . .

A surreal haze of shock accompanied Chey and Sander back to the castle. Details of the death so far were sketchy. The King had been found dead in his chamber. All attempts to revive him failed. No signs of struggle, forced entry, or wounds to the body. Riding in one limousine as a group, the men, voices tense and terse, talked between them the entire ride.

Once more, Chey had no idea what they were saying. She caught a word or two amidst the rest of it, but they spoke so quickly, in such a fever, that she couldn't keep up. One thing she *did* understand, was that Mattias was probably now King of Latvala.

Krislin, wide eyed and in obvious shock herself, said not a word the whole trip.

Arriving at the castle, they discovered it was on lockdown. The number of military present had doubled since the last time Chey was here, providing a hefty barrier at all main entrances and exits.

Inside, men and women milled around the foyer, some in a daze, others hurrying to and fro on business.

Chey hadn't ever seen it so chaotic.

Three men in strict, elegant suits corralled the brothers and guided them toward one of the conference rooms located on the ground floor. Sander, insisting Chey be allowed to sit in on the meeting, wouldn't take no for an answer.

The conference room boasted an enormous oval table with enough chairs to seat twenty people, easy. One wall was for presentation, another fitted with a large screen television for video. Austere and spartan, the room served its purpose.

Sander pulled out a high backed, leather chair for her to sit in.

Chey whispered her thanks, relieved when he took the seat to her right. Mattias and Gunnar positioned themselves so they could make eye contact with Sander and speak easily without wrenching one way or the other.

One of the suited men, of advanced age yet possessing the air of someone in full control of their faculties, stood at the far end of the table.

"In English, please," Sander said, before anyone spoke.

"Very well," the man said. "I am very sorry to say that your father, the King, is dead. Three separate physicians have confirmed this. No announcement has been made due to the fact that your sister and brother, along with Aurora, are still on return from ventures beyond Latvala's borders." He paused to consult his notes, then continued. "So far, the cause of death is a mystery. There are no immediate signs of struggle or injury, no forced entry into the chamber. It was guarded by no less than four men at all times, and each one has given the same account to higher authorities. No one, other than staff, went beyond those doors. The staff are still being questioned in an attempt to narrow down who saw what, and when the King was known to be alive last."

Chey, attempting to gauge what Sander was thinking or feeling, couldn't get a bead on his expression. He hid his emotions well, and she wasn't sure if it was just his way, or if he was being cautious in the presence of the men who had ultimately banned him from the throne.

"Was it suicide?" Mattias asked.

"We just don't know yet," the distinguished gentleman said. "Every possibility will be explored and exhausted until we have answers. As such, we prefer you all to remain here until we know for sure there isn't someone loose on the property."

Chey didn't find it at all odd that there were no immediate clues. Elise, the staff member who attended her room when she first arrived, had meant to kill her with the contents lurking in a harmless bottle of water. Poison or some other deadly thing that was perhaps difficult to detect after the fact. And even if it turned out to be that Aksel took his life—would anyone be able to prove it hadn't been a staged event? A suicide that had really been murder? She remembered, months before, hearing rumors of an assassination plot regarding someone in the royal family.

The gentleman met each of the brother's eyes at that point. "This brings us to the other critical subject of crowning a new King. Over the last two days, our offices have been inundated with phone calls, signed petitions and letters from the public. The people demand to be heard. There are talks of strikes across all manner of government jobs, schools—everywhere. The citizens of Latvala are not used to such upheaval, and news of the King's death will be yet another blow. Yet they have proven steady and true in their aim to have Sander take the title."

Chey glanced from the man to Sander, fretting that they were going to force him into permanent exile so the people would have no choice but to turn their support to Mattias. It made the most sense to Chey to remove the clear obstacle standing between returning the country to more normal footing.

"According to the people, Sander is still of Ahtissari blood, born direct of the King, therefore eligible to take the throne. Even though they realize, as we have explained over the media many times, it is against the laws and covenants of this country, the people view you as successor." The man pinned a look on Sander.

"We've just gone over all this a few days ago," Sander said evenly. His expression was impossible to read.

"Yes, we have. The difference today is that the council met in private early this morning, before all this, to discuss the situation. To put someone, no matter how beloved, on the throne that the people are not fully behind, is asking for revolt. More than we are seeing here. In all honesty, none in the high council expected anything like this. That the citizens would rather shut the country down than bow to pressure from legislation that prevents them from what they consider their due. After several more hours of cautious debate, we have decided that you, Sander Darrion Ahtissari, will be the next King of Latvala should our chosen heir, Mattias, decline his rightful position."

As if on cue, Mattias said, "I relinquish

my right to the throne."

The gentleman withdrew a piece of official looking paper and passed it along the councilmen to Mattias. "Sign, then."

Sander sat up straighter in the seat, jaw tight with tension. He watched Mattias accept the paper, along with a pen, and sign his name with no breath of hesitation. He set the pen down and looked at Sander across the table. A look that stretched into several long seconds before the gentleman interrupted.

"Sander, do you accept the responsibility entrusted to you by this council and the people? Do you accept the title of King?"

Shocked to her core at the turn of events, Chey stared at Sander.

"Yes, I accept the title of King," he said.

The gentleman bowed his head, then removed another piece of paper and walked it, along with a pen, over to Sander, who signed it with a scrawling flourish.

Collecting both papers, handling them with utmost care, the councilman returned to his folder and set them inside. "Per tradition, your coronation will take place seven days after the burial of the late King. You will be expected to make another statement, as you know."

"I'm aware," Sander said.

"Excellent, your Majesty. The council will reconvene and I will present the official papers, informing everyone of the decisions here today. Once we have news of your father, we will release a joint statement and declare your status," he said. The remaining council members rose to their feet and bowed their heads to Sander.

"Thank you. Call a meeting with the council for later this evening as well. I have a few things to discuss," Sander said, stepping straight into his role as if it was natural as breathing. "Such as my impending wedding and the birth of our first child."

A collective ripple of shock passed through the room.

"What? You're to be a father?" Gunnar asked.

"Now *that* I didn't see coming," Mattias said with a quick look at Chey.

"Your Majesty," the man said, echoed by the others, who all wore their surprise in the open. "It will be welcome news after the recent tragedies. Congratulations, Miss Sinclair." The councilmen departed the room with a quiet click of the door.

Chey, stunned at the whirlwind changes, inclined her head to the councilmen as they departed, then glanced at Mattias, Gunnar and Krislin. It had been a long day. A day filled with sorrow and the trauma of death. To cast a little shining light, just for a moment, didn't seem out of place.

She said, "As far as I can tell, he or she will be born in the fall."

Chapter Twenty-Four

Euphoria spread throughout the country on the heels of mourning the death of the King. In a state of exultation at achieving their goal, the people of Latvala gathered en masse on Sander's coronation day, crowding pubs, restaurants with rooms for television, and in the streets to celebrate. They realized the power lie with the people when they chose to flex their collective muscle.

Thousands had turned out for Aksel's funeral services, paying their respects despite the circumstances. Sander, his siblings and the former Queen Helina displayed varying stages of grief. Although Aksel had plotted and condoned murder, he was still their father and his passing, ruled a suicide due to effects eventually found in his chamber, hit them all hard.

The official story, of course, was spun much different in the media. Aksel perished from a heart attack, not suicide by poisoning, and that's the way the story would stay. Some of the King's more dastardly deeds would never see the light of day, buried beneath leaden tongues and the burden of keeping secrets.

Chey would have preferred the entire world know every horrible detail. It wasn't her place to decide, or to say, so she remained cordial and quiet and supportive of her intended. In the course of ten days, everything changed: their movements were tracked to and from all locations, they were never without escort, even outside to the bailey or for short walks to the stable and back. Someone was within sight, ready to defend the new King. Chey hadn't understood just how suffocating it could be until she experienced it firsthand.

By the third day of it, she'd wanted to ditch the lot of them, steal Sander back to Pallan, and hide away until his coronation.

It wasn't to be.

For two days before the event, Natalia had thrown a tantrum of all tantrums, inconsolable about the death of her father and the knowledge Chey would one day become Queen. The walls shook with her wrath until finally, fed up and disgusted, Sander stalked the halls to her room and had it out.

In the aftermath, a pall fell over the castle.

Sander, shouldering meeting after meeting and interview after interview, sought Chey's company whenever he had the chance, burying himself in her softness and sweetness, relinquishing his tension and brooding nature for the Sander she'd met in the woods one fall day. He made no secret of the joy he took in her pregnancy, a joy he exposed in the quietest of times, only to her.

Worried about the image she presented to the world, Chey chose her attire for his coronation carefully. The dress, beige in color, with ivory embroidery on the collar and wide cuffs, buttoned down the front and had a hem that reached her ankles. Of a heavy material, the dress flattered her figure and disguised the faint thickening at her waist. She chose low heeled shoes the same color as the embroidery and fastened her dark hair away from her face, a classic style of twists ending in a small clasp of pearls.

The effect, she hoped, was elegant and cultured without being too droll. Tomorrow, she knew, a thousand critics from a thousand cities would pick apart everything from the application of her make up to the color of the dress to whether or not her lips were too thin.

As ever, the truest test was Sander, who paused to stare after attendants came and went to 'polish' his uniform. They had made sure no lint hung anywhere it shouldn't, that all wrinkles were gone, and that his shoes bounced his reflection back.

Sander's open praise was all the confirmation Chey needed that she'd chosen well. A handful of her own attendants—a thing Chey was sure she would never get used to—had argued endlessly about every detail. In the end, she made all her own decisions and stuck to her guns even when the head attendant complained there wasn't enough color.

Chasing everyone from his chambers, Sander stood before Chey and held her eyes for long minutes. Hair combed back into the usual low tail, he exuded a regal air fitting for today's ceremony.

"What?" she finally asked, lifting a gloved hand to smooth back her hair. Maybe a piece was sticking out.

"Nothing. Just admiring. You wear that color very well," he said.

"Thanks. I'm glad you like it. You look really," Chey paused to run her gaze along his military uniform. "Noble. The most handsome King I've ever seen."

"You're biased," he said, a note of humor in his voice.

"Of course I'm biased. You're still the man who tackled me off a horse and then taunted me about it, you know. Long before you were a King, or even a Prince, you were a thorn in my side."

He laughed. The first real laugh she'd heard out of him since before Laur's death.

"Now I'm just a--"

"Don't get coy and cocky," she said, cutting him off. The corner of her lips trembled with a subdued smile. It was good to banter a little, take the edge off the tension.

He arched a brow, imperious. "Are you deigning to tell your King what he can and cannot do?"

A laugh bubbled in Chey's throat. Sander pulled off imperious well. If they hadn't just been bantering, she might have been a little intimated. "Yes, and I'll be telling you what to do again later, when we retire for the night."

It took him no time to discern the

lascivious tease in her 'threat'.

He barked another laugh and scooped her closer with one arm, lowering his mouth to within a breath of her own. "Little minx. No wonder I love you like I do."

Chey basked in his attention and the sentiment, which made her heart soar. A sentiment she had waited so long to hear. Trailing a gloved finger along the smooth angle of his jaw, she said, "That's right. Don't you forget it."

He tilted his mouth to her cheek and brushed a warm kiss there. Then he whispered, "Lipstick."

"You're so afraid someone is going to see you with color and gloss on your mouth. You have a lipstick phobia," she said with an amused smile.

"PeachyKeenPerfection", he said, obviously making up a fake lipstick name. "Doesn't go with primary colors. What will all the fashion experts say?" Sander struck a feigned look of horror.

Chey gave in to another bubble of laughter. "Did you ever stop to think you could just wipe it off?"

His brows arched, as if her suggestion had only dawned on him right that second. The gleam in his eyes gave his game away. Then he swooped in to claim her mouth with a kiss, so thorough that he transferred some to his lips and smeared the rest off her own.

Either way, Chey wasn't complaining.

. . .

Hung with royal blue silk, a gilt throne front and center on a shallow dais, the throne room was a sight to behold. Chey, standing in her spot to the side of the elaborate chair, surveyed the sparkling chandelier that hung from a high ceiling, the rows of chairs lined up like pews to either side of an aisle, and the collection of faces, cameras and photographers hovering both in the seats and along the sides of the seating. Many council members, ambassadors and other people of importance were in attendance. The royal siblings sat front and center, dressed immaculately for the occasion.

Feeling conspicuous and on display, Chey wished she was one of the photographers standing out of the spotlight behind a piece of equipment. Sander, after their heated kiss in his suite, had easily agreed to pose for her later in his royal uniform and crown so that she could snap a few shots of their own.

The historical importance of what she was about to witness, and become a part of, did not escape her. She found it all but impossible to wrap her mind around what it meant, and what her future might hold. Not just her upcoming wedding to Sander but their child and his role in the Latvala lineage.

A hiss of doors opening pulled Chey from her reverie. Sander, framed in the arch to the throne room, entered as he was announced by a liveried man standing next to an official carrying a pillow with a crown nestled in the center. Another bore a scepter, and still another a long blue cape with silver trim and a silver crest embroidered on the trailing hem. Those men stood in front of the throne, awaiting while Sander made his way to them.

He went to a knee as the ceremony got under way, head bent, looking as regal as any King should. Chey regarded the proceedings with no small amount of awe, tears stinging the back of her eyes, stomach tight with pride and anticipation. To bear witness to one of Sander's greatest moments was a highlight of her own life, an event she would never forget.

Lifting his head at the end of an intonation, he went still as the cape was draped around his shoulders and clasped across his throat. The next man handed him the scepter, a beautiful thing with jewels along the shaft and the complicated wolf's head at the top.

Last came the crown, stunning with its carved silver peaks and blue sapphires inset at intervals. The piece glittered as the man placed it on Sander's head. In the final gesture, a silver sword with matching sapphires in the pommel and rune carvings on the blade touched Sander's shoulder one time each. His coronation ritual complete, the blade passed off to one of the attending officials, Sander rose to his feet.

In English, coming after the Latvala verse, the official ended the ceremony.

"I present to you the new King of Latvala, Sander Darrion Ahtissari."

Applause broke out in the room as Sander passed between the officials, who stood aside with their heads bowed, and took a seat on the throne. He dominated the high backed, ornately carved chair with the sheer power of his presence and charisma.

Chey, a bundle of nerves, wasn't sure if she was supposed to applaud or not. Was it proper? Or was she supposed to remain still, as if she knew this was his due? A glance at Mattias proved the siblings were not applauding with the rest. Taking her cue from that, she held her hands together before her, as demure as she knew how to be.

Flashbulbs popped from both sides of the room, had been for the last twenty minutes, immortalizing the event for all time. Video rolled, people cheered, and the officials signed a document that must have had to do with the coronation. They displayed it aside the throne when they were done, then carefully placed it before Sander, who signed last.

Removing the document, they posed for more pictures with Sander's signature scrawled across the bottom, before carrying it away through a small, guarded door at the back.

Ten minutes was all the military allowed the guests to remain. Row by row, people filed out of the throne room until there was only Chey and Sander left. As the door closed and silence descended, Chey met Sander's eyes.

"Was I supposed to go out with the rest of them?" she whispered, worried cameras were rolling somewhere and that she might have breached protocol already.

Sander laughed. He stood up from the throne, scepter in hand, the cloak trailing behind his feet. Descending the shallow steps, he came her way. "No. This was my first order as King. I told them all to leave us when the ceremony and the pictures were done."

Chey couldn't tear her gaze from his face. Even in low heels, he towered over her, taking her breath away. If not for the wicked twists and terrible turns it took them to get here, she would have thought this was all a fairy tale. Too many memories of funerals and the recent pain of loss assured her it was anything but.

He cupped her jaw with a gloved hand, the cloak whispering around his body as he came to a halt.

"I'm at a loss for words," she confessed, embarrassed.

"Don't be. I'm still the same man you read the riot act to, the same man whose face you've slapped—what? Two times now? Three? I've lost count."

A startled laugh escaped before Chey

could contain it. Of all things for Sander to say. "You're not supposed to bring that up at a time like this."

"Of course I am. You know what comes next, right?" he asked, dragging his thumb over her lower lip.

"I'm not sure, but I suspect it involves redoing my lipstick again, and you washing your glove," she said. There was a peachy stain across the pristine white.

The grin he bestowed on her was riddled with rakish charm. He handed her the priceless scepter, which Chey was hesitant to take. Wrapping her hands around the middle, she held it aloft like it might shatter any moment.

Sander scooped her up in his arms, cradled her against his chest, and struck out for a different door to the side of the room.

Laughing, helpless with amusement, she tucked the scepter against her body and put her lips on his jaw.

Let the sweet torture begin.

. . .

About the Author

Born and raised in Corona California, Danielle now resides in Texas with her husband and two sons. She has been writing for as long as she can remember, penning works in a number of genres. To date, she has published twenty novels and nine short stories. Her interests vary wildly: reading, traveling, photography, graphic art and baking, among others.

There is a black cat named Sheba involved who thinks Danielle's laptop is her personal grooming station.

Check her website for trading card offers, giveaways and announcements!
www.daniellebourdon.com

More books by Danielle Bourdon:

Romance:
Heir Untamed (Royals Series 1)
King and Kingdom (Royals Series 2)
Heir in Exile (Royals Series 3)
The King Takes a Bride (Royals Series 4)
The Wrath of the King (Royals Series 5)

The Royal Elite: Mattias (Royal Elite 1)
The Royal Elite: Ahsan (Royal Elite 2)
The Royal Elite: Chayton (Royal Elite 3)

Fantasy/Romantic Suspense:
Sin and Sacrifice (Daughters of Eve 1)
Templar's Creed (Daughters of Eve 2)
The Seven Seals (Daughters of Eve 3)

Thriller/Romantic Suspense:
The Society of the Nines (Society Series 1)
Violin Song (Society Series 2)
Vengeance for the Dead (Society Series 3)

Young Adult/Fantasy:

The Fate of Destiny (Fates 1)
The Fate of Chaos (Fates 2)
The Reign of Mayhem (Fates 3)
A Crisis of Fate (Fates 4)

Paranormal Romance:
Bound by Blood

Fantasy:
Dreoteth

32604122R00214

Made in the USA
Lexington, KY
26 May 2014